BETTY GOSSELL

Lizzy's Journey
Copyright © 2024 by Betty Gossell

ISBN: 979-8989686391 (sc)
ISBN: 979-8991517904 (e)

Riverview Press

info@riverview-press.com
www.riverview-press.com

Contents

Dedication

I believe we owe much of who we are to our ancestors. I am very fortunate in that my paternal grandmother was the keeper of her family's genealogy -- countless pictures, newspaper clippings, and even an old German Bible filled with names and dates. But beyond just a listing of names and a filled-out genealogy tree, I wanted to know more about these people. What were their lives like? Why did they move from place to place, or immigrate from Europe? How did they adjust to living in a foreign country? When did they truly feel like Americans, or did they ever?

I have always been fascinated with the Civil War, in which many of my ancestors participated, and yours may have as well. Imagine my surprise when I found that my 2x great grandfather Henry kept a journal (in German) during his time in the Army! What a wealth of information and history that was!

This book is a fictional story based loosely on Henry and his wife Lizzy, along with other members of my extended family. Names have been changed and characters combined a bit, but the basic story is their story --- a story of immigration, danger, hard work, love, and loss. And therefore, their story is part of mine.

As such, this book is dedicated to all my ancestors who went before me to blaze a trail into the new world, and whose rich heritage still impacts my life today.

Prologue

Lizzy stared out the bedroom window at the gray skies and drizzling rain pattering against the glass. Such a dreary day–a perfect match for the sadness of her heart. It was late November, and the chill in her bones suggested upcoming snow. In 1914, St. Paul, Minnesota, was a growing city and even in the bad weather, there was a lot of hustle and bustle on the streets below. She was rocking slowly in her favorite rocking chair, a large black cat curled comfortably in her lap. Lying in the bed beside her was her husband of 60 years; 60 amazing but difficult years. He had never been a big man, but the ravages of his chronic illnesses had reduced him to a mere shadow of his former self. His breath was ragged, and his groans of pain were coming more frequently.

"Lizzy?" he moaned softly. "Are you here?"

"I'm here, my dear husband. The doctor is here, too. Rest now - I'm not going to leave you." She brushed his gray hair from his eyes and pressed a cool cloth to his temples. He seemed to relax again, knowing she was near.

"It won't be much longer, Lizzy," Dr. Thiele said softly. "But just keep talking to him -- he seems calmer when he can hear your voice. I truly believe he can recognize you, even at this stage of his passing."

Lizzy studied the doctor sitting beside her–a handsome young man she had met just a few years ago when their regular doctor had moved away. He was about the age of one of her grandsons, which could have worried her, but instead she had been instantly comfortable with him.

"Thank you, doctor. We've had such a long time together–60 years! So many struggles mixed with so much joy. I'm not sure what I will do without him. Is it wrong that I want this final time for just us–leaving the children in the parlor downstairs?

"No, of course not. I understand they have already said their goodbyes. You know, I've only heard part of your life story together–how did you two meet?"

"Oh, that was so very long ago. But our real story starts many years before that."

"Really? Tell me, please–I would like to know more about the two of you and the love story that you share."

"It's a pretty long story. Do you have the time?" she asked.

"I have all the time you need."

Lizzy sighed and looked around the small room filled with pictures and other memories of their time together. Glancing back at Henry, she began, "It all started many years ago in Germany … "

Chapter 1

The piercing cry of a newborn baby shattered the stillness of the quiet night. Jakob Kruse was sitting on the stairs outside his bedroom while a doctor and a neighbor tended to his wife Margaret. They had been so nervous during this entire pregnancy–after the loss of their first child Anna at just three days of age and then experiencing several miscarriages, neither was sure if this pregnancy would have a happy ending.

Jakob rose to his feet just as the bedroom door opened. "You have a baby girl, Jakob," Dr. VanGruber said softly. "Margaret had a bit of a rough go for a while, but everything is fine now. That baby has a mind of her own, though, I tell you! She came out upside down and backwards and wailing at the top of her lungs. You can go in and see them now, but please make it brief. Margaret really needs her rest. I'll be back in the morning to check on them both. You know how to reach me before then if you need to."

The doctor descended the stairs and went quietly out into the dark night. Jakob pulled out his pocket watch and saw the time was 1:27 AM. Margaret had been in labor for more than 30 hours, and Jakob had been worried he would lose them both. He moved quietly into the room and glanced at the tiny baby being tended to by his neighbor Clara.

"Do you want to hold her?" Clara asked gently.

"Oh, yes please," Jakob answered quickly. "I was not sure this day would ever happen."

"She is pretty small, but really feisty. I think you will have your hands full with this one!" Clara beamed. "I'm going to step outside for a little while to get some fresh water and clean linens. But the doctor is right—Margaret really needs to rest for a while."

Still holding the baby, Jakob went to the bed and picked up Margaret's hand. Her sleepy eyes fluttered open and she smiled. "Isn't she beautiful?" Margaret whispered. "Did the doctor tell you about her birth? Did he say that she is ok?"

"Yes, she truly is lovely. And such a miracle, especially since…" his voice trailed off as he thought about the other babies he would never see again.

"I know we never settled on a name," Margaret said tenderly. "I think neither of us wanted to get ahead of ourselves, to get our hopes up. But I was thinking about Hattie Elizabeth. We could call her Lizzy."

"Hattie? Where did that name come from? I've not heard it before."

"It's actually an old family name on my mother's side. I always thought it sounded pretty, but I'm not sure I can cuddle this tiny baby and call her Hattie. But Elizabeth is also a family name, and Lizzy sounds perfect for our spunky, special girl."

"Hattie Elizabeth it is, then. I'll wait here with both of you until Clara gets back. You need to rest. I love you, my dear."

"I love you too, Jakob," she said softly as she drifted off to sleep. Jakob sat in the chair next to the bed and looked closely at his tiny daughter. Even in the nearly dark room he could see her strong features and a mass of coarse auburn hair. She had his nose and high cheekbones, but everything else looked like his beautiful wife. She squirmed a little in his arms, and he rocked her gently back and forth.

"My little Lizzy," he said with a tiny smile. "Welcome to the world."

He watched his daughter for several minutes, thinking about her future and what life would bring to her, until Clara came back into the room with a pitcher of fresh water and some soft towels. "I'll finish cleaning her up, Jakob, and get her settled. Why don't you try to get some sleep? It's been a long several days–and months–for you, too."

"Thanks Clara. I'll just be in the room next door–please come get me if you need me."

"Of course. I know you are anxious, but everything looks good now. She's strong and healthy, and going to make a mark on this world, I just know it. Rest well."

Chapter 2

Life in northern Germany was difficult in the early 1800's, especially for peasant farmers like Lizzy's family. Food shortages and the lack of a fair legal system meant that farmers were left to fend for themselves when issues arose such as a neighbor's cows grazing on their garden or their sporadic (and often ill-equipped) medical care. Things were always tough, but then the potato famine happened.

A son, Adam, had been added to the family in the past few years, and Lizzy's mother Margaret was pregnant again. It was 1845 and life suddenly became 1000 times more difficult when everyone lost their main food source–the potato. Men like Jakob ate between five and ten pounds of potatoes each day, with the women and children eating lesser amounts. This was crucial so they had enough calories for their grueling farm work and other very physical labor in factories. Starting in Ireland and then spreading across Europe, the potatoes became infected by a blight that rotted them from the inside. Suddenly, this source of nutrition was gone, and many people were dying of starvation. Lizzy went to bed hungry most every night. Margaret went into labor two months early, and likely due to her poor nutrition, both she and the baby Louisa passed away. Jakob was left with no wife, very little food, and two small children under his care.

Lizzy was eight years old when her mother died, and she felt very scared and alone.

After Margaret's funeral, Jakob took his small family home and with despair, sank into a chair by the fireplace. Friends stopped by with what little food they had, and his neighbor Clara offered to stay the night to help with the children. Lizzy cried herself to sleep that night–worried about her family and missing her mother. A few days later, Jakob offered Clara a permanent job as caregiver for the children–he could not give her much in the way of pay but provided a little food and a place to live. She agreed, but only if they got married, because she was worried about what the neighbors might think. Jakob agreed, and soon they were married. Before long they had two more children of their own, Rosina and Hannah. And while Lizzy appreciated having a female influence in the house, Clara was *not* her mother, and never would be.

One day in July of 1851, Jakob was visiting with a friend who had heard that boats were sailing regularly from nearby Bremen to America, where there was plenty of farmland and food, and where immigrants were welcome. He had also recently received a letter from his old friend George Augustine who had moved to Minnesota and established a thriving farm along with a successful lumberyard making railroad ties and fencing. George strongly suggested Jakob bring his family to America and find a better life. Without even discussing it with Clara or the children, Jakob sold the few possessions they had and used the money to book passage to New York City. Within just a few weeks, it was time to go. Lizzy tried to understand his reasoning and the sudden decision. She was sad to say goodbye to her friends and the only home she had ever known. Packing a small bag with a few changes of clothes and the Bible her mother had given her at her sixth birthday, she climbed into the wagon for the day-long trip to Bremen. As they left town, they passed the small cemetery and the graves of her mother and the babies. She felt guilty leaving them, wondering if anyone would ever remember that they were buried there.

The drive to Bremen was uneventful. The family spent the night huddled up in the wagon. It was crowded and uncomfortable and no one slept much. The next day Jakob sold the wagon and the pair of oxen that pulled it, and then they boarded a ship named The *Charlotte Reed* along with close to 200 other passengers. Lizzy was now seventeen years old and felt like nothing in her life would ever be the same. Like cattle, they were herded down to the lower levels of the ship into a large area with a few partitioned sections for families or women travelling alone. Lizzy and her family huddled in a corner and did their best to endure the nearly two-month trip to America. It was crowded and noisy, and she had very little privacy. She cried as she watched the shores of her homeland fade from view. A few weeks after leaving Bremen, the ship was tossed about by a large storm. The fierce waves beat against the ship, and the boat creaked loudly as it rocked side to side. The storm raged for two days, with many of the passengers becoming ill. Large waves crashed over the railing, and everyone was cold and wet. All the families prayed fervently for safety, but many people on board started to worry that they had made the wrong choice–to leave their homeland only to die at sea.

Life was very stressful on the ship. In addition to the crowds and noise, there were fights between the passengers and crew, and there never seemed to be enough food or fresh drinking water for all the immigrants. Lizzy felt hungry and dirty and exhausted. Elsewhere on the ship, one small child died on the trip, and two more were born. Things felt very strange, and the future seemed uncertain.

Somewhere in the middle of August, Lizzy was taking a walk on the upper deck, enjoying the fresh air and breeze on her face. Her father had warned her about going anywhere alone, but the crowds and smells in the hold were overwhelming. The blue waters of the Atlantic spread out ahead of her, and it was easy for her to feel overwhelmed by the vastness of the ocean. No land could be seen in any direction. Suddenly, she was approached by a group of four young men who called out to her in a vulgar way. They surrounded her and pushed her back to the railing. The one who seemed to be the leader started grabbing at her clothing while another held her hair and tried to kiss her.

"Please, leave me alone," Lizzy said with as much bravery as she could muster. "Don't do this."

The group laughed and continued their assault until they heard a loud voice coming toward them.

"Get away from her, you creeps!" a much older man yelled loudly in German. "Put one more finger on her and I will break them all off! SCAT!"

The group ran off, and the man stood next to Lizzy, making sure not to touch her or scare her further.

"Are you ok?" he asked. "Did they hurt you?"

"No, they didn't have a chance. Thank you so much for saving me from them."

"Do me a favor, ok? NEVER come back up here alone. Is your father traveling with you?"

"Yes, he's with the rest of my family in the hold," she told him.

"Good. Get yourself back down there and stay with your family. I assume you don't have much experience on your own?"

"I was often by myself back home, but I guess things are different here."

"Very! Those guys have been roaming all over the ship, looking for trouble. It's lucky for you I came along."

"I'm very thankful. My name is Lizzy."

"Take care of yourself, Lizzy. Not everyone is looking out for your best interests." And with that, the stranger moved down the deck and into an interior room. Lizzy looked nervously around her and then dashed down the steps to the lower level. She was afraid to tell her father about the incident, though, not wanting him to worry or scold her for her disobedience.

Finally on September 30th, they pulled into port in New York City. Standing with her family on the upper deck, Lizzy was amazed at the huge city spread out in front of her. Never had she imagined anything like the tall buildings or the sheer number of people hustling up and down the streets. It took most of the day for everyone to leave the ship, as they each had to be questioned and their names put on a list along with their ages, occupations, and town they were from. Since very few of the immigrants spoke English, they had to wait for someone to help with translation, and it was late in the afternoon when Jakob finally finished their interview, and they were free to leave.

Because no one in the Kruse family spoke English, it was difficult for them to try to figure out where to go or what to do next. Jakob had a letter from his friends the Augustines who had contacts in the city and the name of a boarding house that would welcome them for a few days while arrangements could be made for their trip to the small town of Oliver's Grove, in the Minnesota Territory. Lizzy could barely pronounce *Minnesota* and had no idea where it was or why her father was so intent on taking them there, rather than settling at a multitude of other places in this huge country. The family was huddled together on the sidewalk as the crowds rushed past them.

"*Sprechen Sie Deutsch*?" he asked over and over in German to the people hustling by. After several minutes, an older woman approached them. "*Ich spreche Deutsch*," she answered in a friendly tone. Relieved, Jakob asked for directions to the boarding house where he was assured that the owners spoke German and would be able to help with their travel details. Lizzy listened intently while the woman gave detailed instructions. They walked twelve blocks until they found a well-kept house in what was a community of German immigrants. Two rooms were available for the family—a small one for Jakob and Clara, and a larger one for the children. They enjoyed a dinner of sausages, sauerkraut, and rice pudding -- something Lizzy had never seen before but instantly fell in love with. It had been such a long time since they had a real meal that included meat—Lizzy savored every bite. After dinner, the homeowners Hans and Susanna Walz helped the family get settled and heated pails of water so everyone could have a warm bath, another luxury that Lizzy had missed during their long voyage. Susanna gathered up all the dirty laundry from the family and made sure they had clean night clothes and linens to sleep on. Lizzy had the best night of sleep since her mother passed away, although she was still nervous about the future and their upcoming trip to Minnesota.

She awoke just before dawn the next morning, confused about where she was and the unusual sounds and smells. Looking around the room at her sleeping brother and sisters, she pulled the covers up to her chin and then recognized the tantalizing aromas of fresh bread and bacon. She softly tip-toed to the door and opened it quietly. Just outside was a neatly folded pile of clothes that looked like they would fit her and the other children. She heard her father and Clara's voices downstairs, along with several others she did not recognize from dinner last night. She could also hear noises from the street below her window—horses and buggies, people talking and laughing, the rattling of carts and the barking of dogs. It was early morning, but the city of New York was already alive and bustling.

Lizzy took the clothing from the hallway and placed it on her bed. On top were trousers and a shirt for Adam, and lovely little dresses for Rosina and Hannah. At the bottom of the pile was a beautiful blue and white plaid dress with lace on the bodice and sleeves. There were undergarments for everyone as well. Lizzy had no idea who would have loaned such beautiful clothing to her, or how they knew her size. It certainly was the nicest thing she had ever worn.

After helping the younger children dress, they all filed downstairs to the dining room. A veritable feast was waiting for them—bacon, bread, strawberry preserves, boiled eggs, and apple pancakes! Lizzy was overwhelmed with all the new sights and smells and ate slowly as if to memorize every taste. She wanted to be able to cook this well once she had a home of her own, and intended to learn all she could while she was here.

Once the meal was done, Lizzy offered to help clear the table and wash dishes, but Susanna refused her assistance. "You have had such a rough time these past few months, and years for that matter. Why don't you go sit in the parlor and I'll have some of the other women help me. I think my daughter Gretel is going to be attending English lessons in a bit, if you want to sit in."

"Yes, thank you," Lizzy said nervously. She hadn't really thought about how difficult it would be living here and not being able to speak the language. "I did want to ask you about the clothes, if I may? I've never worn anything like this -- where did they come from?"

"They are all donations from people who have stayed here over the years," Susanna replied, "along with gifts from neighbors who want to be helpful. I'm glad you like the dress - it does fit you perfectly."

Clara took the younger children out to play in the courtyard behind the house and Lizzy moved shyly into the parlor. A young girl of about twelve was playing a piano and a small group of adults were gathered around a middle-aged woman who was teaching English. Words such as 'wagon,' 'horse,' 'money' and 'family' were being spoken in both German and English, along with phrases such as "Do you speak German?" and "Can you help me, please?" Several of the women seemed to speak this new language well, and Lizzy found herself desiring to learn it, too. This was her life now and fitting into this new world included being able to communicate clearly. There was so much to learn about this new land–she wanted to learn it all.

Later in the afternoon Jakob gathered his family into the dining room to give them the news that he had met someone who would be travelling to Chicago next week, and they were free to follow along if they wanted. This would probably be the last wagon trip out this fall due to the upcoming winter, so they either needed to go now or wait until Spring. If they left now, they could winter in Chicago and then travel up to Minnesota once the snow melted, probably in March or April. He had been hoping they could make the entire trip this fall, but it was just too late in the year and too risky. The other options were to take a train or boat, of course, but Jakob didn't have enough money for their fares.

"What will be do in Chicago, Father?" Lizzy asked. "I heard some of the men on the boat talking about how cold it gets there during the winter."

"Yes, I'm sure it will be cold and there will be a lot of snow. But if we don't leave now, we will lose most of next year to get to Minnesota and settled. I want to be able to find the right farm for our new life and plant some crops next summer. The time in Chicago will give me a chance to study American farming and learn which plants grow best here."

After dinner, Lizzy and a few others went back into the parlor where the young girl was again playing the piano. "Do you play" Susanna asked.

"Oh, no," Lizzy answered sadly. "We didn't have a piano, and there was no money for lessons anyway. Maybe someday I will get the chance to learn."

"I hope you get that chance, Lizzy. Maybe it will happen in Minnesota?"

"I would love that," Lizzy sighed. "But Minnesota seems so far away."

Chapter 3

The next several days were busy times for everyone in the family. Jakob found a sturdy wagon and a team of oxen for a reasonable price, and Clara and Lizzy worked to find food and clothing for the trip to Chicago, which was estimated to take three to four weeks depending on the weather. There was also worry that some of the river crossings might be flooded due to some heavy fall rains. Finally, the day came for them to leave. Lizzy helped Jakob and Clara carefully load the wagon with as much as it could carry and still not be too heavy for the oxen to pull. The children piled into the back and settled in between bags of flour and sugar and boxes of smoked meat. Waving goodbye to Hans and Susanna and her other new friends at the boarding house, Lizzy once again found herself on a journey to somewhere new and uncertain.

They met up with four other wagons that were travelling to Chicago, along with the group leader Fritz Pulcher. No one but Fritz was fluent in English, so the group trusted him with their safety and their lives. Their route took them through Pennsylvania, Ohio, Indiana and then Illinois. Travel was uneventful with crisp fall weather and starlit nights, except for a few river crossings with water higher than Fritz was hoping for. They slept each night in their wagons and made good progress during the days, but the roads were rough, and Lizzy was soon very stiff and sore. Arriving on the outskirts of Chicago on October 20th, Fritz led them to the boarding house where they would stay for the winter. After unloading the wagon, Jakob sold it and the oxen, so they had money to pay for their rooms for a few months. Lizzy and her parents knew their money would run out long before springtime, so each needed to find some sort of job to pay for their room and board and provide money for the rest of the journey.

The boarding house was noisy and crowded, and there was only one room available for the family to stay in. After unpacking and trying to organize the family of six, Lizzy went downstairs to look around and explore. As she entered the dining room, she met a girl about her age who was setting the table for dinner. She introduced herself as Lydia, and said she was the daughter of Johannes and Eva Kohler, who owned the house. Lydia motioned for Lizzy to sit, and she brought her a cup of warm cider.

"My family and I welcome you to our home. You just arrived, right? Where are you from?"

"Thank you for having us. I'm Lizzy. We just got here from New York City, after our long trip from northern Germany. Things are so very different here—so many new sights and sounds and foods. I have so much to learn!"

"I'm sure you are overwhelmed. And Chicago is very different from New York. How long were you there?"

"Just a few weeks, until arrangements were made to get here. In the spring we will be on the road again, this time to Minnesota."

"Minnesota? Why Minnesota?"

"My father has friends who moved there, and they say the farming is wonderful, along with other good opportunities in town. Father plans to farm; that's all we know. Farming and raising animals. But it is so far away—I wonder why he doesn't choose to stay here in Illinois or any of the other states we just drove across. We passed a lot of beautiful farmland."

Eva poked her head from the kitchen and called to her daughter, "I need help in the kitchen, Lydia—there will be time for talking later."

Soon others started arriving in the dining room, and Lydia carried platters of pork chops, fried potatoes, stewed tomatoes, and fresh bread. There was even a large bowl of fruit on the table and an apple cobbler for dessert. Once again, Lizzy was in awe of the amount of food available. After so many years of struggle in Germany and the rough seas during their trip on the ship, to have *plenty* of anything was foreign to her. Conversation was lively and loud, and Lizzy found herself laughing at the jokes and enjoying herself for the first time in a very long while.

After dinner, Lizzy helped Lydia carry dishes into the kitchen and they quickly fell into the early stages of friendship.

"Frau Koehler?" Lizzy asked shyly. "I'm going to need to find a way to make some money while we are here. Do you know of anyone who is hiring? I don't speak any English, and I know that might be a hindrance."

"As a matter of fact, I just might. It's hard work and not much pay, but it might be sufficient for you."

"What type of work is it?"

"There is a hotel a few blocks away that needs someone to work in their laundry room. It's hot and tiring work, but the pay is $2.00 per week, which would be a great help to your family. I know the woman who is in charge, and I would be happy to introduce you to her."

"Oh, that sounds great," Lizzy smiled. "I could make quite a bit of money over the winter! My parents will be so excited!"

"If they give their approval, I'll take you over there in a few days."

"Thank you so much, Frau Koehler."

"Please call me Eva. I'm very happy to help."

Lizzy rushed to tell her father and Clara about the job at the hotel. Both were pleased and gave their blessing for her to start as soon as it could be arranged. Jakob had found work unloading boats on the fishing docks and Clara would be watching some of the children during the day so their parents could work. Lizzy found a scrap of paper and figured out how much money each of them could make between then and March 1st. She was excited to find that this would be enough to pay for their lodging, find winter clothing for everyone, buy a new wagon, and even have a bit left over for when they got to Minnesota. She reported her findings to Jakob who was able to relax a bit and smile. Lizzy did not remember many smiles from Father, and this eased her fears about the future a bit.

After breakfast a few days later, Eva took Lizzy to a hotel about ten blocks away. The weather was quite cool with a strong wind blowing in off the lake. "We will need to get you a better coat," Eva said with concern. "That thin sweater you are wearing will not help you in our Chicago winters."

"Are they really that cold? I've heard some people talking but wasn't sure what to believe."

"Oh, yes–winters here are brutal. We often get several feet of snow that pile up taller than you, and we are battered by unbelievably cold winds."

"Then why did you stay here, if I can be so bold as to ask?"

Eva laughed as she pulled her scarf tighter around her neck. "I ask myself that every year in January when the lake is mostly frozen, and we have a big blizzard." She smiled at the look of horror on Lizzy's face. "But then springtime comes and it's so beautiful. I feel God put us here to help fellow immigrants and travelers like your family. It makes all the tough times and cold weather worth it.

They turned a corner and Lizzy was amazed with the impressive architecture of the Tremont House hotel. It was nine stories tall, and Lizzy had never seen such a large building other than in New York City. Eva led her around to the back and they descended a narrow flight of stairs to the dark basement. After going down a long hallway, they entered the hot and steamy laundry room. Piles of sheets and towels filled most of the room, and a large hearth covered the back wall. Pots of water were being heated, and several women were working to wash the linens in the steamy water. They were then moved to another pot of clean water for rinsing and then sent through a set of large rollers that would squeeze out as much water as possible. The clean linens were then loaded into a wagon and moved to a different room to be hung on clotheslines to dry. Eva introduced Lizzy to Gertrude Johannson - a big muscular woman who had been barking out orders to her other employees.

"Gertrude, this is Lizzy, the girl I told you about. She and her family just got here from a farm near Bremen. Isn't that near where you were from?"

"Bremen? Yah. It's been many years since I was there. So, Lizzy–are you willing to work hard? I treat my workers fairly, but I expect them to earn their pay and be here every day. This hotel is always open and needs clean linens. You are seventeen?"

"Yes. Is that a problem?"

"No, I just don't want anyone under sixteen. How long will your family be here?"

"Only until the spring. We will head to Minnesota once the snows melt."

"Well, I'm happy for the help for as long as you are here. Can you start tomorrow?"

"Yes, that would be great!" Lizzy was anxious to start earning some money and feeling productive, instead of sitting around watching others come and go from the boarding house.

"OK, be here at 8 AM and bring your lunch. You will work until 5 PM with one short break in the afternoon. Come the back way, like you did today -- you are not allowed to be upstairs with the guests. Any questions?"

"No, I don't think so. Thank you so much -- I'll be here at eight tomorrow."

Lizzy and Eva made their way back to the boarding house and gave the news to Jakob and Clara. Father had already started his job at the docks and would be able to walk her part of the way to the hotel. Eva was able to find a warmer coat for her to wear, although it was a size or two too small. Everyone agreed that finding her a better coat was top on the list of important purchases.

The next morning Lizzy put some bread, a piece of cheese and an apple into a small bucket that would serve as her lunch pail. She tried to eat the breakfast that Eva and Lydia had fixed but didn't feel very hungry -- she was too nervous about starting this new job in a new country. Frau Gertrude did not seem like a woman who would tolerate lateness or incompetence, and Lizzy was determined not to disappoint her. This job would play a big part in her family's ability to pay their bills and afford to move to Minnesota in just a few months. She was proud to be able to help her family in this way.

Jakob kissed Clara goodbye and then he and Lizzy left the boarding house to head toward the lake. The sun was barely up, and the wind was howling off the water, sending a chill down Lizzy's back. The sidewalks were crowded with hundreds of people–young and old–on their way to work or setting up their booths to sell items right on the sidewalk. Fruits, vegetables, fish, and flowers were for sale from carts along the road. Several young boys were rushing up and down the road, calling out "Today's paper! Get your paper here!" Everyone seemed to be in a big hurry, and Lizzy struggled to keep pace with the others so as not to get trampled.

They soon reached the corner where Jakob would continue toward the docks and Lizzy was to turn toward the hotel. "Good luck, Lizzy," Jakob said as he gently patted her shoulder. "I'm sure you will be great. Just do whatever Frau Gertrude asks. You will have to walk home by yourself–don't talk to anyone, ok? I'll work as many hours as they let me, but I hope to see you at dinner."

"Goodbye, Father. I'll do my best today, I promise. Be careful on the docks and keep warm!" Lizzy pulled her scarf tighter around her neck and walked the last few blocks to the hotel. She was nervous about walking home by herself this afternoon–why had she not thought about that before? Here she was–a young girl in a strange country, alone, and unable to speak the language. She prayed for safety and protection. Quickening her pace, she was soon going down the dark stairs at the rear of the hotel. She could hear voices coming from the laundry room and hoped that she was on time. Her father had a pocket watch, but she did not have any way to know what time it was. Perhaps she could find an inexpensive watch somewhere?

"Right on time, Lizzy," Frau Gertrude said as she opened the door to the steamy washroom. "Are you ready? Take off your coat and put your things in that back corner. I'll introduce you to the others once everyone is here."

Lizzy struggled out of her too-small coat and folded it neatly near the others stacked on the floor. She set down her pail, noticing that most of the other women had similar lunches. She looked around the room at the women and girls she would be working with, and hoped they would be friendly. This was her first experience doing anything like this on her own, and since she spoke no English, she was worried about communicating with everyone.

She was soon able to put her fears to rest, however, once she learned that the other women were in situations much like hers. As they were all recent immigrants, most only knew a few words of English and Frau Gertrude was able to address them all in German.

"Everyone, this is Lizzy. She and her family just got here from Bremen, by way of New York City. She'll be here through the winter. I'll let you all introduce yourselves as soon as you get a chance. Augusta, I am going to put her with you in the drying room to start, ok?"

"Sure, that's fine," Augusta answered. "Come with me, Lizzy, and I'll show you want to do."

"Thanks," Frau Gertrude said. Addressing the rest of the women, she said, "Ok, time to get started. The water's hot so let's get busy!"

Lizzy and Augusta went across the hall to a very large room full of clotheslines and stacks of folded sheets and towels. "Ok, Lizzy–here's what we do. After the linens are washed and rinsed, you will load them into these carts and bring them here. We will hang them to dry and once they are ready, we will take them down and fold the towels. The sheets will go in a pile back here to be ironed and sorted by size for the housekeepers to retrieve. Have you ironed before?"

"Yes, some. Mostly just Father's shirts and our dresses."

"Well, I won't start you with ironing until you get the hang of everything else. But eventually we will need you to iron as well. Understand?"

"Yes, I'm sure I will be fine," Lizzy said with more confidence than she felt.

"Ok, one last thing. There is an outhouse across the back alley–use those same stairs as before and whatever you do, do NOT enter the main part of the hotel. Only Frau Gertrude is allowed there, and only in an emergency. Normally the housekeepers come down and load the linens into the dumb waiter to be pulled up to the other floors. We take our lunch in shifts somewhere around noon, but we cannot let the water get cold or allow the process to stop. Any questions?"

"No, I don't think so."

"Alright, take these wagons across the hall and bring the first batch of linens over. They should be about ready by now."

Lizzy grabbed the handles of two small wagons and pulled them across the hall to the washroom. It was very hot and steamy in there now, with several women at the wash tubs and others doing the rinsing. Frau Gertrude and one of the other older women were working the wringers and starting to fill wagons they already had beside them. There were other young girls who were carrying water or wood for the fireplace. It seemed to be a very organized process, and Lizzy could see that everyone's job was important.

"Here, Lizzy—bring one wagon over here and take the one I have filled. And get the one from Florine at the other wringer. Go hang these linens and then bring the empty wagons back. Back and forth - this is your primary job for now—understand? We can't have anyone falling behind or slacking on their job."

"Yes, I understand. I'll do my best for you."

Chapter 4

Lizzy lost track of the number of trips she made between the two rooms; it all became a blur after just a few hours. Her shoulders were aching as she hung the linens on the lines, and even a short lunch break and even shorter rest break around 3 PM did little to help her painful back and feet. She had worn the most comfortable shoes she owned, but there were blisters on her heels and sweat running down her back. It was a long, hot, and uncomfortable day. At 5 PM Frau Gertrude announced that they were free to go home. Lizzy limped over to the corner where her coat was and almost cried as she bent down to pick it up. Everything in her body hurt.

"Lizzy–how are you feeling? I know it's probably more than you were expecting."

"I'm ok, Frau Gertrude" she lied while smiling wearily. All she could think about was getting home and crawling into bed.

"Well, you did great for your first day. Be careful walking home, and I'll see you tomorrow."

"Goodnight," Lizzy sighed, as she walked toward the back staircase. Placing one aching foot in front of the other, she slowly climbed the stairs and stepped out into the cool afternoon air. It was such a shock to go from the steamy washroom to the frigid October winds! Keeping her head down, she focused on getting home as quickly as she could. The masses on the sidewalk pressed against her, jostling her aching body from side to side–she felt like she was just being carried along by the crowds. But eventually she was home and let out a giant sigh of relief as she pushed open the boarding house door. She struggled out of her boots and coat and collapsed into a chair in the foyer.

"Lizzy?" Clara asked gently. "Are you ok?"

Lizzy fought back tears as she opened her exhausted eyes to look at her father's wife. "I'm not sure, to be honest," she answered. "It was by far the hardest physical work I have ever done. I just wish I could take a hot bath and go to bed."

"Well, dinner is almost ready, and then I suggest you get some rest. I'm sure your muscles will hurt even more in the morning, so extra rest is a good thing."

"I'm not sure that is possible. The linens are very heavy, even with most of the water wrung out. And the clotheslines are just an inch or so too high, so I had to reach up more than was comfortable. Everything hurts."

"I have some liniment you can rub on your back before you go to bed. But come to dinner now."

Lizzy moved gingerly into the dining room and sat stiffly in the nearest chair. Eva and Lydia came from the kitchen with platters of boiled potatoes, sauerbraten, roasted carrots, and biscuits. Already on the table were fresh strawberry preserves and apple butter, pickles and a new food called cottage cheese. Lizzy had never seen it before and was a bit skeptical–it looked like lumps of sour milk. Was this edible? Everything on the table smelled wonderful, but Lizzy was so exhausted that she doubted she would be able to eat more than a few bites. But once she started, she realized how famished she was and that her little bits of meat and cheese from lunch were long gone.

They were about finished when her father walked in the front door, exhausted from his long day working on the docks of Lake Michigan. After washing up, he sank wearily into his chair and closed his eyes. It was obvious that his day was difficult as well. He and Lizzy gave each other weak smiles, and then he filled his plate with steaming food.

After dinner she slowly climbed the stairs to the bedroom the whole family shared, and gingerly pulled off her work clothes to slip into a nightgown. She rubbed a thick layer of the liniment Clara gave her onto her back and legs, then crawled into her cold bed. She was asleep almost instantly,

The days at the hotel turned into weeks, and then into months. She was able to find a warm coat that was the correct size, along with some gloves and a hat. One of the other immigrants gave her an old pocket watch so she could keep track of time. She also purchased some boots to keep her feet dry as she walked through the rain and mud and increasing snow each day. She had seen snow in Germany, of course, but nothing like this. The temperatures kept dropping and the snow kept accumulating. The walk to and from work each day continued to get more difficult and uncomfortable. She usually walked with her father in the mornings, but in the afternoons, she was alone.

Three days before Christmas, a ferocious storm blew in across the lake and dumped more than twenty inches of snow throughout the city. Lizzy had been told that there were no days off or holidays at the hotel and that she needed to be there no matter what. She opened the front door of the boarding house and was met with a wall of white snow blowing left to right; she was instantly disoriented. How in the world was she going to find the hotel when she could not even see across the street? There were very few people outside at the time, or if there were, she couldn't see or hear them. She struggled and stumbled her way down the road that headed toward the lake, and into the howling wind. She had gone only a few blocks before she was chilled to the bone and becoming disoriented and scared. She didn't have her father to walk with this day, as the docks were closed because of the storm. Of course, hotels never closed and there was always a need for clean linens and sheets.

She continued to push herself forward into the wind and blinding snow, each step becoming more difficult. Finally, she was at the corner where she could turn and go the last few blocks to the hotel. Relieved to have the snow and wind out of her face, she hustled along, anxious to get out of the cold. Suddenly she heard a loud noise behind her -- the rattling of a cart and the stomping of horses' hooves. Over the howling wind she could barely hear the voice of a man yelling "get out of the way!" She quickly turned to see two giant horses bearing down on her, running totally out of control and unresponsive to the frantic pleas from the man driving the wagon. Lizzy jumped to her left just in time to avoid being trampled by an enemy she could barely see in the blinding snow. The cart continued careening down the road as Lizzy finally reached the back alley of the hotel. Rushing toward the stairwell that led downstairs, she struggled over mounds of snow and thought she would never be warm again.

Once in the basement, she heard the voices of Frau Gertrude and several of the other women, already hard at work. "I'm sorry if I'm late," Lizzy said as she entered the laundry room. "The weather is so bad, and it took me a lot longer than usual."

"Oh, don't worry," Frau Gertrude answered warmly. "I'm just so relieved you got here safely. I've never seen a storm quite like this one. I don't suppose you brought other clothes to change into. No? Well, I imagine you will dry out soon."

Lizzy went right to work and was quickly warmed by the fires and steamy laundry. After lunch, one of the maids came down and said the snow had finally stopped and the skies were blue again. Lizzy was surprised to see the snow had piled into drifts several feet high in many places. There were still not many people out and about when she walked home, but at least she could see them this time. After trudging for what seemed like hours through thigh-high snow, she was finally back at the boarding house, soaking wet and exhausted. Clara met her at the door with a warm blanket and a cup of spiced cider. "We are so relieved that you are home, Lizzy," Clara said tenderly. "It must have been just horrible for you."

"It was pretty tough," Lizzy replied. "The worst part was when I almost got run down by a team of horses pulling an out-of-control wagon!"

"What?" Clara cried. "Are you ok?"

"I saw and heard them just in time, but it was pretty scary."

"I'm sure it was! Well, just warm up here by the fire and dinner will be ready soon."

Most of the boarders—and all the children—had been trapped in the house all day, so tempers were a bit short and many of the babies were crying. Too many people had been cooped up all day, and emotions were high. The dining room was overly crowded, and Lizzy noticed a few extra chairs pulled up to the table. Soon a new family walked in -- a husband and wife with two sons about Lizzy's age.

Johannes Kohler stood and addressed the group. "Ok everyone, I know you are all tired of being in this small house all day, but I have an announcement. I'd like to introduce a new family that will be with us for a while. This is Emil and Antonia VanDussen, and their sons Kurt and Erik. They were on their way to Iowa when they got stranded by the storm. I know the house is very full right now, but I just could not turn them away. We've done a bit of juggling and found a room for them—let's all extend kindness toward our fellow immigrants, ok? Is anyone here working at a job that is hiring? Emil and the boys are all willing to work for a few months until they can get back to their travels."

"The docks are always hiring," Jakob said. "I can introduce you to the foreman in the morning if you want?"

"That would be great," Emil said enthusiastically. "We got a late start on this leg of our trip and had hoped to get to Iowa before now. We had to ditch our wagon and walk the last few miles. Thankfully we could bring the horses with us."

"We'll put together a party to dig your wagon out tomorrow," Johannes said before asking for volunteers to help. Several men and boys raised their hands, and Emil was thankful.

"We only have what we were able to carry, which isn't much. Retrieving the rest of our things would be a Godsend." Emil was emotional when he said, "Thank you all so much. Jakob, I'll go with you to see about jobs for us, and the boys can stay and help dig out the wagon."

Lizzy looked across the room at the two new boys -- Erik was tall and thin, and Kurt was a bit shorter and more stout. She tried to smooth out the wrinkles from her dress and pushed a few stray hairs behind her ears. She wished she had taken time to freshen up before dinner.

Eva and Lydia came from the kitchen bringing platters of bread and cheese, and a large tureen filled with vegetable soup. Johannes continued, "As for dinner tonight, I'm afraid we have a bit less to offer all of you. Between the storm and our four new guests, we are low on a few things. Hopefully we can get out and do some shopping tomorrow, so we can add fresh things like fruit and milk. For now, however, my wife and daughter have done their best. It's warm and hearty, and I'm sure sufficient for tonight. Let us thank the Lord for his goodness to us—keeping us all safe in this storm and allowing us to be warm and well fed."

"Amen." Everyone echoed as the platters and soup were passed around the table. Lizzy noticed that Kurt and Erik took very small portions, probably feeling guilty for taking food away from the others. Lizzy, however, enjoyed her piping hot soup and crusty bread with freshly churned butter.

"So, where in Iowa are you headed?" one of the men asked Emil.

"Just across the big river and south to Ft. Madison. The farmland is supposed to be spectacular, and the fort will help protect us from the Indians."

"We were originally headed to South Dakota," Erik added, "but settlers just aren't safe there now with the Indians burning homes and scalping everyone."

"You do understand why they are doing it, right?" asked another man. "It was *their* land originally and the government forced them to move. Not many of us would be happy about that if it happened to us."

"No, but I wouldn't be raping the women and scalping the men!" shouted yet another of the boarders.

Angry voices erupted around the room, and at first Lizzy felt very uncomfortable. She hadn't thought much about the uprisings from the Indian point of view before. She certainly would not have liked it if someone had come into her homeland and forced her to move.

Johannes rose to his feet once again and begged the men to stop arguing. "Please, I know this is a hot topic for discussion, but not at dinner and not with the women and children present–please!"

The arguing stopped but there was a murmur of discontent among the immigrants. This was the first time Lizzy had been involved in a political/ethical discussion of this magnitude, and while it was uncomfortable, she found it fascinating and hoped she could find ways to listen more often.

Christmas came and went without a lot of fanfare. As struggling immigrants, no one had extra money for gifts. The parents did try to make it a bit festive for the children, and Eva fixed a wonderful Christmas dinner. Lizzy had to work, of course, but Frau Gertrude gave each of the workers an extra dollar and a small bag of nuts and cheeses.

January and February brought more cold days and snowstorms, but Lizzy had fallen into a familiar routine of work during the day and English lessons from Mr. VanDussen in the evenings. He had been a teacher in Germany and volunteered to help anyone who wanted to learn. Her English was rapidly improving, and soon she was able to carry on simple conversations with shopkeepers or other merchants. Erik and Kurt both spoke English very well, so she was able to practice with them or ask questions if there was something she did not understand. Kurt seemed especially eager to help her, and she wondered if he had taken a fancy to her. She found him to be quite handsome with sparkling blue eyes and auburn hair like hers, but certainly didn't want to encourage him since they would be living so far apart from each other in just a few months.

March 1st brought a flurry of activity to the boarding house. Most of the families were making plans to continue their journeys westward and the rooms were filled with boxes of flour, salt, preserved meat along with blankets, farm tools and other items needed for the trip and starting their new lives. The VanDussens were packing as well, anxious to complete their trip to Iowa. Jakob suggested that they travel together as far as Davenport where the VanDussens would head south but Lizzy's family would head north. Lizzy asked Jakob again why they were going to that particular town in southern Minnesota, but all he would say was that he had heard the soil was great and that the government was almost giving land away to anyone who would homestead.

Two weeks later, Lizzy walked home from the hotel one last time. Frau Gertrude was sad to see her go, but totally understood the desire to move away from the city and start over on a new farm in a new state. The other ladies had put together a small gift for her that included two aprons and some new stockings.

Frau Gertrude gave her an envelope that contained $5.00 and a note thanking her for all her help over the winter.

March 18, 1852, the Kruse family set out for the final leg of their journey to Minnesota, along with the VanDussens and two other families–the Millers and the Bauers. They had no guide for this trip, so the men from the four families agreed to work as a group, following a map one of them had acquired. The trip across Illinois took only a few days, even though many of the roads were muddy and traveling was slow. They reached the Mississippi River just south of Davenport, Iowa, and camped in Illinois one last night together as a group. Tomorrow they were to cross the river and head in different directions to their new homes.

As the families were settling in for the night and the women were fixing dinner, Jakob asked Lizzy and Kurt to look for firewood. The sun was setting quickly, and as Lizzy reached for a small stick, she heard the *hisssss* of a snake. She froze, afraid to move in any direction. Suddenly, Kurt was at her side and stabbed the snake with a small knife he had in his pocket.

"Are you ok?" he asked nervously, so afraid that she had been bitten.

"I'm fine, I think, but my hand stings a little. I did not see him at all, hiding among the other sticks and leaves. Thank you so much for saving me!"

"Let's get you back to the others and make sure your hand is ok. I'm just glad I was here, or this could have been much worse."

Kurt grabbed her right hand and wrapped it in his handkerchief. "Hold your hand up near your chest," he said as he gently led her back to the others. "That will help, hopefully."

"Mother! Father!" he yelled. "I think Lizzy might be hurt! Come help me!"

Jakob and Clara, along with the VanDussens and a few others, rushed to find out what was going on. Jakob picked Lizzy up and carried her to the wagon as Kurt explained what had happened.

"She says her hand hurts. I'm not sure if the snake got a good bite or not. But I took care of him—he won't be biting anyone else."

"Bring her closer to the fire so I can get a good look," Mrs. VanDussen said. "Erik, find my medicine bag, ok? And hurry!"

Jakob sat Lizzy on a box near the fire as Erik came back with a small basket full of various herbs and lotions.

"I've done a bit of nursing in my day, and even helped a doctor as a midwife. Before we left Berlin, I was able to gather a few medical supplies. I have an ointment that should help if this truly is a snake bite."

Everyone watched nervously as she examined Lizzy's hand. "Can you bend your fingers? Does it hurt anywhere else? How do you feel otherwise?"

"It's a little sore, just like I scraped it on a rock or something. I feel fine elsewhere."

"There is a break in the skin, but I'm not sure if it is from the snake—it's hard to tell right now. Let me rub some ointment on it, and I'll wrap it to help keep it clean. Try not to use it for a day or two, and we'll keep an eye out for infection. You are one lucky young lady."

"Kurt was the one who saved me," Lizzy whispered. "I honestly didn't see the snake until after he attacked."

"Thank you, Kurt," Jakob and Clara said in unison. "You saved our little girl's life!"

"Kurt," his father asked, "did you see what kind of snake it was? It will help us know how to treat Lizzy if she doesn't get better."

"Not really, but I could go back and get it. It all happened so fast."

Kurt went back to where he had killed the snake and put it in a grain sack. Back by the fire, he dumped it onto the ground, and everyone gasped.

"I'm not exactly sure, but it looks like a type of rattlesnake to me," Jakob said. "That brown and tan coloring certainly blends in with the other brush and leaves - no wonder she didn't see it. But the diamond pattern on his back sure gives us a clue. Lizzy -- this would have been very serious if he had bitten you more severely."

"Thank you again, Kurt, " Lizzy said softly. She felt a stirring of affection for him that was different from her usual interactions with boys. But she could not let herself get swept away since they would be saying goodbye tomorrow, and she would probably never see him again.

Chapter 5

Lizzy opened her eyes and immediately felt pain in her hand and an ache over much of her body. She remembered the incident from last night and was worried that her snake bite was more serious than they originally thought. The sun was just peaking over the horizon, and she tried to move quietly so as not to awaken the others. One glance at her hand was enough to know that it was swollen to about three times normal size, and the pain was throbbing down to her elbow. She tried to climb out of the wagon but winced in pain and let out a small groan. Her father immediately sat up and asked what the problem was.

"I'm sorry to wake you, Father," Lizzy whispered, "but my hand is so sore and really swollen. I'm worried the snake got more venom into it than we had hoped."

"Let me see," Jakob said worriedly. "Oh dear, this is not good at all. I need to see if Mrs. VanDussen has anything to help. Clara -- wake up. Lizzy's hand is swollen, and we need to get her help before we cross the river today."

Clara quickly got a strip of cloth and some cold water and re-wrapped Lizzy's hand until Mrs. VanDussen arrived with her medicine bag.

"Oh no, I was worried about this," Mrs. VanDussen said. "I'm afraid we need to find a doctor in Davenport just as soon as we can. She needs more treatment than I can provide."

The original plan had been for the men from the four families to help each wagon across the river. They were camped very near a ferry crossing and had already arranged for their passage. But with Lizzy's serious illness, they all agreed that Jakob should make the trip across first and then rush her and the rest of the family into the city to a doctor.

After re-loading their wagons, the group lined up at the ferry, with Jakob at the front. The ferry-master, George Blakley, led the wagon onto the ferry and everyone climbed aboard. Jakob sat up front and tried to keep the oxen calm, while Clara was huddled in the back with the children. Lizzy was wrapped in a blanket, wedged between some boxes and the side of the cart. After assuring that everyone was situated, George confirmed that his team of horses were securely attached to the barge and then led them into the river. George had warned everyone that the river was running a bit high and fast due to some early warm weather and extra snow melting to the north. The ferry rocked from side to side as George tried to keep the horses focused on reaching the Iowa side of the river where his partner Albert Lee was working. Step by step, George guided the horses to deeper water. About halfway across the river, one of the horses stumbled and scared the rest of the team into frantic pawing and straining at the reins. Jakob's oxen reacted as well, and tried to pull the wagon from the ferry, which tipped precariously to one side. Water lapped over the side and drenched everyone on board. George was able to calm the horses, however, and they continued their slow trek toward the other side. After what seemed like an hour, the horses reached dry land and pulled the barge onto the shore. Albert was there to help unload the wagon from the ferry and to make sure everyone was safe.

It was then that Lizzy realized that this was the last time she would see Kurt or any of the other travelers. She stood up in the wagon and waved weakly back across the river toward her new friends. Jakob and the rest of the family did the same, and then he turned the wagon north in hopes of finding a doctor in Davenport.

Lizzy returned to her corner of the wagon and tried to get comfortable as they bounced along a rough and dusty trail toward the town. It was just a mile or so, and as soon as they entered the town, Jakob pulled the team up in front of a general store. Rushing inside, he frantically asked in German where they could find a doctor to help with Lizzy's snake bite. The shopkeeper didn't speak German, but one of the customers could speak a little and she said they were in luck, that the town doctor had an office upstairs. She told Jakob to pull his wagon around to the back and to bring Lizzy up the stairs to the second floor. Doc Parsons was usually in his office at this time of day. She said she would go with them to help interpret.

Jakob thanked her and rushed back to his family. Lizzy was slumped in a corner of the wagon and Clara believed she was running a fever. He pulled the wagon to the back of the building and after picking Lizzy up, carried her up the stairs. The woman from the shop downstairs was already there and talking to the doctor. After carefully examining Lizzy's hand, he took out a scalpel from his bag and disinfected it with whiskey. He asked if they knew what kind of snake it was, and Jakob said he thought it was a rattlesnake of some sort. The doctor made a small X across the wound and a copious amount of pus began draining. He gently cut away some skin that looked like it had been too badly damaged, and then applied a salve made of ground herbs and buckeye nuts. He explained what he was doing to the woman who translated for Jakob, although Lizzy found she could understand most of it.

"I've opened the wound so it could drain and then removed some dead skin. This salve I am applying is something I learned from the local Indians. I'll wrap the wound and give you some herbal tea for her to drink for at least the next two weeks. I'll put her arm in a splint, and she needs to keep it elevated as much as possible. Where are you folks headed?"

"The Minnesota Territory, near St. Paul," Jakob answered.

"That's quite a long journey. Stick to the main roads and don't hesitate to get more treatment for her if she doesn't improve in the next few days. You are one very lucky young lady, Lizzy. Rattlesnake bites are very serious."

"Thank you for your help," Lizzy said slowly in English. "Did I say that right?"

"You did great! Be sure to get lots of rest and drink plenty of water. I know the trip will be long and hard on you—I wish you well."

"How much do we owe you?" Lizzy boldly asked. "We have a little money."

"Only $1.00, " Doc Parsons said. "My parents were Irish immigrants, so I know how difficult this journey is for all of you."

Jakob pulled a small bag from his pocket and handed some coins to the doctor.

"Thank you," Jakob said in English, one of the few phrases he had learned. He fought back tears as he thought of how differently this situation could have ended.

"Good luck to you all," the doctor said as he watched Jakob lead Lizzy carefully down the stairs and into the waiting wagon below. He saw a woman in the back with several children and all their belongings.

"I hope Minnesota treats you well, my friends," he said as he closed his office door. He should have charged them much more than $1.00 for his treatment and medicine but didn't have the heart. They had already been through so much, with so much more to come in the days and years ahead.

Chapter 6

Using the directions he had received from a dock worker in Chicago, Jakob drove the wagon north a few miles through Davenport and then turned west. The plan was to continue west until they reached a well-traveled road that would go north into Minnesota. This leg of the journey was about 350 miles, which would take about four weeks if they didn't run into any trouble. This would have them arriving in Oliver's Grove at the end of April. Jakob hoped they could quickly find some land and he could even start a few crops this year.

Jakob pulled the wagon to a stop and turned around to address his family. He was nervous for the first time since they had left Germany.

"I wanted to stop and talk to you a bit, and explain again what the plan is, or was. My hope was to get us settled in or near the town of Oliver's Grove before the end of April. As you know, I have an old acquaintance, George Augustine, who moved there a few years ago and who recommended it as a great place for us. He has been looking for good pieces of land for us nearby and has narrowed it down to a couple for me to check out and then make the final decision. It's not much of a town–more of a township to be exact, without anything but a small trading post for the Indians and a tiny country church. George runs the lumber yard and has offered to let us stay with his family for a few months while we get settled and put up at least a bit of a shelter that would be sufficient until a better home can be built. However, after the events of the past few days and what has happened with Lizzy's hand, I feel that we need to be a bit more flexible with our schedule. Lizzy, if you start feeling worse, you have got to tell us right away. No more being brave, ok?"

"Yes, Father. I know how close I came to losing my hand or even my life. I'm sorry for the delays this might cause us–I know you are anxious to get a crop planted. I should have been more careful."

"Don't you worry about that–we'll figure something out. We just need you to be healthy! Ok, here we go–we'll go west about 150 miles and then turn north for the rest of the trip. I have no real way to contact George if we get delayed, but God has protected us this far, and I know he will protect us the rest of the way."

It was almost noon at this point, so they were only able to travel about 10 miles before they reached a nice place to stop for the night. Parking near a stream, there was plenty of water and grass for the oxen and a quiet place for them to rest. Jakob went looking for firewood while Clara got a few things ready for dinner. Lizzy sat off to the side with her hand elevated on the side of the wagon.

"I feel so helpless," Lizzy complained. "I should be helping you make our camp comfortable or fixing dinner. Why did this have to happen now?"

"Lizzy, it is not up to us to know God's plans, but I do know that I have been praising him all day for keeping you as safe as possible and thanking Him for having Kurt with you. I hate to think what would have happened if you had been alone!"

Soon the fire was going, and Clara had hung a pot in which she was boiling some dried beef and vegetables. "Jakob," she said quietly, "I believe we have enough food for the four weeks to our new home, but if we have any delays we will need to stop along the way. Do we have much money left?"

"There is a bit, beside what I have saved to purchase our land. I hope the price has not increased since the last time I heard from George."

"I have a few dollars, Father," Lizzy said. "At least let me pay for any more doctors or medicines, ok? It's the least I can do."

"I'm sure it won't come to that, Lizzy. How is your hand feeling? Did you have that herbal tea Doc Parsons gave you?"

"I'm just now fixing it for her, Jakob," Clara said. "I looked at her wound earlier and it is so much better than this morning. Finding that doctor was such a Godsend. Lizzy, drink this, then gather the children around for dinner. Make sure they wash their hands."

The soup and bread were sufficient to fill their hungry stomachs, and as they finished, a chilly wind started blowing from the north. Jakob quickly put several logs on the fire while Clara helped to get the children situated in the wagon. Wrapping each in a warm blanket, she spoke softly as she made them as comfortable as possible. She helped Lizzy brush her long hair and then re-wrap her hand.

"How is it feeling tonight? Do you hurt anywhere else?"

"It's so much better than before. I will confess, I was pretty scared this morning. When the doctor cut it open, so much fluid rushed out. I almost fainted."

"I am so thankful he was in his office and able to help you. I know this is not comfortable for you at all, with all the boxes and supplies, and then all the children trying to rest. I promise when we get our new home, I will find a way for you to have a room or space of your own. It might not be large, but I know it's time you had some privacy. You will be turning eighteen soon—where has the time gone?"

Once the children were situated, Clara fixed a pallet on the ground for her and Jakob, using the wagon as a bit of a shelter.

"It's not the most comfortable bed, I'm afraid, " Clara whispered. "But at least the ground is dry and it's not horribly cold."

"I want so much more for you Clara," Jakob said tenderly. "For you and all our children. Just a few more weeks, and we'll have warm beds and a roof over our heads. I am so thankful that George is allowing us to stay with him!"

"Yes, a real bed would be wonderful. So many weeks sleeping on the ground has been difficult, especially since …"

"Since what?" Jakob asked.

Clara hesitated a minute and then said, "since the weather has been so cold."

Lizzy had a hard time falling asleep and listened to the whispered conversation below her. Her hand was getting better but was still quite swollen and stiff. And every muscle hurt from so many miles bouncing roughly along in the wagon. She ached for a real bed, for warm water to take a real bath and wash her hair, and for some semblance of normalcy again. But how long had it been since she felt normal? She wasn't sure.

Chapter 7

The days quickly fell into the rhythm of an early breakfast, about seven hours of travel, and setting up camp near a stream or small lake. After six days, they reached the bustling town of Iowa City, which was the new state capitol. Lizzy's hand was doing well, but Jakob knew he would feel better for the last leg of their journey if he found a doctor to look at her again. He still did not know enough English to have a lengthy conversation with anyone, so Lizzy volunteered to ask for directions.

The wagon pulled up alongside a well-dressed woman in a carriage waiting outside a hardware store. "Excuse me, but could you direct me to a doctor?" Lizzy asked carefully.

"Yes, of course," the woman answered. "The closest doctor is just two blocks down and to your left. His office is next to the new post office. Are you not from around here?"

"No, we are on our way to Minnesota. We have just come from Germany."

"Wow—you have come a very long way. Is someone sick? Doctor Nilan is a very nice doctor."

"I hurt my hand last week. We just wanted someone to look at it again. I'm still learning English—I hope you can understand?"

"You did great. I pray your hand is better and that you have a safe trip to your new home." Just then a man came out from the store and climbed into the carriage. "This family is on their way to Minnesota," the woman told him.

"More stupid immigrants!" the man fumed under his breath. "Soon this country will be over-run with them! I don't know why the government doesn't send them back to where they belong!" and he drove away quickly, as if he was afraid just talking to Lizzy would make them sick.

Lizzy was shocked at the man's attitude. "Maybe I misunderstood him," she thought to herself, still unsure of her English skills.

"What did they say?" Jakob asked.

Still a bit rattled, Lizzy gave him the directions to the doctor, but kept the rest of the conversation to herself.

After finding the doctor's office, Lizzy asked Clara to come inside with her. Somehow, she was nervous about leaving everyone in the wagon without Jakob to watch for trouble. This was the first time since their long ship ride that she had been afraid of the people here. What if that man came back and started yelling at Clara and the other kids? No, she wanted Jakob to watch out for them.

Doctor Nilan was as nice as the woman had said he would be. He was patient with Lizzy's halting English and was pleased with the treatment she had already received.

"It looks to be healing nicely," he said as he applied some more ointment and re-wrapped her hand. "Whoever did the original treatment did just the right things. You are a very lucky young lady."

"Thank you," Lizzy answered. "We all know that God was watching out for us."

"Well, I'm not sure about it being God, but I think this should heal without any lasting effects. Of course, continue the same treatments you have been doing and keep it elevated as much as possible. Do you still have some of the tea left?"

"I have enough for three more days–do I need more?" Lizzy asked.

"Probably not, but to be safe, let me give you enough for another week. You should be as good as new before long. Where in Minnesota are you going?"

"Near St. Paul–Father has friends who are helping us purchase land and start our new life."

"That's a lovely area, but all of Minnesota is. It does get awfully cold there in the winter–I hope you are all settled by then."

"We just spent the last winter in Chicago," she answered, "so I'm getting used to cold."

"Chicago? Now *that's* a cold place. Hopefully Minnesota will be better."

"Do I owe you anything?" Lizzy asked.

"I didn't really do much, so how about fifty cents?"

"That sounds fine," Lizzy said as she handed him the money from her pocket. "We all appreciate your help today."

"Lizzy, may I ask you one more question?"

Instantly nervous, considering the recent interaction with the man in the carriage, she said "Yes, of course."

"Are there any other men travelling with you besides your father? I ask because, well, I don't want to scare you, but there have been some incidents lately with the Indians and I am hoping you will be safe the rest of your trip."

"No, it's just Father and my younger brother. But we are staying on the main roads, even though it is making our trip a bit longer. And I know how to shoot a gun."

"OK, well, just be careful. I would feel better if you were travelling as part of a group."

"Thank you, Doctor. God will take care of us."

Chapter 8

Lizzy's hand continued to improve, and the group made their way northward through the towns of Cedar Rapids, Waterloo, and Charles City. According to Jakob's map, they were just a few miles away from the Minnesota Territory line. They had driven through many lovely towns and amazing farmland just waiting to be tilled, but Jakob kept pushing them north. About ten miles from the border, they stopped in the small village of St. Ansgar. Lizzy and Clara went into the general store to pick up a few needed items, and Jakob stayed in the wagon to watch the younger children. Even though the town was small, there were a lot of people milling around, including families with children but also numerous Indians. Jakob had not seen many up close and was interested in how they would conduct themselves. Based on the stories he had heard, he expected them to be in buckskin and brandishing axes and arrows and covered in war paint. This group, however, was dressed in western clothes and speaking some basic English. He kept his guard up, though, not feeling like he could totally trust them.

Lizzy looked longingly at the bolts of fabric stacked against the back wall of the store. She tried to smooth the wrinkles from her stained dress, wishing she had something–anything–new to wear. How long had it been? All her things were getting small, and the few things that fit were worn out. She dreaded the thought of trying to make friends in her new neighborhood with such old and ragged clothes.

"I understand, Lizzy," Clara said softly. "All of you children are needing new clothes, and poor Jakob's pants are about worn clean through. I'm hoping that the homestead doesn't take all our money so there is some left for new clothing and shoes."

"You need new things as well, Clara. I've noticed how badly your shoes are looking, and your dresses are so faded."

"Thank you, dear. But as parents we always put the children first."

Clara purchased a little bit of flour and two pounds of smoked bacon, and then they returned to the wagon.

"I'm hoping to camp in Minnesota tonight," Jacob said, "so we best get going. Did you find everything you need?"

"Yes, they were well stocked with a little bit of everything. If we weren't headed to Oliver's Grove, I think this would be a good place to settle."

Jacob helped Clara into the wagon as Lizzy climbed into the back with the three other children. "Here we go—the last leg of our big adventure!" Jakob cheered. "I know it's been a rough journey for all of you, but it's almost over."

It wasn't long before they noticed a crudely carved sign along the side of the road. "Entering Minnesota Territory." Jakob pulled the wagon to a halt and led the family in a prayer of thanksgiving and protection.

Three days later the wagon came to a stop in front of the Oliver's Grove trading post. Jakob let out a huge sigh of relief, then climbed down to stretch a bit. He had really pushed everyone the past few days -- he felt that time was passing, and it would soon be too late to plant a crop this year.

He had Lizzy go inside with him in case he needed help with his English. They had been practicing in the evenings, but there was still so much he did not know how to say.

"Hello, " Lizzy said to the shopkeeper. "We have just arrived in town and are looking for directions to our friend George Augustine's farm. Do you happen to know him?"

"Are you the Kruse family? George stopped by here a few days ago and left a letter for you. He said you were coming from Germany? Welcome!"

"Yes, thank you." She took the letter and handed it to her father. He opened the envelope and saw a roughly drawn map that would lead them east from town towards his farm. Jakob thanked the owner and headed back to the wagon.

"Only another 10 miles!" Jakob said cheerfully, as he urged the oxen forward. "Thank you, Lord, for all Your provisions of safety and good weather. We know there is much hard work ahead of us but are grateful for Your faithfulness."

"Amen," the rest of the family said. It wasn't long before the wagon came to rest in front of a large rock and wooden house with a nice barn beside it. Inside a fenced area were two milk cows and a few sheep and chickens. Off in the distance they could see a man working a plow with a team of horses. There was a newly cultivated garden with the beginnings of spring crops emerging. Jakob had a broad smile on his face as he surveyed his friend's farm and had visions of his own in the near future. They heard the screen door slam as a stout woman came rushing out, wiping her hands on her apron.

"Jakob! So good to see you again!" she said in German. "It has been such a long time."

"Yes, a very long time. How are you doing?"

"It's tough, I won't lie to you. But it is very fulfilling to have a place of our own to invest in the future of our children and the future of Minnesota. There is talk of it becoming a state soon, which will bring us more protection by a state militia and improved roads and services. I know George has a lot to talk to you about and will show you the properties that are available. Our hope is that you will find something close to us—it's been a bit lonely without other German families within ten miles."

"I am hoping that as well," Jakob said. "Clara, children— this is Marie Augustine, George's wife. Marie, this is Clara my wife, along with Lizzy, Adam, Rosina, and Hannah. We are so grateful that you are letting us stay with you for a bit while I get us situated and a home built."

"We are thrilled to have you! I'll let George know you are here, and it will be time for dinner before long. Everyone, come inside and freshen up. I remember from our trip here how I longed for a hot bath and a warm meal!" She then stepped to the edge of the porch and rang a large bell. The sound carried to the far pasture where George heard it and turned toward the house. Seeing the wagon and all the family, he raised his arms in a big wave and started to bring the team of horses towards the barn.

"I'll go help him," Jakob said. "It will be good to see what he is doing and planting."

Marie led the rest of the family inside where they were greeted by the delicious smell of fresh bread and the comforts of chairs with cushions and a carpeted floor.

"Adam, is it?" Marie said to Lizzy's brother. "Would you mind filling this bucket with water from the pump outside? I'm sure everyone would like a chance to clean up. Clara–let me show you and Lizzy around and we'll figure out where everyone can sleep. It will be a bit crowded for a while, with all of you and our own three children, but we'll make it work."

"Where are your children now?" Clara asked.

"They are at school–can you believe it? It just opened this past fall. Grades first through eighth all in one room, and it's about a mile to the north. The teacher does not speak German, and our children speak little English, so it is a struggle, but we are thankful."

"How wonderful," Clara smiled. "It will be good to send the younger children when they are old enough. Perhaps they might let Adam attend for a year or two?"

"I'm not sure, but we can ask."

Adam returned with the water and Marie put it on the stove to heat. She gave Clara and the children a brief tour of the house. There were four bedrooms and a sitting room that could be converted to a sleeping space as well.

"I figured George and I would stay in our room, and you and Jakob could take the other one here on the main floor," Marie told Clara. "Then we could put the little girls in one room upstairs and the younger boys in the other. Adam, perhaps you could stay in the sitting room and Lizzy, I have a surprise for you."

They climbed the stairs to the second story where there were two large bedrooms and a long storage area that ran along one side.

"I thought maybe you might want to convert this storage closet into a room for yourself. I know what it's like to be your age and to want a bit of privacy. If not, there is room for you with the other girls."

"Thank you, Frau Augustine," Lizzy said. "An area for myself would be wonderful, but not if it causes any trouble."

"First off, please call me Marie. We're going to be living together for a while, so there's no need for formalities. Secondly, it's no trouble at all. We can move beds around and make pallets on the floor if needed."

"Thank you, Marie. It does sound lovely."

They heard men's voices downstairs and the sound of laughter. How long had it been since Lizzy had heard her father enjoying himself with conversation and sounding so relaxed?

Before long, the Augustine children came home from school - Fred, Sebastian, and Sarah. Soon the house was overflowing with voices, and Lizzy was happy to be around so many friendly people.

After everyone had a chance to wash up a bit, Clara and Marie started dinner and the men went to the dining table to discuss business. Lizzy took the opportunity to explore outside and soon found herself sitting on a hay bale in the barn, playing with a litter of kittens. She had always wanted a cat—maybe George and Marie would let her keep one, once they moved to their own place? A yellow striped kitten curled up on her lap and proceeded to take a nap, while another tried to untie the laces of her boots. She loved the smell of a barn and animals and hay–her mother had laughed at her about this when she was a small girl. Mother–how she missed her. Clara was nice and all, and she was glad Father found someone to help with his loneliness and to raise the children. But Lizzy wished her own mother had been able to be here.

"Lizzy, where are you?" Clara called. "Dinner is almost ready."

Lizzy stepped out of the barn and into the crisp evening air. Minnesota was so different from any place she had ever lived. Was this really her new home now? What would the rest of her life be like living here? How soon before she was married with babies of her own? She would be eighteen in just a few months–the age that her friends back home would be settling down and forging their own lives. How was she going to do that here, in a new country, with a new life?

Chapter 9

While dinner was cooking, the men and boys unloaded the wagon and took the oxen to the barn. Lizzy unpacked her meager belongings and tried to fashion a bed for herself in the storage closet. It wasn't much, but she had room to stretch out her legs for the first time since they had left Chicago. And she comforted herself that this too was temporary, and soon they would have their own home and she would have her own room with her own bed.

Downstairs again, she went into the kitchen to witness a whispered conversation between Clara and Marie, with Clara near tears. She had rarely seen Clara cry, so she rushed to her side.

"Are you ok, Clara? What happened?"

"I was just explaining to Marie that I feel so badly that we have invaded them with so many people and so little to offer. We are down to the last of our food, and of course we have no money to help pay for anything. I just feel like such an imposition."

Marie clasped Clara's hands in hers and said, "My dear, new friend. What you have given us is sufficient. We have all been placed on this earth to help others. When we first arrived here, we had only what we brought with us, but God provided helpers for us. Now we are able to help others and are thrilled to do so. And if I may be so bold, when are you going to tell him?"

"Him? Jakob? What do you mean?"

"Yes, Jakob. Does he know that you are expecting?"

Lizzy's eyes went wide as Clara admitted, "No, he doesn't know. I didn't have the heart to tell him while we were on the road. He already had enough to worry about. How did you know?"

"You just have that look, I guess, and a familiar way you walk. But it was especially dangerous to travel in your condition, with all the rough roads and other dangers. How far along are you?"

"I'm three months, I think. I know it was dangerous, but it was worth the risk. I just could not add that stress onto him these past weeks."

Lizzy gave Clara a quick hug and then helped carry food to the dining room. Jakob and George had found every chair and box they could, so they could all sit together. Eleven people gathered around the table to give thanks for the bountiful food, for safe travel, and for friendship. After the prayer was over, Marie nudged Clara and gave her a wink. Clara cleared her throat and stood to her feet.

"There is one more thing to be thankful for. Jakob, we'll be adding a new member to our family this fall."

Jakob almost dropped the platter of meat he was holding. "What did you say? A new member? Are you…?"

"Yes, dear husband. We are having another baby before Christmas."

Everyone cheered as Jakob gave his wife a tender hug. "Why didn't you tell me sooner? All those miles we travelled—all those nights sleeping on the ground under the wagon. It must have been so uncomfortable for you!"

Dinner was a noisy affair with the four adults and seven children talking and laughing at the same time. Lizzy ate until she felt her stomach would burst—the first time she was truly full since Christmas dinner in Chicago. It was only four months ago but seemed like years. So much had happened in such a short time.

Lizzy helped clear the table while Clara and Marie washed the dishes. It was almost dark, and George was lighting a few oil lamps. The little girls rushed upstairs to play, and Adam was telling the other boys about life in Germany and their trip to Minnesota. Marie pulled Lizzy off to one side.

"Now that things are calming down, would you like me to fix a hot bath for you? We can set the wash tub up in my bedroom and you would have total privacy. I have some lavender soap that I got at the trading post last week, and if you are anything like me, a warm bath and a chance to wash my hair would be heavenly."

"Oh, Marie! Yes, that would be amazing. How kind of you to ask."

"I also have a few clothes you can borrow until we get a chance to make you more. How about a nightgown and a different dress for tomorrow? I usually do laundry on Monday, but since we have a double batch now, I don't think the Lord would mind that I washed on Saturday, too. I do hope you are planning to attend church with us in the morning. We just got a new pastor and although the attendance is small, the people are friendly."

"Marie, you are so good to us. You are truly a blessing from God. Yes, I am sure Father will want all of us at church, probably in the front row."

"Let me get the water heated and I'll let you know when it's ready. You will have total privacy and can stay in as long as you wish."

Lizzy let down her braids and brushed her long auburn hair until Marie called her again. She gently opened the bedroom door to find a large wash tub in the middle of the room, along with soap and towels. Laying on the bed was a lovely cotton nightgown and robe. Marie gave her a hug and then left the room, pulling the door tightly behind her. Lizzy heard her instruct everyone to stay out and to leave Lizzy alone. How sweet of her.

Lizzy removed her clothes and gingerly climbed into the tub. The water was quite warm–almost too hot -- but felt so wonderful on her tired and aching body. She slid down until the water was almost to her chin, then she dunked her head under. How she wanted to stay like that forever!

But of course, she knew she couldn't, and after a brief soak she washed her hair and then climbed from the tub to dry off with the fluffiest towel she had seen since the hotel in Chicago, and then slipped into Marie's nightgown. Lizzy couldn't help but be a bit envious of all of Marie's nice things. Life must really be treating them well here in Oliver's Grove.

Leaving the bedroom, she handed her laundry to Clara and thanked Marie again for the wonderful bath. The little girls were already in bed when she climbed the stairs and then stretched out in her little separate space. Minnesota–finally they were here and getting settled. She was content and comfortable and could not help but feel excited about the future.

Chapter 10

Lizzy awoke to the sound of a rooster crowing just outside the bedroom window. One of her favorite things to do each morning was to listen to the sounds and try to recognize any new smells. This morning, she smelled bread and bacon, along with something different --- cinnamon? Even though they had been here for less than twenty-four hours, she had learned that Marie was an excellent cook and Lizzy was hoping to learn from her.

Lizzy came from her little 'closet' to find that everyone else was up and downstairs already. Noisy conversations, laughter, and the rattling of dishes were mixed in a way that she was sure would become very familiar. Lizzy skipped down the stairs and into the dining room. She wished she had a nicer dress to wear–she felt bad going to church this morning wearing such a tattered and ill-fitting frock.

"I hope you slept well?" Clara asked as Lizzy pulled a chair up to the table. "I wish we had a real mattress for you to sleep on. Hopefully we can fix one for you at the new house."

"It's fine, Clara, really. I loved being able to stretch out and not be bumping into boxes or flour sacks or other children!"

"Lizzy, dear, could you come into the bedroom for a moment?" Marie called from the front of the house.

"Of course," Lizzy answered. She walked into the bedroom to find Marie arranging several dresses across her bed.

"I believe you and I are close to the same size. I could not help but notice while doing laundry yesterday just how worn and tattered most of your things are. Would you be interested in borrowing any of these for church today? I think the yellow one would look especially lovely on you this perfect spring morning."

"Really? It's lovely–but I don't want to …"

"Yes, I want you to have it. It doesn't fit me quite right anymore and would be perfect for you. Hurry, though–the men are about ready to load up the buggies."

Marie left the room and Lizzy quickly changed into the yellow pinafore. The dress was edged with white eyelet lace and looked simply stunning on her. She left the bedroom and started to climb into the back of their wagon.

"Oh, no, you don't–not in that beautiful dress!" Clara exclaimed. "You need to sit up front with Father and I."

"You knew about this?" Lizzy asked.

"Of course. Marie talked to me about it yesterday while we were doing laundry. She truly is a lovely woman."

"Yes, she is. This is the prettiest dress I have ever worn."

The drive to the church was quite short, and Jakob helped Clara down from the wagon. "Help your sister down, Adam," he said sternly. "Don't let anything happen to that dress!"

Adam came up next to Lizzy and teasingly said, "Let me help you, Fraulein Elizabeth!" He held his hand up to help her and she gave him a smirk.

'Don't be rude—we don't know these people. Please don't make a bad impression on them!"

Lizzy walked into the tiny country church to see the Augustine family already settled in the front pew and Father was lining their group up in the row behind. Someone was playing the piano and there were about 35 other people in attendance—mostly families with young children. There were a few people her age, though. The pastor walked to the front of the church, and everyone found a seat and waited for the service to begin.

Lizzy watched the man playing the piano and soon realized that he was probably the best pianist she had ever heard. How she wished she had been able to take lessons when she was younger. Everyone stood to sing a few songs, then the pastor stepped behind the pulpit to begin his sermon about loving your neighbor. He was quite a young man and Lizzy wondered how long he had been a minister. She also noticed that the pianist had left the piano and was now sitting on a chair next to it so he could see the pastor. He looked to be in his late 20's or early 30's and had dark brown hair and large brown eyes. He was nicely dressed, but not overly so. She tried to focus on what the preacher was saying but felt like she was being watched. She glanced toward the piano and found the man looking at her. Their eyes met for a brief moment, and he smiled. She blushed and went back to reading her Bible. The sermon was in English, and she wanted to use the time practicing her new language skills. But honestly, she was not listening to a word that was said.

At the conclusion of the sermon, the pastor announced that there would be a picnic next week after church, and then welcomed Jakob and the family as new residents from Germany. Lizzy felt very self-conscious as everyone stared at them, but she was extremely glad she had on Marie's dress and that her hair was neatly braided. As people started to leave, she walked to the wagon but felt a hand touch her arm.

"Hello –I think I heard your name is Lizzy, right? My name is Henry, Henry Sauter. You have recently come from Germany? I immigrated here myself just two years ago."

"Hello, Henry. My name is Hattie Elizabeth, but everyone calls me Lizzy. Where in Germany did you come from?"

"Berlin. I played in the symphony there and gave private lessons–not just piano but also French horn and trumpet."

"Oh, that is so interesting. I always wanted to learn to play piano, but my family could not afford it."

"I would be honored to give you lessons, if you are still interested."

"Thank you for the offer, but I'm sure that's not possible right now. Perhaps sometime in the future after we have had a chance to get established."

"I would like that. Well, I see your family is about to leave. I hope to see you next week?"

"I believe so. We will be living with the Augustines for a while until we purchase land, and our home is ready."

"See you next week, then," he said as he politely bowed, and then he helped her into the wagon.

On the way home, Clara said softly, "He looks like a nice young man. And he seems very intelligent and talented."

"Yes, he seems to be," Lizzy said with a slight flush to her cheeks. She had never really felt like this before, not even after Kurt saved her from the snake. No, this was different—a more mature attraction. She was anxious for the next Sunday to come.

After a large Sunday dinner, Jakob called his family to the dining room for a discussion. He wanted to share with them the land that George had told him about and ask their opinion about the two best options. The first was fifty acres about a mile away from the Augustines with a small stream and lots of timber. There would be plenty of wood for a nice log home, but quite a bit of clearing would be needed before they could plant crops or a garden. The price for this was 75 cents per acre. The second property was 35 acres with not as many trees, so the land would be easier to clear and plant. There was a tiny creek at the far west side of the property—the farthest from the timber. The soil was about the same in both places—fertile looking but filled with hundreds of small rocks that would need to be picked up before planting could begin. No wonder they had seen so many rock fences and barns and houses! Rocks were everywhere! The cost for this land was $1.00 per acre.

"We have the money for either property," he continued, "so that will not be the determining factor. Clara, I would like to take you, Lizzy, and Adam out to visit both places. Marie said she would watch the smaller children. I have an opinion but would like your input."

"Of course, Father," Lizzy said. "Although the decision is totally yours."

They loaded into the wagon and drove to the first property— the fifty acres of mostly timber.

"I've been meaning to ask, Father. What are those white trees with the bark peeling off? They are everywhere here."

"Those are called White Birch and only grow here in the north. The wood is pretty good for building things, and the bark is a great fire starter. I understand deer and moose eat the bark and leaves, and the Indians have ways to weave the bark together into boxes and even clothing."

"Well, this parcel of land sure has a lot of them," Lizzy said. "I think it's lovely, but an awful lot of work to clear them all before planting fields."

"Pretty tough work," Adam agreed.

The smaller property with more open farmland was beautiful and got Lizzy's vote right away. "Would you put the house near the stream, Father, or closer to the stand of trees?"

"Probably near the edge of the trees. They would provide shade in the summer and protection in the winter. I just hope we can find water close by and not have to haul it too far."

"Well, I know it's not up to me, but I think I prefer this one. Although there are many more rocks, I just like the lay of the land better."

"Adam, your thoughts?"

"I agree–this place just has a better feel about it. The number of trees on the other place was a bit overwhelming."

"I'm glad you both agree. Clara?"

"This one is great, as long as we can find water. I'm not up to hauling it from the other side of the field every day for the rest of our lives."

"Then we are in agreement–this is the new Kruse homestead! I need to go into St. Paul next week to file the deed, but I prefer this place as well. We just need to pray that we can find a well quickly and then we can start planting."

The next hour was spent deciding on a place for the house and barn and imagining their first harvest. Jakob and Clara already had a rough plan drawn for the house and were pleased to see that since the land was relatively flat, it would be fairly easy to build. Adam picked up some rocks and they marked out the approximate location for the house and outbuildings. It was finally becoming real to Lizzy, and she could not help but be excited.

"Our first challenge will be to move enough of these rocks that we can plant a garden and get at least a small crop of hay and corn in the field," Jakob continued. "Then we need to start on a house. I worry that it won't be livable before fall, which means a whole year with George and Marie. I am exceedingly thankful for their help but hate imposing on them for so long."

"What if we build something small to start with," Lizzy asked, "enough for us to live in but then could be used for chickens or sheep after we build something bigger? That way, we would not be overstaying our welcome quite so much."

"I like that idea, Lizzy," Clara said. "Marie is a wonderful woman, but living with them for a year and not being able to contribute financially makes me very uncomfortable. However, we would be very crowded again–and I know I promised you your own room."

"Clara, you are ok with this, even with the baby coming?" Jakob asked with worry in his voice. "This would be awfully primitive living with a new baby."

"I'm sure it will be fine. What have women done for the past thousands of years?"

"OK, it's settled. Let's get back and I'll plan to get to St. Paul as soon as possible."

Chapter 11

Jacob left the next morning for his trip to St. Paul to purchase the 35-acre parcel of land. It would take him two or three days to get there and back, and this was the first time for him to be away from his family that long. He wasn't sure what all would be involved at the land office, so planned to stay overnight and also pick up some much-needed supplies with any leftover money he had. George promised him that everyone would be fine, and that they would celebrate when he got home with the deed.

The women kept themselves busy with cooking and washing for the seven children, and Clara continued with plans for the new home. She also discussed with Marie what crops she could plant this late in the spring at the new property, once they got the rocks moved and the land plowed. Marie suggested lettuce and squash–both would grow well in the newly-tilled soil.

Each morning while Jakob was away, George drove all the children to the new property, and they started moving rocks, piling them along what would be the fence rows and near the new house. It was a bit of a risk to do a lot of work on property they did not officially own yet, but neither man wanted to waste productive time. "These will be perfect for steps up into the house and also flower beds," George told them. Each day they worked until it started getting warm and the littlest ones were tired, and then he drove them back to his farm. After lunch he worked in his own fields with Adam helping.

On the third day, George broke a piece of his plow and sent Adam into the barn for some tools. Just as he was about to enter, Adam noticed some movement along the back wall. Peering inside, he saw three Indians rummaging through the toolbox, removing an axe and some rope.

"Hey! What are you doing?" he yelled at them in German. "Get out of here!"

The Indian closest to him jumped to his feet and pulled a gun from his leather belt. Aiming at Adam, he pulled the trigger. Suddenly, Adam felt intense pain in his shoulder. The other Indians started yelling but grabbed a few other tools and ran out the back of the barn. Adam fell to the ground as blood poured from his wound. George heard the commotion and was soon at his side. He scooped Adam into his arms and then carried him quickly toward the house.

"Marie! Clara!" George yelled. "Adam has been hurt— hurry!"

Marie was the first out the door, with Clara and Lizzy close behind.

"Bring him inside quickly," Marie ordered. "Was that a gunshot we heard? What happened?"

"It was Indians," Adam whispered, feeling weak from the loss of blood. "They were trying to steal things from the barn when I found them."

"Fred, run and get my medical bag," Marie said urgently. "We've got to make sure the bullet is out so we can stop the bleeding. Sebastian–put some water on to boil. Hurry!"

George carried Adam inside and sat him in a chair in the kitchen. Marie pulled a chair up next to him and gently started exploring the shoulder wound. Lizzy kept her arm around Clara while the younger children stood in the corner of the room, their eyes wide with fear.

Fred quickly appeared with the medical bag, and Marie pulled out a small knife and some rolls of gauze. "How is the water, Sebastian?" she called into the kitchen. "Lizzy, go help him and bring me a bowl of cool water for now."

Adam was trying to be brave, but the pain in his shoulder was excruciating. "George–put him on the floor and prop up his feet–he's losing too much blood."

Marie gently cleaned the wound with the cool water Lizzy brought and was pleased to see that the bullet was not lodged in the shoulder but had passed clean through. She packed the wound with gauze as Lizzy squeezed Adam's other hand and told him how brave he was. Rosina brought a pillow from the sofa and propped it under his head. Sebastian arrived with a bowl of warm water and George helped hold Adam down while Marie attempted to irrigate the area. She then poured in some strong-smelling liquid that Lizzy did not recognize, and Adam yelled in pain.

"I've done all I can do, I'm afraid," Marie said to Clara. "He really needs to see a doctor, but I don't know who to send. George needs to be here in case the Indians come back, and it's not safe to send Lizzy by herself, plus it's much too far. We just need to pray that Jakob gets back soon."

As if in an answer to prayer, the rumble of a wagon was heard coming down the road. Lizzy rushed outside to tell Jakob what had happened. He bounded up the steps and ran in to find his only son lying in a pool of blood on the dining room floor.

"What do you need me to do?" he asked, his words directed at no one in particular. "Adam, are you ok?"

"It's a pretty serious wound, Jakob," Marie answered. "I've done all I can, but he really needs a doctor."

"Where is the closest one? Is there one in town?"

"No," George interrupted. "The closest one is several towns away. There is a doctor who will be moving here soon, but he is not set up yet. But I know of someone who lives nearby that I think can help. Marie–you know who I mean, right?"

"Yes, but are you sure? It's pretty risky."

"Risky? How?" Clara asked. "What are you talking about? Just do whatever you need to do to save our son."

"It's risky because he is a runaway slave. He's been hiding at the Baker's farm for the past several months. His name is Amos and if he gets caught, he'll be sent back to Missouri where they won't be kind to him."

"But why him?" Jakob asked. "Is there no one else?"

"I'm afraid not. I only suggest him now because we need help quick, and he is the only one in the area who is qualified."

"Qualified? How?" Lizzy asked.

"He was a medicine man for his tribe back in Africa. He used his skills while enslaved in Missouri and has even helped a few times here locally. There really is no other option, I'm afraid. Do you have an issue with a black man, a runaway slave, trying to save your son?"

Jakob and Clara glanced at each other, both struggling to know what the right thing was. Lizzy pleaded with them to save Adam, no matter the ethics involved. Clara nodded her agreement, and Jakob asked George to bring Amos over as soon as he could.

"I'll take your wagon, Jakob, since it's already hitched. Everyone, stay inside until I get back. Wish me luck."

George rushed to the wagon and urged the oxen back into service. Lizzy was so conflicted–she had never seen a black man up close before, certainly not one who had been a slave. She had always believed that slavery was wrong but had not anticipated that the issue would appear at her front door. Would knowingly having a runaway slave in the home put all of them in danger as well?

Marie and Clara tried to keep Adam comfortable while Jakob kept watch at the door. Knowing that Indians had been on this property was upsetting enough, but the fact that they would try to kill his son made him very angry. How he wished he could chase after them and give them a piece of their own medicine!

It wasn't long before they heard the wagon returning. Marie ordered all the younger children to go upstairs to their rooms. Jakob went to the door to find George with a very tall man wrapped in a blanket climbing down from the wagon. Once inside, he took off the blanket and Lizzy found herself just feet away from a very dark-skinned black man. They walked quickly into the dining room, and Amos knelt beside Adam to examine the wound.

Seeing the concerned look in everyone's eyes George said, "Friends, this is Amos. I'm very grateful that he has agreed to come here tonight and see if he can help Adam."

"Hello," Lizzy said boldly in English. "Please, can you help my brother?"

"I'll sure try ma'am," he said softly. His big hands were gentle as he probed Adam's injury, and then he reached into a jacket pocket for a bottle of liquid medicine. He washed the wound and then asked George to sterilize a needle for him. Once the needle was ready, Amos pulled a piece of thread from a small bag and made a few stitches deep in the wound, and then a few more on both the front and the back of the shoulder. He then dressed the wound and put Adam's arm in a sling. Adam tried to be brave, but it was obvious that he was in tremendous pain.

"Let me get you back home, Amos," George said, "before it gets much later. I'll tell you all more of his story when I get back, OK?"

"How can we thank you?" Jakob asked tearfully. "Is there any way we can help?"

"I have a little bit of money," Lizzy whispered. "It's all I have but will never be enough to thank you for saving my brother."

"I am just happy to help. I don't need your money, but thank you," Amos replied softly. "Yes, George, we had better be going."

"Thank you," Adam whispered. Amos squeezed his hand, and then he wrapped himself again in the blanket and climbed into the wagon.

"I'll be back soon, and then we will talk," George said as he walked out the door. "I know all of you have questions, and this is something we wanted to tell you, just not quite so soon."

The sounds of the departing wagon faded into the early spring evening. Lizzy and Jakob silently stared at each other while Clara sat next to Adam on the floor and cradled him in her lap. Marie went to the kitchen for more water and rags and began scrubbing the blood from the floor. Lizzy rose to help her, but Marie motioned for her to get a drink for Adam and then to go check on the younger children. When Lizzy returned, they had gotten Adam into a chair, and he was drinking an herbal tea similar to what she'd had after the snake bite. Jakob was pacing back and forth, peering out windows to look for any sign of George's return, or perhaps more Indians, or both. Looking at his family—his wife in tears, his son injured, and his other children in hiding -- maybe he had made a huge mistake coming here. And now there was the knowledge of a runaway slave living nearby. Perhaps he wasn't cut out for life in such a rugged and hostile place.

They heard the wagon return, and George went straight to the barn to unhitch the oxen and bed them before entering the house.

Gathering the others around him, George said "I know this has been a very strange experience for you. Since you just recently arrived here in America, I'm not sure how much you know about the country's slavery situation. Emotions are running high on both sides, and no one knows how it is going to be resolved."

"We've heard a bit," Jakob said. "It is something that none of us would condone or support. That is one of the reasons I insisted we move this far north and away from areas that are more intolerant."

"I'm glad we agree on this issue. Have you ever heard of the Underground Railroad?" Judging by the puzzled looks on their faces, it was obvious that they had not. "The Underground Railroad is a group of people spread across the country that aids slaves in escaping and making their way into safe areas. I heard it was started by a runaway slave. There are abolitionists scattered along select highways or rivers that will hide the slaves and assist in passage to the next safe area. The Bakers are part of the Underground Railroad, and so are we."

Chapter 12

"Tell us more about this railroad," Jakob said. "What all is involved? And does it put both my family and yours in danger?"

"Absolutely," George said. "If we were caught harboring or aiding a runaway, it would be very serious. But knowing you were coming, and not being totally sure of your beliefs in this matter, I asked the Bakers to take over our share of the duties, at least until I had a chance to talk to you. Obviously, I did not want you involved in any way at this time."

"So, how do the slaves get away, and get this far north?" Lizzy asked.

"Most of the ones we have seen managed to stow away on riverboats and then escaped into St. Paul. There are a lot of free blacks in the territory, and one of them works as a barber and who is instrumental in our cause. He helps to get them out of town, and they are led to us here in the country where we assist them on their way to Canada."

"When was the last time you helped someone?" Lizzy continued with her questions, finding the topic so interesting.

"We actually had a mother and her young son here just a month ago. Amos arrived about the same time, but he has already helped several supporters with medical issues. It's too bad that he is not a free person, because I would be proud to have him as my doctor and for him to be able to treat others out in the open. We've helped dozens of runaways over the past two years. I don't have to remind you that this entire situation *must* be kept secret!"

"Of course!" everyone echoed, but Lizzy also felt a bubble of excitement to be part of such an important work to end slavery.

"Lizzy, dear, could you go upstairs and help the young ones get ready for supper?" Marie asked. "It's not much, I'm afraid, as I've not cooked anything. But there is bread and cheese and the last of some pears that I canned last fall. It will have to do for today."

After dinner, Clara helped Adam get situated on the sofa and the rest of the family talked quietly around the table.

"In all the excitement, Father, I forgot to ask. How did things go in St. Paul?" Lizzy questioned Jakob.

He reached into his jacket pocket and withdrew a large piece of paper. "I got it—here's the deed. Stamped 'paid in full' and totally ours now! The only requirement is that we put up a permanent shelter within the next year and improve the land in some way. They don't want speculators buying up huge parcels of land and then raising the prices to gouge new settlers. But our plan is to live on and work the land, so I don't foresee a problem."

"We've been working over there since you left, Father, moving rocks and large branches from where you want the garden and house to be," Lizzy said proudly. "The white birch trees are quickly becoming my favorite, especially in such numbers so close together. I can see why they are popular with the natives—the bark is unusual, and the trees are so unique."

"That's wonderful, Lizzy. Maybe we'll be able to get a garden planted in a few weeks. I need to feel like I am providing for my family, not taking advantage of the Augustines' generosity."

"We are happy to help, as I've said before," George interrupted. "Don't think any more about it. I've about got the last section of my field tilled, and then you are welcome to borrow the plow. I need to start spending more time in town at the lumber yard, anyway. Orders are really starting to pick up. But from what I saw this morning at your place, it won't take many more days of 'rock picking' before you can turn the ground over for the first time. How exciting!"

"We will miss Adam's help, of course," Lizzy said. "But his recovery is most important. I was lucky to find Doc Parsons in Davenport to help me, and Adam is lucky to have found Amos."

"Do you need help finishing your fields, George?" Jakob asked.

"No, I'm in pretty good shape. Why don't you take the children over each morning as I have been doing, and then if I need help in the afternoons, you will be here."

"Perfect plan. I'm anxious to go over tomorrow and see what all the children have accomplished."

"Trust me, Father," Lizzy said. "We have moved a ton of rocks, but we saved a few for you!"

The next day Jakob took all the children except Adam to the new land, and they spent the morning moving rocks from the garden area and marking out the property line for fencing.

Saturday afternoon and evening was spent giving the children baths and preparing food to take to the picnic after church the next day. Lizzy had just finished washing her hair when Marie knocked on the bedroom door.

"Lizzy, dear–may I come in?"

"Of course, Marie. I just finished. I'm sorry if I took too long."

"No, you are fine. We just want to talk to you about tomorrow."

Lizzy opened the door to find both Marie and Clara waiting for her.

"With all of the excitement of this week, I have neglected to find any new things for you, or to even purchase fabric so we could make something," Clara apologized. "I figured you would want something nice to wear tomorrow. At least, nicer than your current clothes."

"We all saw you talking to the pianist, Henry," Marie said with a twinkle in her eyes. "Would you like to pick something else from my closet? George and I have known him for a few years, and he is a fine young man, talented and hardworking."

"A very suitable suitor," Clara said with a smile.

"Suitor? Oh, I don't know about that. I'm only seventeen, and we just met."

"But you like him?" Clara asked. "A girl could do a lot worse, trust me."

"Well, yes, I mean… he is quite handsome and very talented."

"I think this lavender dress would be lovely on you," Marie said as she showed Lizzy a simple pinafore with clusters of dark purple fabric flowers around the waist and on one of the shoulders. "It's not overly fancy, but it brings out your lovely coloring and would be stunning with your auburn hair. Want to try it on?"

"Of course, thank you so much. I was a bit worried about what to wear tomorrow. This is so very generous of you."

Lizzy slipped into the dress which fit her perfectly. Her long hair went almost down to her waist, and as she started to braid it, Marie had an idea.

"I recently saw a woman in St. Paul with the most beautiful hair. I would love to experiment with her braid style, if that's ok? We can take it down if you don't like it."

"That sounds like fun," Lizzy said. "I'm pretty bored with the way I have been doing it for the past few years."

Sitting on a chair in the kitchen, Marie brushed out Lizzy's long hair and complemented her on how beautiful and healthy it looked. She then set out to weave the hair into a lovely crown, leaving a few tendrils to frame Lizzy's face with softness. Rosina walked into the kitchen and gushed, "Lizzy, you look like an angel!"

Lizzy looked into a small mirror that Clara held up for her and was shocked at how lovely she looked.

"I think you will gain some attention tomorrow, especially from a certain young musician we know."

"I don't know anything about him, really, other than he seems several years older than me. How is it that he is not married, or pledged to someone already?"

"I'm not totally sure," Marie answered. "Just waiting for the right one, I guess."

"Thank you again for letting me borrow such a lovely dress, and for fixing my hair. I'll be very careful with both, I promise."

The next morning, everyone but Adam and Clara loaded into the wagon for the short trip to church. Even though Adam insisted that he felt well enough to be home alone for a few hours, Clara refused to leave him. Lizzy sat up front next to her father, who looked handsome in his freshly washed but tattered suit.

As they pulled into the yard next to the church, Lizzy noticed that several makeshift tables had been set under some shade trees for the food. Children were running and playing, and the air held the feeling of fun and friendship, something she knew she needed, especially after this difficult past week. Several people came to help Jakob unload the food from the wagon and take it to the tables.

"Good morning, Lizzy," a soft voice said behind her. "May I be so bold as to say you look particularly lovely this morning?"

Lizzy turned to see Henry standing beside her, smiling with his big brown eyes. He was several inches taller than her, and somewhat thin. She blushed a bit and said, "Thank you so much, Henry. You look handsome as well."

The bell rang loudly from the steeple, and everyone turned to go inside. "You are staying for the picnic, I hope?" he asked sweetly.

"Oh, yes. My family would not miss this for anything. It's all that the little ones have talked about all week, and both Marie and Clara have been cooking for days."

"I don't believe I saw Clara this morning?"

"No, she is at home with Adam. He had a bit of an accident earlier this week and she wanted to keep an eye on him."

"Yes, I heard something about an incident at the Augustines'. I do hope that he will recover soon. I'm sure he is needed to help clear your new property."

"You know about that?"

"News travels fast around here–everyone knows everything. May I escort you inside? The pastor always wants church to start on time."

Lizzy shyly placed her hand on his arm, and they walked the few yards together until they reached the church door, which he opened for her. He walked with her down the aisle to sit with her family, and then he took his place at the piano. Many people turned to admire the young couple together, and to smile their approval. Lizzy tried to pay attention to the songs and the sermon but found herself very distracted. At the conclusion of the service, the pastor asked Jakob to stand again and to introduce each of the children.

"This is Lizzy, my oldest daughter. My wife Clara was unable to be here this morning as she is at home taking care of my son, Adam, who is not feeling well. These two other children are Rosina and Hannah. We are also expecting another child in the fall. We are happy to be here, and anxious to get acquainted with all of you."

"Thank you, Jakob," the pastor said. "Let's all stand together for our closing hymn and then head outside for the excellent food I know is waiting for us. Jakob, I would like your family to go first, as you are our guests of honor."

After the close of the service, Lizzy and the smaller girls followed Jakob outside and she found herself trying to juggle her plate along with Rosina's and Hannah's.

"Here, let me take one of those," a gentle voice said behind her. Lizzy turned to see Henry offering to help. "Which of you lovely young ladies would like me to help you?" he asked with a big smile.

"Me!" they both yelled.

"Hmm, how about I take Rosina this time, and then Hannah, I'll bring you back for a dessert?"

"Thank you," Lizzy whispered. "I sure do miss Clara and Adam at times like this!"

After filling their plates, Lizzy led the group to a blanket that Jakob had put on the ground.

"Here you go, Rosina. Sit carefully—I would hate to see you spill your lunch all over that pretty dress," Henry said.

Rosina smiled at him, and Lizzy knew he had a new friend. Henry stood up to find somewhere to eat and Jakob said, "You are welcome to eat with us, unless you have family or friends that are expecting you."

"Thank you. I would love to eat lunch with you and to get to know all of you better."

Lizzy blushed again and wondered how many people heard him or were staring at her.

"Herr Kruse, please tell me more about your trip from Germany and across the country. I hope it was more pleasant than mine was a few years ago."

"Please, call me Jakob. I am not sure it was more enjoyable than yours," he said, and then proceeded to recount the trip across the Atlantic, their time in New York City, and their winter in Chicago. He mentioned that he and George Augustine were old friends from the homeland, and he had recommended that they move here to the Oliver's Grove area.

"What about you, Henry? Did you come here alone or with other family?"

"I came with my parents and younger brother Levi with his new bride. My parents died last winter from a mysterious illness, but Levi and his wife Gladys purchased some land not far from here. They had a son, Reuben, who died shortly after birth. They now have a daughter Audrey who was born just a few weeks ago. That's why they are not here today."

"Oh, so much sadness in such a short time," Lizzy said softly. "I am truly sorry for you and your family."

"Thank you," Henry said. "I live in town in a small apartment above the feed store. I have plans to purchase half of Levi's property once I…well, when I feel it is time to build a home of my own. I've worked out there some, getting the land ready. It's a lovely place with a small stream and lots of shade trees."

"White birch?" Lizzy asked. "I had never seen them before we came here. Such interesting trees. I'm glad we have plenty at our new place."

"Yes, lots of white birch. It makes good firewood and has other uses as well, such as furniture. Plus, it just looks so unusual."

"So, what do you do in town, since you are not farming?" Jakob asked. If this man was going to be a potential suitor for his daughter, he wanted to be sure he could provide for her.

Before Henry could answer, Hannah tugged at his sleeve. "Dessert, please," she said softly, with a pleading look in her eyes. "Chocolate!"

Everyone laughed as he got up, taking Hannah by the hand and almost running to the dessert table. "Just one, Hannah!" Jakob called to her.

"Oh, Father, two? May I have two?"

"OK, but Henry, make sure they are small pieces. We don't want to waste any of this wonderful food."

Hannah returned, proudly carrying a plate with a chocolate cookie and a very small piece of strawberry pie. Jakob nodded in approval and Henry helped Hannah get situated on the blanket.

"Now, to answer your question," Henry said with a smile as he brushed cookie crumbs from his shirt. "I'm a musician by trade. I was in the symphony in Berlin, which was wonderful. I do teach music lessons in town, but that's not enough to keep me busy or support me, so I also work at the feed store which has a livery in the back. I have learned a lot about caring for horses and other farm animals which hopefully will come in handy once I start a farm of my own."

Jakob nodded in approval, then said, "Well, I think I will go mingle a bit and meet a few other folks. Hannah and Rosina, let's find you some other children to play with." Jakob gave Lizzy a little wink and then left.

Lizzy suddenly felt very shy and awkward. She was sitting alone (although there were plenty of people nearby) with an unmarried man who seemed to take an interest in her. Was she ready to think about a serious, grown-up relationship? She knew that this was the logical next step for girls her age, but Lizzy never was one to abide by all society's expectations.

Chapter 13

Lizzy glanced nervously at Henry and her hands trembled a bit as she tried to tuck some stray hair back into her braid.

"Your hair is lovely that way," Henry finally said. "And such an unusual color. It must be quite long to make such a lovely braid."

"Yes, almost to my waist. And thank you, Marie did this for me last night."

"So, tell me more about *you*," Henry urged. "I know about your trip here, but what was before that? Did you always live on a farm?"

"Yes, for as long as I can remember, my father has been a farmer. My mother's name was Margaret, and I am the oldest child, and then Adam. She passed away several years ago, and then Father married Clara. She is the mother of Rosina and Hannah. I love her dearly, but I have never called her *mother*, and she understands. I turn eighteen in a few months."

She waited for that last bit of information to register with Henry. If he felt she was too young to carry things further, it was best that he knew now.

After a brief pause, he said, "I'm so sorry about your mother. You must have been quite young when she passed?"

"I was eight," she answered simply. "It was worse for Adam, since he is two years younger than me."

"I'm sure it was hard on you both. So why did you decide to come to America, if I may be so bold?"

"Life was pretty awful for us–very little food, no money. We were a growing family and Father had no real way to take care of us. When he heard from George Augustine about all the opportunities here, he jumped at the chance to come. It's still a struggle–very little money and living with the Augustines until we get a house built and the land cleared enough to plant a few things. But the future looks so much brighter here than it did back home."

"But things are much different here, too–the climate, the lifestyle," he replied. "How do you feel you are adjusting? You speak English quite well for someone in this country such a short time."

"We spent the winter in Chicago, as Father mentioned. One of the other boarders had been a teacher in Germany and he spent many evenings working with me. He also had two sons about my age who helped me, too."

"Things are very different here politically as well," he mentioned, "with the Indian situation and slavery. If the country cannot come to some sort of agreement on these issues, I'm worried for what might happen."

"Slavery is such a barbaric institution!" Lizzy said boldly, then realized she was not sure of Henry's stance on the issue. "How can someone buy and sell another person? It's horrible."

There, she said it. If he disagreed with her, there was no way she would continue spending time with him. She was very convicted on this issue.

"I'm so happy to hear you say that," Henry quickly responded. He glanced at the other picnickers and said, "Barbaric is the correct word. How about we take a walk over to the creek? There are too many prying eyes and ears here."

She laughed and agreed to walk with him a few dozen yards to the stream. There were plenty of people to act as unofficial chaperones, and she felt safe with him. After finding a suitable log for them to sit on, he softly said, "I have a question—what do you know about the Underground Railroad?"

Her eyes flew open, and she was afraid to admit that she had learned a lot last week but didn't want to get anyone in trouble.

"It's ok," he said. "I know that Amos was the one who helped Adam with his wound. I was the one who helped get him out of town and to the Bakers."

"YOU?" she said loudly, then quickly switched to a whisper. "You are part of the Underground Railroad?"

"Yes, I'm the main contact who lives in town. And since I have access to horses in the livery, it helps me to get the runners to safety. That's another reason I have not moved to Levi's farm. And to answer the question you were too shy to ask, I just turned thirty in January."

"That's a long way from eighteen," she said with her eyes to the ground. "Maybe you would rather spend time with someone closer to your own age?"

"It's not an issue for me—is it for you?"

"No," Lizzy whispered, afraid to meet his eyes.

"Lizzy, look at me, please?" he asked gently. After she did, he continued, "I know that we barely know each other and you are just starting your adjustment to living here, but if it is ok, I would like to call on you some evening. Of course, Jakob and Clara would need to approve, but I really would like to get to know you better. Would that be alright, or am I being too forward?"

Lizzy felt herself blushing again–she had blushed more today than she had in the rest of her life. "Yes, Henry–I would like that."

Henry grasped her left hand and gently lifted it to his lips. Kissing her fingers gently, he smiled and said, "I'll be around soon to talk to Jakob. Now I had better get you back to the group before people start talking."

Chapter 14

A week after Adam's injury he was able to help with the smaller rocks and branches at the new property. George finished plowing his land and Jakob quickly tilled an area for their large new garden. Lizzy, Clara, and Marie planted row after row of lettuce, cabbage, carrots, and beans. They also found room for potatoes and squash. They still had to carry water from the creek on the other side of the property as Jakob had not dug a well yet. But things were coming along, and each day they started to feel more comfortable there.

Several days later, George told Jakob that they had arranged transport for Amos most of the way to Canada. Not long now, and he would be safe. The Bakers said that Amos had sent a message hoping that Adam was doing well. Jakob and Clara wrote a 'thank you' note and Lizzy placed a handkerchief embroidered with "sleep well" in German into the envelope. George promised to give the gift to Amos before he left in a few days.

The next Sunday, Henry was not at church, and Lizzy had a hard time hiding her disappointment. She didn't feel comfortable yet asking the pastor about him, so she went home and then to her room, stating she had a headache and didn't want any dinner.

Alone in her tiny closet/room, she tried to understand her conflicted feelings. Henry had only just recently expressed a desire to court her, and they had certainly made no promises to each other. For all she knew, he was sick or injured somehow, but she could not help but let her imagination run away with her. Maybe he had time to think about it and decided that she was too young and inexperienced? She had never felt quite this way before and came to the realization that she had started to develop feelings for him that were foreign to her. Was she just a silly young girl with her first crush, or could these feelings be real?

Clara called up the stairs, "Lizzy, dear—can you come down? There is someone here to see you."

Lizzy sprang from her pallet and tried to smooth the wrinkles from her dress. She splashed a bit of water on her face and patted her hair. "Yes, Clara—I'll be right down."

She tried to calm her nerves as she descended the stairs. She knew very few other people here, so it had to be *him,* right?

She entered the dining room to find everyone about to enjoy a huge Sunday dinner, and Henry was standing off to one side, his hat in his hand, looking a bit tired and dusty.

"Hello Lizzy," he said softly. "I hate to interrupt your meal, but I was hoping to speak with you for a few minutes."

"Have you eaten today, Henry?" Marie asked.

"No, ma'am, not since before dawn."

"Then please sit down and eat with us. Anything you wish to speak to Lizzy about can wait." Jakob said with a smile. "Go wash up, and Adam, find us another chair. Lizzy, your place is waiting for you, too."

Henry returned from the kitchen to find Lizzy seated at the table with an empty chair next to her. Jakob rose to offer the blessing as everyone around the table held hands. Lizzy shyly offered her hand to Henry and felt his warm hand envelope hers.

"Our dear Heavenly Father," Jakob began. "We gather today around this table with our family and friends, to offer our thanks to You for this meal and blessings upon those who prepared it. We thank you for your guidance this past week and trust You for blessings for the week to come. Amen."

"Amen," everyone replied, and soon platters of chicken, boiled potatoes, coleslaw, and roasted carrots were passed around the table. Henry gave Lizzy's hand a soft squeeze and then joined the conversation.

"We missed you at service this morning," Clara said slyly, knowing that his absence was the reason for Lizzy's discouragement earlier. "The pastor's wife is a fine pianist, but not nearly as proficient as you."

"Thank you so very much. I had to be out of town for a few days and tried to make it back in time but ran into trouble with one of the wheels on my buggy, so it took a bit longer."

"I hope all is well," Jakob added. "Do you need me to look at it?"

"No, thank you. I was able to get it fixed, so it's better than before."

"Well, let me know if you ever need help. I have had a bit of experience with wagons over the years."

"Thank you, I will."

The meal continued with pleasant conversation, but Lizzy found herself too nervous to eat much. Henry ate with enthusiasm—an obvious sign that wherever he had been, food had been scarce.

After the dishes were cleared, Marie returned to the table with a large cobbler that Lizzy had never seen before. Clara followed along with dessert plates and forks.

"Is this rhubarb?" Henry asked with a smile.

"Yes—my first crop this spring. None of our new friends have had it before. Do you know what rhubarb is?" she asked Clara.

"Not until you picked this yesterday. What an odd and sour plant! And you made it into dessert?"

"Yes, with the help of a lot of sugar, it's wonderful. Rhubarb is a plant you either love or hate. George, here, is not much of a fan, I'm afraid, so I don't do this often. But our children love it. I'm curious what the rest of you will think."

"Well, I for one love rhubarb," Henry said, as he scooped out a large helping. "Lizzy, would you like to try?"

"I'm all for trying new things, but this does look strange," she said as she placed a small spoonful on her plate. She took a bite and tried to be polite when she said, "Well, it's different!"

Laughter erupted around the table as the dish was passed. Most everyone liked it, but those who didn't just said, "Well, it's different!"

After dessert was finished, Henry turned to Jakob and asked, "Jakob, it is such a lovely spring afternoon. Would it be permissible for me to take Lizzy for a walk along the stream? We won't leave the property. That is, if you would like to go, Lizzy?"

She tried to hide her excitement as she turned to Jakob and said, "Father, I would like that, if you approve."

"Yes, that would be fine, just stay within view. I'm sure the fresh air will help your headache, Lizzy," he said with a smile.

"Oh, I'm sorry," Henry said. "I didn't realize you were not feeling well. Another time, perhaps?"

"I'm fine, really. I'm sure some fresh air would be wonderful," she said, glaring at her father. "I'm already feeling better, after such a wonderful lunch."

The adults all tried to stifle their amusement as Lizzy led Henry out the door. He held out his hand to assist her down the steps and they strolled toward the garden.

"Lizzy, I'm so glad I have this chance to see you and tell you where I was this morning. I hope I did not worry you."

"I was a bit concerned, but you really don't owe me an explanation."

"But I want to tell you. I was gone for several days because I was the one escorting Amos on the next leg of his journey."

"You went all the way to Canada?" she asked in amazement.

"Well, close but not quite. I handed him off to another family who had plans to complete the journey with him."

"Was it dangerous for you? Did you run into any troubles?" she asked nervously. It was one thing to believe in the abolitionist cause, but another thing to think of the danger and risks he faced.

"There was one time that I was a bit nervous, but I'm getting better acting nonchalant, even when I have a fugitive slave hiding in the back of my buggy. The only real problem I had was with the wheel about 20 miles back."

"I'm very proud of you for doing this. I wish there was more that I could do to help the cause."

"You never know—God may be planning something for you in the future. You just need to be open to the opportunities."

Lizzy smiled to herself, content with his answers and thrilled that he wanted to share this part of his life with her. She imagined that he did not have many people he could trust with this secret.

"You have a birthday coming up soon if I recall correctly?" he asked.

"Yes, the 27th of June."

"Not far away at all. I am hoping that I will be included in your celebration?" he asked gently.

"I imagine that can be arranged," she said with a smile. There was more she wanted to say but was suddenly very shy. Henry noticed a change in her demeanor, and asked if anything was wrong.

"No, nothing is wrong. It is just that this is all very new to me. There are still so many things I wish I knew about you."

"My life is an open book—what do you want to know?"

"Ok—I'll try. You are a handsome, talented man. Why is it you are not married or pledged to someone? Thirty seems...... well........."

"Old?" He finished her sentence for her. "I guess in conventional circles it probably is. But in Berlin I was very involved in the Symphony, and we travelled a lot. I met many interesting women, but each seemed to be lacking something I was searching for - a certain spark. I just wasn't going to *settle*, as was expected of me. I wanted something grander–something unique. And then you rode into my life. A beautiful young Fraulein from my home country with auburn hair and the face of an angel. I know we have not known each other long, but I cannot think of my life without you in it."

Lizzy nervously glanced up the hill toward the house, where she saw Clara and Marie sitting on rockers, shelling peas but also keeping an eye in their direction. "I'm not quite sure what to say," she answered shyly. "I'm new to this, but cannot imagine my life without you in it, either." Not caring about the women watching, she stood on her tiptoes and planted a gentle kiss on his cheek. Unbeknownst to her, the women at the house looked at each other and smiled.

Chapter 15

They spent the next hour strolling across the property, arm in arm. Henry was quite knowledgeable about many things, including gardens and flowers. He told her more about the share of Levi's land that he planned to purchase and the dairy cows he wanted to raise. He hoped to produce enough milk to sell in town, along with butter and cheese. He also wanted chickens and pigs for personal use, of course, but was hoping for the main source of income to be milk, which was in somewhat of a short supply in town.

Lizzy listened with fascination but admitted that she knew almost nothing about dairy cows. She did know how to churn butter and Marie promised to teach her to make cheese. Henry offered to take her for a ride to the farm someday, and perhaps Adam could come along as chaperone. There was no way Jakob would let her go anywhere in a buggy with a man alone, they were both sure of that.

"Well, I suppose we have been gone long enough, Lizzy, "he said a bit sadly. "I don't want to give your father anything to be worried about and want to do this correctly. You say you are new to this—well so am I. I've never taken a relationship further, and I certainly don't want to do it wrong."

They returned to the house to find that the women had gone inside, but Jakob and George were playing checkers on the porch.

"Thank you for the walk, Lizzy, and I'm glad your headache is better," Henry said formally. "I hope we can do it again soon sometime."

"I would like that," Lizzy said boldly. She kissed her father on the cheek and skipped into the house.

"Henry, can you stay a minute?" Jakob asked.

"Of course. I was hoping to have a chance to talk with you, sir."

"Then I'm sure you know that my first concern here is my daughter. What exactly are your intentions?"

"They are purely honorable, I assure you," Henry said. "In fact, I would like to ask for permission to court her, with plans to ask her to marry me at her upcoming birthday." He explained his plans for the dairy cows and building a house on the land he would buy from Levi.

"I am in love with your daughter, Jakob, and will do my best to provide a safe and comfortable life for her."

George rose to his feet and said, "I had better get Clara for the rest of this conversation."

Soon Clara came out, wiping her hands on her apron. "George said you needed me?"

"This young man wants to court our daughter in hopes of asking for her hand in marriage. What is your opinion?"

"I think Henry is a fine man who would treat Lizzy well, and I am comfortable giving my blessing for now–and you? I imagine you are confident with his ability to provide for her?"

"My Lizzy–growing so fast. But I doubt there is a finer suiter than the man standing here in front of us. Yes, I approve."

"Thank you so much," Henry said with a sigh of relief. "I'm hoping to keep any talk of marriage a secret for now, until I can ask her later?"

"Of course," Clara said. "Something this special needs to come from you!"

Not many days passed before Lizzy realized she could recognize the sound of Henry's buggy even when it was a quarter mile away. His presence was becoming more frequent at the dinner table, and he often arrived with gifts from town such as flour or sugar. Once he carried in a large ham and another time a bushel of peaches that had been brought up from St. Paul. Of course, he did not mention that a large shipment of peaches had been accompanied by a runaway slave named Ruby, who he then escorted to a safe house. He told Lizzy about that later, and she was quite proud of his continued involvement with the railroad.

Many evenings Henry spent playing games with the little girls and checkers with the men. And of course, the two of them enjoyed a bit of time separated from the others, discussing life and plans and cows. Lizzy shared again her desire to learn to play piano and Henry promised to teach her as soon as he could find a used one for her.

"Oh, Henry–no. That's too much. I cannot allow you to spend that kind of money."

"We'll see," he answered with a smile. "I have connections all over the world, you know."

The night before Lizzy's 18th birthday, Clara came to her with a surprise gift wrapped in a piece of cloth. "I know your big day is not until tomorrow, but I wanted you to have this early."

"What in the world? You know you didn't need to do this. It's just a birthday."

"I disagree. I have been working on this for a week. I really do hope you like it."

Lizzy untied the fabric and saw the most beautiful soft pink dress with a satin ribbon at the waist and lace on the sleeves.

"What? How? Did you do this?"

"Yes, I've been up late many nights working on it. Do you remember a week or so ago when Marie and I made a trip to town? That's when I saw this fabric and knew it would be perfect for you, for your birthday. And it's not just a birthday–turning 18 is a big milestone. You are a young lady now, ready to take on the world. I know you wish that your real mother was here, and I wish that for you as well. But thank you for letting me be a stand-in for her this past ten years."

"I love you, Clara. Yes, I miss my mother, but Father was blessed to find you, along with all of us. This dress is amazing–thank you so much."

"Is Henry coming for dinner tonight or waiting until tomorrow? I always need to cook a bit extra when he is here–that young man sure can eat."

"No, I don't think so. He said he has a special gift for me tomorrow and doesn't want to run the risk of ruining the surprise. I don't suppose you know what it is?"

"My lips are sealed!" she said with a smile.

Lizzy awoke the next morning to the sound of gentle rain tapping on the windows. She washed her face and admired the dress from Clara. It was so beautiful, and she wanted to put it on right away. But knowing it needed to be saved for later, she slipped on an older dress before skipping down the stairs.

"Happy Birthday!" everyone sang as she walked into the kitchen. Lizzy found that Marie and Clara had fixed her favorite breakfast foods including bacon and warm rice with cream and cinnamon.

"Thank you. Each of you are special to me in your own way, and I am happy to spend this day with you."

"I'm about to start your cake, Lizzy," Clara said "but wanted to make sure it's ok. How does pound cake with fresh strawberries and cream sound?"

"Heavenly," she said. "Everything is heavenly today."

"Lizzy, after I put this cake in the oven, why don't you ride with me to the new place, and we can pick some lettuce and radishes for dinner and check the rest of the crops. I think it is about done raining, and Marie can watch the cake for me. I think a fresh salad with dinner sounds lovely."

"What else are we having?" Lizzy asked.

"Only more of your favorite foods—sauerbraten, spaetzle and roasted carrots."

"Oh, wonderful!" she answered excitedly. "Yes, a salad would be nice, and the cake would finish the meal perfectly."

After returning from the garden and helping start dinner, Clara urged Lizzy to go upstairs and rest a bit before Henry arrived. "And I know you want a chance to freshen up, so go relax and I'll let you know when he gets here."

Lizzy kissed her on the cheek and then went up to her room. She tried to lay down and rest but was too excited. It wasn't like any birthday she had had before–there was an air of excitement and anticipation.

Eventually she put on the new dress and re-braided her hair. She was almost done when she heard Henry's buggy in the drive. She was lacing her boots when Clara called her, "Lizzy, Henry is here. Come on down whenever you are ready."

Giving herself one last glance in the mirror, she tried to descend the stairs in the most mature and graceful way she could. Henry had been talking with Adam but looked up to see her enter the room. A smile lit his face, and he was almost in tears when he saw how lovely she looked. Any fears he had about proposing marriage this afternoon had been whisked away.

Just before they started eating, Jakob rose to give the blessing, and everyone joined hands. Lizzy remembered the first time–not all that long ago–when she had held hands with Henry and how shy she was. Today she confidently held her hand out to him, and he took it gently into his. Their eyes met for a second, and she could not believe how fortunate she was to have such a handsome, talented, and caring man beside her.

"Dear Heavenly Father," Jakob began, "We come to You this day of celebration to thank You for the wonderful food You have provided for us, and for the loving way it was prepared. Today we celebrate Lizzy, Hattie Elizabeth, and ask You to bless her today and all her days to come. Help us all to do Your will and spend our days serving You. Amen."

"Amen," everyone echoed. Dinner was filled with laughter, with Jakob and Clara telling Henry stories about Lizzy when she was younger. The food was excellent, and by the time she had a piece of her birthday cake, she wondered if she could eat it all. Henry continued with his large appetite, eating seconds of most everything. Clara and Marie teased him, saying it must have been hard to keep him full when he was a child.

Once dinner was over, it was time for a few presents. Clara and Marie had helped the younger girls make her a new apron, while the boys had taken some white birch and made a candle holder. Finally, Jakob and Clara presented her with a beautiful locket that could be opened, and pictures put inside. She thanked everyone and then noticed that the room had gotten very quiet.

"Lizzy, it's such a beautiful evening, " Henry said finally. "Would you like take a walk with me? I'd love to watch the sunset with you."

Lizzy looked back toward her parents, who were both nodding in approval. "Adam, I think Marie's garden needs watering," Jakob said with a smile. "How about you take care of that while these two take their walk?"

"Sure," Adam said, giving Henry a wink.

Lizzy held Henry's arm as they descended the steps in front of the house and began their stroll past the garden and toward the creek. Adam followed along with a bucket in each hand, and they chatted about the weather and the latest news from St. Paul about the Indian uprisings. After Adam's buckets were full, he turned back to the garden and Henry led Lizzy to a small stack of rocks nearby. He found a good one to use as a bench for them and dusted it off with his handkerchief so as not to get her new dress dirty. He then helped her to sit down.

"Lizzy, I wanted to tell you how lovely you look. I've not seen that dress before–pink is such a pretty color on you."

"Clara made this just for me. I really love it."

They sat in silence for a few moments; the only sound was some birds chirping off in the distance and the little girls chasing the cats in and out of the barn.

"Lizzy," Henry's soft voice was like a whisper. "Lizzy - I usually don't have trouble finding the words to convey how I feel, but tonight is very different." He paused, searching for just the right words. "I think I fell in love with you the first day I saw you in church. You are the woman I have been looking for, and I cannot imagine my life without you. I know that I do not have a lot to offer at this time–I don't have a real home or a lot of land, but I would be the happiest man in the world if you would agree to be my wife."

The last word seemed to hang in the air as Henry looked at Lizzy expectantly. He could not tell if she was happy or scared or a little of both, and wished that she would say something.

"My dear Henry–when we arrived here a few months ago I had no intentions of looking for a husband or even a suiter. I had been on such a long journey from Germany to America and then to Minnesota, and it was a huge adjustment for all of us. But when I saw you looking at me that Sunday in church,

I knew that my life was about to continue a journey that I was eager to be a part of. So yes, yes, of course yes! I will marry you!"

Henry reached into his pocket and pulled out a small wooden box. With trembling hands, he opened it and retrieved a lovely band with a small dark red stone in the center. "I wanted this to match your lovely auburn hair. May I place this on your hand?"

"Yes," Lizzy whispered as he slid the beautiful ring onto her left hand. "It's the most beautiful ring I have ever seen."

Henry lifted her hand and kissed it gently. "Only more beautiful now that it is on your hand. I love you, Lizzy Kruse."

"And I love you, my dear Henry Sauter. I am so looking forward to our life's journey together."

Adam was coming down toward the creek to refill his buckets when he saw his sister lovingly lift her face toward Henry and they shared their first real kiss. Quietly turning around, he went back up the hill and sat beside a tree where he could satisfy his duty as chaperone but not interfere. He watched a glorious sunset over the valley below and wished his sister all the happiness in the world.

Chapter 16

Lizzy and Henry walked back to the house just as the sun was setting. Marie and Clara were busy lighting a few oil lamps, and Jakob and George had just set up the board to play Chinese Checkers. The younger children were playing with wooden blocks, and Adam was settling down to practice his English reading. He wanted to be ready for school when it opened in the fall, since he had gotten special permission to attend for just one year. All attention was turned toward the couple when they heard the screen door shut.

Standing nervously in the dining room, Henry cleared his throat and said, "Everyone, I need to be heading back to town before it gets much later, but I wanted to let you all know that tonight I asked Lizzy to be my wife, and she has graciously agreed. I have a lot of work to do at my new homestead, but I am the happiest man in Minnesota tonight, that's for sure!" Lizzy gave his arm a soft squeeze and looked at him lovingly.

Everyone was cheering and sharing congratulations, while Clara and Marie admired Lizzy's ring.

"That is such an unusual stone," Clara said. "Where did you find something so beautiful?"

"Actually, it's from one of the Indian traders that comes to the store regularly. He had brought in something similar a while ago, and I asked him to be on the lookout for a lovely deep red stone. He found it in one of the streams nearby, then I had the blacksmith fashion a band for me. It's truly one of a kind, just like my Lizzy."

"Well, it certainly is," Jakob added. "Henry, you best go before it gets too dark. Be safe, and I'm sure we will be seeing a lot of you in the future."

"Yes, sir," Henry agreed with a smile.

Lizzy turned to her father and said, "May I walk Henry out?"

"Of course. Before long, you won't need to ask permission," he said with a wistful smile.

Lizzy and Henry descended the steps again and stood by his buggy for a minute.

"This is the best birthday anyone could ask for," she said lovingly. "I love you, Henry."

"And I love you, Lizzy, more than I can ever show or say. I'll see you soon, I promise." He gave her one more tender kiss and then climbed into the buggy. "Goodnight my sweet girl."

"Goodnight," Lizzy whispered as she watched him disappear into the dark evening. With a peaceful sigh, she turned and went back into the house, ready to bask in the glow of her love and approaching wedding. A wedding! She was getting married to a wonderful man she loved!

The next several months were a flurry of wedding planning, working on the cabin at the new homestead, and preparing things for Clara's baby who was expected to be born in late October. Jakob and George had enlisted a few men from the church to help with the framing and putting on the roof, Lizzy split most of her time between tending the garden and working on the cabin.

They had good weather until the end of September when the days started getting shorter and cold winds were blowing in from the north. Jakob was hoping to be able to move in before the first snow, but it didn't work that way. On October 9th, three inches of fluffy white snow covered the ground and there was at least a week's worth of work yet to do. Levi took time off from his work to help with the finishing details but didn't quite get things done before baby Casper entered the world very unexpectedly. Clara did well, even delivering him before Doctor Hampton could arrive. He examined both Clara and the baby and declared them in good health, but the baby was quite small. When Clara explained that they planned to move to the cabin in just a day or two, he counseled against it, stating it was way too cold and remote for her to be with a newborn, and advised that they stay with the Augustines for at least a month, maybe longer. Jakob agreed but did not think he should leave the new property vacant, since there were continued rumors of increased Indian activity in the area. Jakob wanted to spend nights at the new cabin, and Henry volunteered to stay with him for a few weeks, leaving George and Adam as the older males to watch the big house. Henry had just started working on his own home on the property he purchased from his brother Levi but was willing to help Jakob out during this unusual circumstance.

Clara understood the reasoning, but she and Jakob had spent only a few nights apart since they were married. She had Marie and Lizzy to help with the baby, though, and she understood why she needed to stay where it was safer for everyone.

Henry brought a satchel with a few changes of clothes and his gun, which Lizzy was not even aware that he owned. Marie packed a box of food including bread and cheese, and the little bit of fresh fruit she had left. Lizzy promised to come over each day and work in the garden, along with taking care of her new brother in the evenings so Clara could rest. Wedding plans got put on hold–everyone agreed that finishing the family's cabin and taking care of Clara took top priority.

Four days later, Dr. Hampton returned to check on both mother and child. Clara explained that things were going well for her, but the baby did not seem to be very alert and didn't eat much. The doctor asked if Clara had been resting and eating well. She admitted that it had been difficult, as she was too worried about Jakob staying out at the cabin with only Henry to help protect the property, and each other. Just as the doctor finished his exam, Adam came running in the door, back from one of his first days at school.

"Clara–Lizzy!" he called loudly. "Did you hear what happened today?"

"No," Lizzy whispered, "but please keep your voice down. We just got the baby to sleep."

"Oh, sorry. We were in the middle of class today and an Indian boy maybe eight years old showed up at the door–looking very dirty and hungry. We weren't quite sure what to do, and of course he did not speak English or German. He did, however, point to his mouth and then rubbed his hand across the stomach, indicating that he was asking for something to eat. We each dug in our lunch pails and gave him what we could. His eyes grew wide, and it really looked like he hadn't eaten in a very long time. It makes me wonder how many of our interactions aren't because the Indians are savages as we have been told, but they are just looking for food for their families because they have been pushed off their land?"

"Did he leave peacefully?" Clara asked. "Was he alone?"

"Yes, he was peaceful. We did not see him again, and no one else was around that we could tell."

"I've heard of this happening quite a bit lately," Dr. Hampton said. "Seems you are right, Adam, and the confrontations have mostly been driven by the need for food, not from other hostilities. I heard about what happened to you a few months ago. I wish I had been here to help but I was in the process of establishing my practice here, having just moved here from Iowa."

"OK, well, I'm going to the barn to talk to George about it. I think we should be on the lookout,"

After Adam left, the doctor went back to discussing baby Casper. "I'm worried that he's not getting enough to eat. How was it with the older children?"

"Everything was fine–they were hardly sick and grew like weeds."

"But you are a bit older this time–well, whatever the reason, we need to find a way to help him eat more. Why don't you try to feed him a bit of cereal, very watered down of course, and see if we can't perk him up. How is he sleeping? Does he seem to be in pain?"

"He's sleeping more than my other babies did, and he doesn't cry much."

"He seems a bit lethargic. Let's go into the bedroom and I'll watch him feed, if that's ok?"

"Whatever you need, doctor. Please, help my baby."

Clara and the doctor took the baby to the bedroom where she attempted to nurse him. Casper did not seem very interested, and Clara said that it had been that way for the last 24 hours or so.

Lizzy and Marie remained in the kitchen, starting dinner, and worrying about the baby.

"I've never known her to have problems before," Lizzy said sadly. "I sure hope the baby perks up and starts eating better. He's so tiny."

"We must remember that he came several weeks early. It might just take him a little extra time to figure it out."

"I hope so," Lizzy whispered. "Both Clara and Father were so excited about this surprise addition to the family."

About 20 minutes later, Clara and the doctor came into the kitchen. "I told Clara but will tell you ladies also. We really need to keep a close eye on him --- with him being so small, it wouldn't take much for him to become dehydrated and emaciated." Clara was on the verge of tears, and Lizzy didn't know what to say. How would she deal with this if this was her baby? Does a mother ever stop worrying?

"Dinner is about ready, doctor," Marie said. "Would you like to stay?"

"No, thank you, I have another patient to see, but I'll swing past here before going back into town. I'll sleep better if he's eaten again before then and has a bit more energy."

"Adam, I need a favor," Clara called to him.

"What do you need, Clara?" Adam replied.

"Please ride over to the new house and get your father. Pack an overnight bag and offer to stay in his place. Henry is there, so you won't be alone. But I need your father here."

"Of course," Adam said as he hurriedly packed a bag and ran toward the barn.

"Take one of my horses, Adam," George called.

"Thanks --- I'll have Father back in just a few minutes."

Less than 30 minutes later, the horse raced into the yard, and Jakob dismounted before the animal had come to a complete stop. He rushed up the steps and into the bedroom where he found Clara and the baby. Clara was crying and trying to explain what the doctor had said, and Jakob picked up his tiny son.

"The doctor will be back to see us before going back to town. But I'm so worried."

"Of course you are, we all are. He's not very active, is he?" Jakob said worriedly.

"No, and it seems to be getting worse," and she started crying hysterically.

Lizzy appeared at the bedroom door and offered to help.

"Would you mind taking him for a bit?" Jakob asked. "I need to talk with Clara."

Lizzy took Casper and carried him to the living room. She sat in the Augustine's family rocking chair and gently rocked him back and forth, whispering encouraging words to him. A few minutes later she stopped and looked at him closely. She could not see his little chest rising and falling, and he was not responding to her at all.

"Clara! Father! Come quickly!"

Clara rushed into the room and grabbed her newborn son. She listened to his chest and then let out of sob. "Jakob! Our son is gone!"

Jakob placed his ear near the baby's heart and then rubbed his back but got no response. Casper was dead.

There were no sounds in the house except for Clara's crying and Jakob trying to soothe her. Dr. Hampton knocked on the door and Marie answered it, her face wet with tears and her eyes puffy and red.

"I'm too late, aren't I?" he asked softly.

All Marie could do was nod as she directed the doctor to the bedroom where Clara was still cradling her baby, her heart broken.

"I'm so sorry, Jakob and Clara–I know there are no words that are adequate at a time like this. Can you tell me what happened?"

Clara pointed blindly toward Lizzy, afraid to let go of her son.

"I was holding him and rocking him, talking to him. Then I happened to notice that I could not see or feel him breathing, so I called for Father and Clara to come check on him."

"He was gone when we got out here. It had only been a few minutes after you left," Jakob stated with difficulty.

"Clara, I'd like to look at him and check him over, if that's ok. Maybe identify a cause?"

"My baby………..my beautiful baby boy. How could this happen to him?"

Dr. Hampton gently took Casper from Clara's arms and laid him on the bed. Clara's sobs filled the room as he tried to do a quick examination. Nothing looked outwardly wrong, except he was very tiny and appeared malnourished.

He turned back to the parents and said, "I know this is hard to think about, but we need to make some arrangements. Your family has only been here a few months–do you have a preference for a place for burial?

Clara collapsed on the bed beside her baby, her body shaking with waves of grief.

Jakob thought for a moment, then turned to Lizzy. "What do you think about burying him at the new place? You know, on that pretty hill filled with birch trees, overlooking the creek?"

"I think that would be lovely," Lizzy whispered, "if it isn't too painful for Clara to have it so close to the house?"

"No, I want him close," Clara finally said between sobs. "If we have to put him in the ground, I want to be near him."

"Then that's what we'll do," Dr. Hampton said. "I have some contacts in town that can help with the details. And of course, you will want to talk to Revend Clarke."

"Yes, he must have a Christian burial," Clara insisted between sobs. "My sweet baby–you are in God's arms now."

Chapter 17

Two days later, the family and a group of friends stood beside a small open grave with Casper's tiny coffin next to it. The weather was overcast with a strong, raw wind blowing from the north. Most of the leaves from the birch trees had already fallen, and the black and white trunks and branches stood out against the gray sky. Pastor Clarke began the service with readings from Matthew and then Lamentations. *"At that time the disciples came to Jesus, saying, 'Who is the greatest in the kingdom of heaven?' And calling to him a child, he put him in the midst of them, and said, 'Truly, I say to you, unless you turn and become like children, you will never enter the kingdom of heaven. Whoever humbles himself like this child, he is the greatest in the kingdom of heaven. Whoever receives one such child in my name receives me."*

"My soul is bereft of peace," the pastor continued. *"I have forgotten what happiness is; so I say, 'Gone is my glory, and my expectation from the Lord.' Remember my affliction and my bitterness, the wormwood, and the gall! My soul continually thinks of it and is bowed down within me. But this I call to mind, and therefore I have hope: The steadfast love of the Lord never ceases, his mercies never come to an end; they are new every morning; great is thy faithfulness. 'The Lord is my portion,' says my soul, 'therefore I*

will hope in him.' The Lord is good to those who wait for him, to the soul that seeks him. It is good that one should wait quietly for the salvation of the Lord."

The pastor turned to Henry, who then led the small group in singing *"Blest be the tie that binds our hearts in Christian love. The fellowship of kindred minds is like to that above. When we asunder part, it gives us inward pain. But we shall still be joined in heart and hope to meet again."*

"Amen," the crowd responded. George and Henry placed the coffin into the ground and started to lay dirt on top. Clara was sobbing and threw herself onto the grave. Jakob lovingly helped her to her feet so the men could finish. A crude wooden cross with Casper's name was then pounded into the ground nearby. One by one, the mourners turned to leave, until all that was left was the immediate family and the pastor.

"Again, I want to tell you how very sorry I am, we all are," the pastor said softly. "If any of you need anything, or just want to talk or cry, please come see me. Or send word and I'll come to you."

"Thank you, Pastor." Jakob said. "We will, I promise."

The family loaded into their wagon and Lizzy climbed into Henry's buggy as they all headed to the Augustine farm. Clara turned to look behind her as the gravesite faded from view. The new cabin was almost completed, and soon the family would be moving here permanently. When she could no longer see the grove of birch trees, Clara turned to look straight ahead—staring nowhere in particular, her face swollen with her tears.

They arrived at the Augustine farm to find Marie and her children setting the table and arranging dishes and platters of food brought in by some friends. No one was very hungry, of course, but the kindness was deeply appreciated.

"Father, I need to get some fresh air," Lizzy said. "I'll just be on the porch."

"May I sit with you?" Henry asked while glancing toward Jakob.

"Of course," Lizzy answered, and Jakob nodded his approval. "Be sure to put on a warm jacket–can't have you or anyone catching a cold."

Lizzy put on her heaviest coat and she and Henry went to sit on the rocking chairs on the porch.

"How are you doing?" Henry asked gently. "I know this is very hard on you as well as Jakob and Clara–especially since you were holding him when he died."

"Yes, it is. But I must admit that my feelings have been all mixed up. How does a mother ever get past losing a child? I don't think I could bear it."

"I know it's hard, and I doubt we will ever understand. Losing a child must be devastating to all the family."

"I didn't tell you that I am not actually my father's first child. Before me was a baby girl named Anna that only lived a short while. Then there were several failed pregnancies before I came along. Then after Adam was born, mother died in childbirth with Louisa. I know Father took it very hard."

"Oh, I had no idea. I'm sure they just had to trust God and keep trying, if that is what He wanted for them."

"I had always imagined myself with a large family, but after this week…"

Henry reached for her hand and gently placed it in his. "My dear Lizzy, the sadness will lessen and when the time is right, we will have our own family of happy, healthy children. How many were you planning on, anyway?" he said with a smile.

"At least five–maybe ten That is, before today. I'm not sure I'm strong enough for the heartache."

"Ten? Well, we'll see. And if there is heartbreak, you would not be facing it alone, remember that. Now let's get you back inside. I can stay a bit longer, then need to ride back to your new place. I know you haven't seen the inside for a while–are you anxious to see it finished?"

"Of course! I know that it is not really meant to be a house, and that was the plan all along. But I am curious."

"We did the best we could with the small size of the cabin. And it will be a perfect chicken house or goat shed once the real house is built."

"I'm sure it will be fine. Compared to what we had in Germany, this will probably feel like a palace."

"It was really tough for you there, wasn't it?" Henry asked softly.

"Yes, more than I can convey. Always hungry, always tired, always worried about the future. And then after Mother and Louisa died…as afraid as I was, I'm glad Father decided to leave and search for a better life here. I'm not sure how much longer any of us would have lasted."

"Well, I am very glad that you are here with me now. And before many more months, we will be together forever. But I'm afraid I need to leave for now." He kissed her gently then escorted her back into the house. Clara was lying down, but the rest of the family was sitting quietly in the living room.

"I'm ready to head back over to the cabin," he said to Jakob. "Come whenever you are ready or send Adam instead. I want to try to get things finished so you can move in next week."

"Henry, we never would have been able to do all of this without you. You truly have become like a son to me. I'll send Adam over in a bit–I don't think I should leave Clara just yet."

"That's fine. It's actually closer for him to get to school from there. Marie–may we take some of the food with us?"

"Of course–take whatever you want. There is plenty."

After gathering up several boxes of food, Henry said goodnight to Lizzy and climbed into his buggy for the short ride to the cabin. Adam was just a few minutes behind on one of George's horses. Arriving at the cabin, Henry was relieved to find everything as he had left it this morning. Indian sightings were becoming more frequent, and he knew the family could not take much more stress right now.

"We really don't have much left to do, Adam" he said with a sigh of relief. "I have been happy to help here, of course, but it has put me way behind on the things I need to do at my own new homestead. Do you think you all will be ok here until Jakob can build a bigger house?"

"Well, we have to be. I know he and Clara are very insistent about not staying with the Augustines any longer than necessary."

They worked until dark, stopping only to eat the food Marie sent. Their hands were cold and chapped from the wind, cut and scraped from splitting logs for the flooring. Finally, they made a pallet on the floor with some old blankets and Henry added logs to the fire. With a sigh, he tried to get comfortable for the night.

"I think we can finish tomorrow," Henry said tiredly. "I must go to work for a few hours but can come back after lunch. And you will be here after school. Maybe we can both sleep in our own beds tomorrow night?"

"That would be wonderful. This weekend I can help Father bring our things over, and hopefully move Clara and the girls on Monday."

"That sounds like a good plan. I just hope Clara is up to it."

Chapter 18

Jakob, Adam, and George spent most of the weekend moving the family's belongings to the cabin. It only took a few trips since they had not accumulated many new things in the previous months. Marie and Clara had preserved as much food as they could. This would be stacked into a cave Jakob dug into the side of the hill that would act as a root cellar until the official house could be built.

Monday morning, Jakob loaded the wagon one last time to take his family to the new property. George and Marie promised to come over later but wanted the family to have a chance to get settled first. The four children were in the back along with more food that Marie insisted on sending with them. It only took a few minutes until the grove of white birch came into view. Clara had not been back since Casper's funeral, and she let out a quiet sob. Jakob directed the wagon off the road and across the field to the cabin. He had just recently had a well dug that was about halfway between the cabin and where the new house would stand next year. An outhouse had also been placed behind the cabin, along with a three-sided lean-to for the oxen so they could stay out of the winter weather as much as possible. Jakob had purchased several bales of hay and some grain that he hoped would last the winter.

Jakob helped Clara down from the wagon. She was still recovering from her recent childbirth and needed assistance getting up and down. He asked the children to wait in the wagon for just a few minutes while he and Clara had some time alone inside.

Jakob opened the door and led his wife inside. The cabin was split into two rooms–a larger one in the front that would be for the two of them to sleep in, along with being the kitchen and sitting area. It had a fireplace for cooking and a table that George had made for them. They had no chairs, but they had saved various shipping crates and boxes that would have to do for now. The smaller room would be for the children to make pallets on the floor and for other storage.

"I know it's not much, especially since we got used to roomier accommodations these past few months. But it's sturdy and should keep most of the cold winds out. What do you think?"

Clara looked around and let out a sad sigh. "It will be fine. It just won't be the same without our baby…"

"I know–we all miss him. But I think if we can make this work over the winter, we will be ready to start on the big house as soon as the snow melts. We have other things to keep us occupied–you have the two smaller children to tend to and along with Adam, they will be in school a good part of the day. Lizzy can help with the cooking and laundry, plus be a help to you. I will be chopping trees and moving rocks, and Adam will also help with fishing and hunting. Are you ready for the children to come in?"

"Yes, it's time. I don't want them sitting outside in this cold."

Jakob opened the door and motioned for the others to come in, bringing the food with them. After explaining the close quarters they would have for the next five months or so, the family got busy putting the food into the cave and making the beds in the second room. Adam and Jakob brought in armloads of firewood and then started chopping more to stack outside.

"Lizzy, I want you to think about things we really need over the winter," Clara said. "I'm afraid my thoughts have not been really clear lately, and I feel like we are forgetting some necessities."

"The only thing I can think of now is a large pot that we can do laundry in. And I'm sure we will need more oil for our lamps.

They worked until lunch, then took a break to eat some of the food from Marie. Clara looked around the room at her family, and then the modest amount of food that would have to last several months. A look of concern came over her face, and Jakob caught her eye and smiled. They had been through tough times before, and they could do it again, he was sure. But his children were older now, and Adam was a growing boy with a big appetite. He prayed they would be able to find enough rabbits, deer, and other wild game to tide them over until they could plant crops in the spring.

They had just finished their small lunch when they heard a buggy approaching. And then they heard another one—and then another! Confused, Jakob opened the door to find the Augustines along with Pastor Clarke and several other families from the church. Each buggy or wagon was loaded with food, blankets, or an occasional piece of furniture. Clara's eyes filled with tears as her friends provided their help and friendship.

"Henry was the driving force behind this," Pastor Clarke said. "But it did not take much persuasion–we all wanted to help, of course. It's not much, but hopefully will be of benefit over the winter."

Jakob was fighting back tears also as he answered, "We thank God for all of you–you are angels to us as we start our new lives here. We thank each of you–truly."

Some of the men carried the furniture inside --- two chairs and a small steam truck to use for clothing storage–and Jakob led the others to the cave where some perishable food could be stored. The women inspected the cabin and agreed that it was warm and sufficient for the winter.

"When we lived in Lewiston," Pastor Clarke's wife Lillian said, "our home wasn't much bigger than this, and we were there for three full years with our children. I know it will be challenging, but you will come out of it stronger. God will be faithful–and the rest of us here will continue to help as we are able."

"There is one more thing, Clara," Pastor Clarke said. "I know of a man in town who does stonework. I asked him to make a headstone for little Casper. Do you have something special you would like inscribed, in addition to his name and dates?"

Clara's eyes filled with tears once again, and she looked to Jakob for his opinion.

"How about this?" Jakob asked. "*He was the sunshine of our home.*"

"That is perfect," she whispered.

"OK, that sounds lovely. I'll have it taken care of for you. He said it would take a couple of weeks. We're going to head on out now and let you all get situated. Jakob—be sure to reach out to Henry or one of us if there is *anything* that you need. We are all family here and take care of each other."

"Thank you, Pastor, I will."

Once everyone had left, Clara told Jakob that she wanted to visit Casper's grave and to go alone. Lizzy and Adam both offered to go with her, but she said she needed this private time to say the things she was too grief-stricken to say at the funeral. Jakob understood and told her to please be careful. If she was not back in 30 minutes, he would be looking for her.

Wrapping herself in one of the blankets she had just received, she slowly started the climb toward the birch trees. It didn't take long before she was standing next to the tiny grave of her infant son. Emotions washed across her in waves as she brushed the leaves aside and straightened the wooden cross.

"Oh, my dear little baby. You were such a surprise to me as we were travelling across the country. But you were so wanted—I do hope that in your short time you were here you felt our love for you—not just mine, but from everyone. Jakob, Lizzy, and all the other children couldn't wait to hold you, play with you, watch you grow. I'm so very sorry if I did something wrong that kept you from staying with us. Did I not eat enough of the right foods? Did I work too hard, and it somehow caused you to come so early? I wish I had the answers..........I wish I knew why you could not stay."

Clara sat on the ground next to the grave and cried silent tears for the time she was not going to have with her son. She would never watch his first step or hear his first words. She would not see him grow, get married and have babies of his own.

The wind had increased, and she pulled the blanket tighter across her shoulders. The limbs in the trees were rattling and seemed to echo her sadness. She thought she could hear a soft cry in the distance but knew her imagination must be playing tricks. It sounded like a baby crying --- was Casper crying for her? No, that was impossible. But she still heard it, and it seemed to be getting louder. Then she heard a rustle in the leaves behind her, and she caught some slight movement. Was it a wild animal? Why was it crying?

She slowly stood from her sitting position and then saw a tiny orange kitten. He was limping and looked very hungry. Clara got back on her knees and held out her hand. The kitten was hesitant at first, but then walked timidly toward her. He sniffed her fingers and rubbed his head against her hand. She picked him up gently and held him to her chest. He started purring and looked at her with grateful eyes.

"Hey, little guy," Clara said softly. "Where did you come from? Is your mom around here? Why are you limping? Well, let's go down to the house and check you over. Your bright orange fur is like sunshine on this cold day. Sunshine, just like my little Casper was."

Clara was almost back to the cabin when Jakob came outside looking for her. She explained how she found the kitten and how he seemed hungry and hurt. The children rushed out to see him, and begged Jakob to let them keep him.

"I have no issue with keeping him, but someone needs to be responsible for him, making sure he's fed and warm. Having a cat will help with any mice problem we might have, and of course, pets can be a source of comfort and company during sad times."

"I found him, and I want to keep him as mine," Clara said quickly, before Lizzy had the opportunity to volunteer. She had always wanted a cat, and her father knew that. But she didn't have the heart to complain since this was the first time Clara had smiled in a long time.

"And I think I will name him Sunshine," Clara continued. "Just like Casper was sunshine in our home for such a short time, this kitten can be our Sunshine now."

"That sounds perfect, Clara," Lizzy said as she reached out to pet the cat. "He sure is cute—and tiny. I wonder what happened to his family?"

Lizzy found a box and an old towel that she put inside as a bed for Sunshine. Hannah took a cup and filled it with water while Rosina gave him a piece of chicken left over from lunch. After he filled his tummy, Sunshine curled up in the box for a nap. Lizzy was sad that Sunshine was not her cat, but also understood why Clara felt the need to claim him, especially since he was found at Casper's gravesite.

The rest of the family soon fell into a routine that would carry them through the next several months. Adam took the younger children to school each weekday morning, and Jakob worked outside moving rocks from the fields and making fences. He continued to clear away bushes and small trees that were in the way of the new homestead or barn. Adam was getting quite proficient hunting rabbits, and rabbit stew found its way onto the menu weekly. Clara and Lizzy did the cooking and washing, along with knitting and sewing in the evenings. Henry came over regularly on Sundays after church, and he and Lizzy would try to find some private space to talk and plan their future.

The week before Christmas, Henry asked Lizzy to share an early Christmas dinner with his brother Levi and wife Gladys. They had met several times at church over the past few months, but Lizzy did not feel that Gladys thought she was good enough for Henry, and the interactions were somewhat uncomfortable. But she knew that in just a few months she would be joining this family and wanted to find a way to make things better. She felt bad that she was not in the position to bring anything for the meal, but Henry said everyone understood. Jakob gave his approval for her to leave unchaperoned but warned Henry not to make him regret the decision. Lizzy put on her nicest winter dress (another one she had been gifted from Marie) and a wool coat that had seen better days. She had never been to Levi's home but had seen it from the road. It was quite large with lots of windows and a veranda that wrapped around three sides. There was a substantial barn and numerous other outbuildings. Lizzy felt very outclassed.

Henry tried to calm her fears as they bounced along the snow-covered roads. "I know Gladys can seem a little cold sometimes—her family is very wealthy, and she seems to prefer people just like her. But deep inside her tough outer shell is a nice person, and baby Audrey is a doll."

After about 30 minutes, the buggy pulled into the drive of Levi and Gladys' beautiful home. Lizzy hadn't seen anything quite this nice outside of the cities of Chicago or New York. It was obvious that they were not just poor immigrant farmers!

Henry helped Lizzy down from the buggy as the front door was swung open by Levi who was wiping his hands on a towel. "Come in, both of you! It's freezing out here!"

He held the door open for Henry and Lizzy, who stepped nervously into the foyer. Her family of six was living in a cabin about the size of this one room. Henry squeezed her hand and then led her into the opulent dining room - the table was set with crystal dishes and loaded with platters of food. There was a roaring fire in the living room nearby with upholstered furniture and paintings on the walls. Lizzy was afraid to move for fear of breaking something.

Gladys entered the room holding nine-month-old Audrey—both were wearing frilly dresses and had matching bows in their hair. Gladys was of medium height but extremely thin and fragile looking. Her skin was flawlessly white and smooth, with no signs of working on the farm under the hot sun or fierce winter winds. Audrey was almost asleep and looked like a little angel.

"Welcome to our home," Gladys said curtly. "Levi, be a good host and take their coats. Lizzy—that dress is an exquisite color on you."

"Thank you—your home is lovely."

"Yes, we love it here. And before long we will be neighbors—how nice."

Lizzy wasn't sure if she was being honest or sarcastic. She felt panicky and looked to Henry for guidance.

"Levi," Henry said to change the subject. "How are things going with the dairy cows? You know that I want to expand on that once Lizzy and I are married and I can start my own herd."

"Actually, I wanted to talk to you about that. Gladys, how long until dinner? I'd like to steal Henry for a few minutes."

"Not long—about 15 minutes. But take your cow talk to the den, ok? You know it's not my favorite subject, especially with company."

The men left the kitchen to talk farming and dairy cows, leaving Lizzy alone with Gladys in the dining room. An awkward silence hung in the air.

"So, Lizzy—we haven't really had much time to get to know each other. And since we will soon be sisters-in-law, I'm curious. Levi said you immigrated two years after he and Henry did. I must say, your English is better than many who have been here for years."

"I was fortunate to have many wonderful teachers this past year. Have you been here in the country long?"

Gladys stifled a laugh and said, "Actually, my family came over almost 100 years ago from England. We have been involved in the railroad industry from the very beginning, and it has been good to us. My father was offered the opportunity to help extend the railroad to St. Paul, which is why we live in the Minnesota territory. I met Levi at a social event shortly after he and Henry arrived. Obviously, my father wanted me to be comfortable living out here in the wilderness."

"Well, my father is not nearly as prosperous, but we have our faith in God and love for our family. And now that I have Henry's love as well—I have all I truly need."

"I heard that!" Henry whispered in her ear as he and Levi had just returned to the room.

"Did you solve the world's dairy problems?" Lizzy asked with a grin.

"You never know," he answered with a wicked smile. "What did we miss? Everything ok in here? Gladys, dinner smells wonderful."

"Yes, it should be ready. Levi–help me in the kitchen?"

After the couple had left, Lizzy turned to Henry and whispered, "You came back just in time. I almost said something I would likely regret."

Levi and Gladys returned with a huge platter filled with the biggest turkey Lizzy had ever seen. "Levi shot this one himself," Gladys bragged. "There are tons of them around here. I'm sure Henry will be providing them for your table soon enough."

The dinner was amazing, and Lizzy made mental notes of all the food and decorations and the atmosphere, since she was sure the little girls would want all the details. Dinner was almost over when Audrey woke up and needed some attention.

"Would you like to come to the nursery with me? It will give the men more time alone to talk farming, which I know they have been wanting to do all evening."

"Of course," Lizzy said as she smiled sweetly to Henry. Surely it was about time for him to take her home?

The nursery was a lovely room with fancy furniture and was filled with toys. Gladys changed Audrey's diaper and then turned to Lizzy. "Would you like to hold her? I need to take care of this diaper and heat some water for her bath."

"Of course," Lizzy said as Gladys left the room, placing a squirmy baby in her arms.

"Well, hello Audrey. My name is Lizzy, and soon I will be your auntie. I hope we can have lots of fun with each other, and maybe soon you will have some cousins to play with."

Lizzy suddenly realized that the last time she held a baby was when Casper died in her arms. She tried not to panic but could not help but relive the feelings associated with realizing that he had died. She started to tremble a bit, and wished Gladys would return.

But it was Henry who appeared at the doorway, and he instantly recognized what was happening. "Hey, Levi—come here a minute?"

Levi appeared at the nursery door and Henry said, "I really need to get Lizzy home. Guess it's time to wrestle your daughter away from her new friend."

Lizzy tried to keep her composure as she said goodnight to their hosts and climbed into Henry's buggy for the crisp ride home. The snow glistened in the moonlight, but Lizzy could barely see for the tears in her eyes.

"I'm so sorry—I know the whole evening was stressful. But holding the baby ---- I'm sorry. Gladys had no idea, I promise."

"Oh, I know. I don't blame her. I know it will take a while for the pain to ease."

They rode along in silence, and just before they reached the cabin, Henry pulled his buggy to a stop. "Lizzy, thank you so much for a wonderful evening. I wanted to tell you while we have the chance that all I could think of during dinner was that next Christmas we would be celebrating together in our own home. It won't be as grand as Levi's, but it will be filled with love and warmth. And it will be the best Christmas of my life."

Chapter 19

Lizzy awoke on the 1ˢᵗ of January 1853, and realized that this was the year of change for her and her family. As soon as the snow melted, they would all be hard at work building the new house. They had spent many evenings pouring over the plans that Jakob and Clara had designed–adding a closet here, subtracting a window there, until they were satisfied that it would be sufficient and comfortable for everyone for many years to come. They would also be planning Lizzy's wedding, and Henry was busy building a home for him and Lizzy, along with a large barn for his dairy herd.

But today it was snowing, and the wind was howling–cold air seeping in between the cracks of the crudely-constructed cabin. Lizzy shivered under her covers and tried to think warm, happy thoughts. She heard her father and Clara talking softly in the other room as Jakob piled more wood on the fire. Sunshine was meowing, demanding breakfast, and Clara was hunting around for something to feed him. Jakob opened the front door to get more firewood, and wind and snow came rushing in. That woke up the other children, with Hannah crying that her tummy hurt.

"That wind is awful, and the snow is really piling up," Jakob said. "I'm glad we have as much wood as we do under the tarp to keep it dry. But if this snow doesn't stop soon, I'm not sure what we will do. We can't burn wet wood."

Lizzy helped Clara start breakfast and heated an extra kettle of water so everyone could have a warm drink. Adam helped Jakob carry in as much dry wood as they had and piled it in a corner. After their last load, they changed into dry clothes and hung the soaking wet ones near the fire. Clara fixed oatmeal for everyone and fried some bacon. "How much more do we have in the cave?" she asked Jakob.

"Several more pounds, but I'm not sure I can find it now with all this snow. Surely it will stop soon, and I can dig us out. We'll just have to make do with what we have for now."

But the snow raged on for hour after hour, and soon it was almost impossible to get out the door. Hannah continued to complain about a stomachache, despite the herbal teas and soft foods Clara gave her. The cabin felt very claustrophobic for this family of six, and soon everyone was restless and bored.

The evening darkness seemed to wrap the little cabin in a black blanket. The wind and snow continued, piling over six feet in front of the door. There was no going to the outhouse, and Lizzy was fighting panic that they were being buried alive. How long were they going to be trapped here? When would anyone find them? Was this the end of the journey for them all?

Shortly before dawn, Hannah cried in pain and was burning with fever. Jakob was helpless to help his daughter, and Lizzy could see the fear on Clara's face. Was she going to lose another child?

The wind had calmed considerably, and Jakob was thankful that they still had a few sticks of wood to keep the fire going.

If that ran out, they would be forced to burn the furniture that had so generously been given to them by their friends.

Again, Lizzy heated a kettle of water and fixed a cup of warm tea for each of them. Everyone was shivering and concerned about getting out of the cabin and finding help for Hannah. There was nothing more Clara could do.

After breakfast, Jakob put one of the last pieces of wood on the fire and gathered the family around him to pray. "Dear Heavenly Father, we thank You today for bringing us safely through the night. Your blessings are new every morning."

Lizzy opened her eyes and looked at her father. Even in this difficult time, he was thanking God for His blessings. She wasn't sure she felt quite as thankful and asked God to strengthen her faith. Her father continued, "Lord, You know the situation we are in, running out of wood and food soon, being trapped inside, and now with Hannah needing medical help. We ask that You provide a solution for us, deliver us from our fears and concerns, and restore Hannah to full health. We thank You for caring for us. Amen."

"Amen," the family said in unison. "Lord, hear our prayers," Clara added tearfully.

Several hours passed, and the cabin got colder and colder. Everyone was wrapped in blankets and hovered as close to the tiny fire as they could. Jakob was forced to use the wooden crates for firewood and was about to start pulling the chairs apart when they heard a noise off in the distance. It sounded like a voice, but it was very muffled, and they could not make out who it was or what it was saying.

Then Lizzy jumped to her feet --- it was Henry!

"Jakob! Clara! Lizzy! Are you all ok? I'm here to help dig you out, and others are coming as well. Jakob?"

Jakob opened the door to find that snow was piled almost to the roof except for about 2 inches at the top. Henry laid down on the snow and peered inside. "Is everyone ok?"

"You are just in time. We are almost out of wood and don't have much food left. But Hannah is sick, and we really need to get her to a doctor. How did you get here? I'm sure the roads are impassible."

"I'm on snowshoes and pulling a sled behind me. Here are a few sticks of wood and some bread and cheese. I'll start digging and then once the others get here, we'll get Hannah out and someone will take her to the doctor. Lizzy—are you ok?"

"I am now that you are here! God has answered our prayers!"

Jakob put the wood on the fire and Clara divided the food between the children. Henry was working frantically outside to clear the snow from in front of the door. Soon several other men arrived, including Levi and the Augustines and Bakers. Before long they had cleared a few feet away from the door, and Jakob lifted Hannah to Henry's waiting arms. George volunteered to put her on his sled and make his way into town. He begged Clara not to worry, although everyone was aware of her fears. Levi had brought a few extra blankets, and he lovingly wrapped one around Hannah.

"The ride will be a bit bumpy," George told her, "But think of the story you will be able to tell once school opens again. Clara—I'll take care of her as if she was my own. Please try not to worry."

The men continued to dig until Jakob and Adam were able to get out and help. Clara and the other children stayed inside, even though Lizzy wanted outside to see the sun and breathe some fresh air. Clara begged her to stay with her to help keep the children calm, but Lizzy knew it was to help her not to worry about Hannah.

Several more men arrived, and soon the doorway was clear. They also dug a path to the outhouse and were trying to find the root cellar. Pastor Clarke came with a sled loaded with firewood and baskets of food packed by his wife. Levi climbed down the ramp of snow and into the cabin to deliver a package to Lizzy. He looked around the tiny rooms in awe, and then quietly said to Lizzy, "No wonder you were a bit overwhelmed at Christmas. I had no idea your place was this… well, compact, with all of you in here."

"It's pretty tiny," Lizzy said with a laugh. She could see a lot of similarities between Levi and Henry. They had the same sense of humor and friendly, dark eyes.

"Gladys wanted me to bring this to you. I think she enjoyed our evening together and hopes we can do it again soon."

Lizzy unfolded a large, beautiful blanket to find several warm scarves and gloves tucked inside. She lifted questioning eyes to Levi, and he said, "She couldn't stand the thought of all of you out here, trapped in the cold and snow. She took this blanket off our bed and the other things were from her closet."

"I'm not sure what to say–thank her so much from all of us."

"She was particularly concerned about Clara," he whispered. "How is she doing?"

"She is struggling, and now so worried about Hannah. I pray George brings her home soon."

"I know Gladys would be devastated if anything happened to Audrey, since we already lost Reuben."

Lizzy patted his arm gently and said, "Grief is so hard. I often wonder if I would be able to survive. But God is our ever-present help in times of trouble–we just need to trust Him."

Levi could not help but be impressed by his brother's fiancé. There was a depth to her faith and an inner strength that Gladys just did not possess. His brother was very lucky.

After an awkward silence, he climbed back out of the cabin and went back to helping the others. Jakob and Adam carried in enough wood to last several days, and other men cheered when they found the opening to the root cellar.

Once they felt they had done as much as possible, the men left one by one to go back to their own homes. George had still not returned with Hannah, and Clara was becoming more distraught as the day wore on. Jakob tried to comfort her but knew nothing would help except to have her youngest child back in her arms. It was almost evening before they heard the now-familiar sound of crunching snow under snowshoes. Clara grabbed a blanket and wrapped it around herself as she rushed up the ramp of snow to see George moving slowly across the field toward the cabin.

"Momma!" Hannah called out when they saw Clara. "I'm all better now, momma!"

George stopped near the cabin and untied Hannah from the sled. "We are fortunate that the doctor was in his office, despite the storm. He thinks it was a stomach infection, perhaps something she ate? He gave her some medicine and sent more home with her. She's doing remarkably well now."

"How can we thank you, George? You and everyone! Things were starting to get desperate."

"We are a family here, I told you. We help each other when we can–that's just who we are. One day it will be me needing help, or Pastor Clarke. I better head home so I can get there before dark. Bless you all and stay warm!"

Clara and Hannah rushed inside and sat beside the fire. Hannah began telling her story to the others, adding exciting details that Lizzy doubted were totally true. Jakob looked at his wife lovingly caring for their youngest, and thanked God for his protection and the provision of good friends

Chapter 20

The winter was long, but there were no more blizzards and the family rejoiced at the first signs of spring. The snow melted and the warmer breezes finally brought songbirds and flowers back to the homestead. The birch trees came back to life and attracted squirrels and other small animals that Adam took great pride in harvesting for the family's dinners. At last, they were free to start working on the new home and plowing the fields. Jakob was up at dawn each day and only stopped for quick meals before returning to work until dark. Clara and Lizzy planted their garden and were soon harvesting some early lettuces and radishes. Sunshine had grown into a fat and happy boy and loved to be out exploring all day.

Adam finished the school year with the younger children and was proud of what he had learned in just one year. His English was almost perfect, and he had excelled in math. But he was the oldest one at the school, far past the others, and would not be returning in the fall.

Henry continued to visit each Sunday after church, and he and Lizzy selected September 30th for their wedding. He knew he would have his new house completed by then, and Lizzy would have her 19th birthday in June. He planned to keep his job in town for a while as this would allow him to do his work with the underground railroad and earn a bit of money at the trading post. Things with the railroad had really slowed down over the winter, with the snow making transport almost impossible. But the springtime had brought renewed hopes for the slaves but increased tensions between the states.

Henry selected Levi to be his best man, of course, but Lizzy struggled with who to select as her bridesmaid. She didn't really have any close friends and had no sisters or cousins of the appropriate age. The only woman she knew about her age was Gladys, but they were hardly friends or even friendly. Did she really want to spend time planning her budget conscious wedding with someone of such wealth and high-class ideas? She knew Gladys would apply pressure to have the ceremony up to society's standards, and this was very unappealing. Lizzy wondered if her vision for a simple ceremony was possible without offending Gladys. She talked to Henry about it one afternoon, and neither could come up with an acceptable option. Henry said he would be sure to talk to Levi and hopefully he could rein Gladys back from her affluent choices.

Just before her birthday in June, Jakob had their new house completed enough for them to move into, and Lizzy was never so glad to move in her life. Seven months in the crowded cabin had stressed everyone. As promised, she had her own bedroom with a door so she could finally have some privacy. It all seemed a bit silly now since she was just three months from getting married and sharing a room with Henry. But Clara said Adam would likely move into it after she left.

The room was on the top floor of the house, away from the noise and clutter of the younger children. She had a bed of her own–finally–and somewhere to put her few belongings. The window looked out toward the grove of birch trees, and she found comfort knowing that Casper was there. Even after all these months, she was still haunted by the memory of him dying in her arms. She could also see the garden with its rows of healthy produce, and if she tried really hard, she could see the road that led to Henry's place–soon to be her place! She was almost giddy thinking about her new life waiting for her just a few miles away.

Jakob still worked from sunup to sundown to raise his first crop to sell in town. The day he brought home his first earnings after selling a wagon load of sweet corn, the family had a big celebration. THIS is what Jakob immigrated for, and even though life was tougher on all of them than they anticipated, Jakob and Clara took this as a sign that they had made the best decision to leave their homeland and start their new life in America.

Clara and Lizzy had gone into town a few times to look for fabric for her wedding gown, but nothing seemed quite right. Clara wanted to take a trip into St. Paul to look further, but Lizzy declined. This was a dress that she would wear for just a few hours and she refused to spend much money on it, especially since that money could be used more appropriately in other ways.

The next Sunday after church, Henry asked if Lizzy could go with him to Levi's home for dinner. Jakob reluctantly gave his permission, stressing again about proper behavior while unchaperoned. Lizzy smiled and kissed him on the cheek–"Just three more months, Father. Everything will be fine."

Dinner at Levi's was a bit more relaxed than the one at Christmas, and Lizzy found herself less anxious about talking to Gladys about wedding plans. Once the meal was over and Audrey put down for a nap, they moved to the living room where they would all be more comfortable. Levi and Gladys kept sharing little glances and winks, and Lizzy had no idea what was going on. Finally, she broke the silence.

"Gladys, I know that you and I have not known each other very long, and we come from very different worlds and circumstances. However, in just three months Henry and I will be married, and you will be my new sister. As such, it would please me for you to serve as my matron of honor."

Gladys broke into a wide smile and grasped Lizzy's hand. "Levi told me that you might ask and told me that I am to be on my best behavior. I love planning parties and tend to be a bit pushy. If I get too pushy here, just tell me, ok?"

"I think this is our cue to go look at your cows, Levi," Henry said with a smile, "and leave the ladies to the wedding talk."

"I agree, Henry. And Gladys....remember what I told you!"

"Yes, dear," she said with a smile. "Now, Lizzy–tell me what all you have in mind? Have you decided on a dress?"

"The wedding will be very small and simple–just family and a few close friends. And I don't want to spend much money on it. I'm putting my foot down about that, understand?"

"Of course, I will be respectful of that. I thought about offering you my gown to wear, but we are very different sizes and I doubt the style is what you are wanting. But I would be happy to let you borrow my veil while we search for a suitable dress?"

Lizzy was surprised how kind and respectful Gladys was being. Maybe her talk with Levi really worked?

"Clara and I found a sketch that I really like, but we've not found the right fabric."

"Well, not here in Oliver's Grove you won't. Have you gone to St. Paul?"

"She offered to take me, but I don't want to spend a lot. I'll just have to settle for something local, I guess."

"Lizzy, listen. I know I just promised not to push or interfere, but I have to say this one thing. This day, your wedding day, is the ONE day in your life you shouldn't have to settle. There will be plenty of other times–where to live, what kind of buggy to drive or who to socialize with. But this one day is YOUR day and you should not ever have to look back with regret. Do you have the sketch with you?"

"Yes, it's here in my pocket," Lizzy said as she pulled out a well-worn slip of paper with a lovely but simple dress drawn on it. "I know it's not fancy, but it seems to fit my modest personality."

"Lizzy, dear, this is lovely, and will look beautiful on you. What if someone was to give you a wedding present a bit early, and it just happened to be enough to purchase fabric for this? Would that be acceptable? I know you want to say 'no,' but please let Levi and I do this for you."

"I don't know what to say–no one has ever offered anything like this before. It's way too generous."

"Please, it would mean so much to me, to both of us. We could take a trip into St. Paul and make a real day out of it."

Lizzy said she would think about it, and then they continued discussing other plans such as flowers and food for the reception. The men came back in from the barn to find the two women chatting like old friends. Henry and Levi smiled, relieved that the tensions were gone between them.

When Henry took Lizzy home, she shared with him Gladys' offer to purchase fabric for her dress and going into St. Paul for a day of shopping. Henry seemed surprised that Lizzy would dream of spending a whole day with Gladys, considering her feelings just a few hours earlier, but was glad to see this side of his future wife. He said he would talk to Jakob about how it could be arranged. It would involve an overnight stay at a hotel–would Jakob give his permission?

As expected, Jakob was not in favor of the ladies travelling to St. Paul to go fabric shopping, certainly not alone. After a lot of persuasion, he finally agreed that Lizzy could go if Levi would be driving, but they would NOT stay overnight. They made plans to leave at sunup the next Monday morning to arrive in town as the stores opened, have a nice lunch, and then return before dark.

Lizzy was excited, of course, but also a bit nervous. This would be an entire day with Gladys in her environment and comfort zone. She put on her prettiest dress and hat and waited for the buggy to arrive. Right on time, Levi's buggy pulled into the drive and Lizzy skipped down the steps. Jakob was close behind, and lectured Levi again about the need to be home before dark and not to leave the ladies unaccompanied at any time.

Gladys sat in the middle of the bench seat with baby Audrey asleep in her lap. "This is going to be a very long day for her–I hope she sleeps most of the way there. But I've never left her for an entire day and won't start now. Have you spent much time in St. Paul, Lizzy?"

"No, not at all. When we arrived here, we pretty much just drove in one side of town and out the other."

"Oh, what a shame. It's not Chicago or New York, but it has most of the things the bigger cities do–restaurants, hotels, theaters, and shopping. I wish we could stay longer so we could go to the theater --- it's been way too long for me. I'm hoping that we can meet my parents for lunch–I'm sure you will love them as much as we do. You have the drawing for the dress? I know just the shop I want to stop at first, and they will help us make sure to get enough fabric."

"Yes, it's right here. I'm still not totally comfortable with you doing this–I hope it doesn't cost too much money."

"Oh, just let me worry about how much is too much. You are marrying Levi's brother–of course we want to help make everything perfect for you."

They had a lovely drive in the early morning sunshine with not many people on the road, and baby Audrey slept most of the way. Once they got close to St. Paul, there were many more people out and about, and there was an air of excitement Lizzy had not felt since they left Chicago.

They pulled up in front of a millinery shop run by Gladys' old friend Emily Dahl, wife of millionaire William Dahl. Gladys went in first and introduced Lizzy to Emily and of course had to show off the baby. Levi found a sitting area where he could watch Audrey while the ladies talked about wedding dress fabrics and design.

Lizzy tried to contain her excitement and the feeling of being completely out of her league. The large store was filled with rack after rack of finished wedding dresses, and one whole wall was lined with beautiful fabrics of all kinds.

Emily invited them to sit at a small table covered with expensive linens and in the middle was a small bouquet of flowers. She motioned for one of the workers to bring them a pot of tea and tiny tea cakes.

"I'm so happy to meet you, Lizzy, and to see you again Gladys. It has been such a long time! Tell me what brings you here after all these months?"

"Emily, you know my husband Levi, but you may not remember that he has an older brother Henry. He has finally decided to settle down and will soon be marrying this lovely lady here, Lizzy. We are here to pick out fabric for her wedding dress."

"Lizzy, dear, how lovely to meet you. How soon is your wedding, and do you have a dress in mind?"

"We are getting married at the end of September and I found this sketch of a dress I like. The ceremony will be very small with just immediate family and a few friends. Gladys is letting me borrow her veil, and I want to keep the cost of the dress to a minimum."

Emily looked at Gladys quizzically, and Gladys interrupted, "The fabric is a gift from Levi and me. It will be Lizzy's choice, of course, but it doesn't have to be from the bargain rack."

"Do you have the sketch with you? Do you have an estimate of the fabric needed?"

"Yes, I have the sketch. I was hoping you could help determine the amount we need to purchase. I've done some sewing, but never a wedding dress."

"Are you sure you wouldn't rather look at the completed dresses we have for sale? Making a wedding dress is a huge undertaking."

"No, as you can see by the sketch, it should not be overly difficult, and I have several months to work slowly on it."

"That's perfectly fine. Let me see the sketch and talk to me about what kinds of fabric you are thinking about."

For the next hour or so, the ladies studied the sketch and then selected several fabrics that would be appropriate. Lizzy had a hard time keeping her eyes off the completed dresses, though–until she saw the prices! Wow–they were more than her father would make selling wheat in an entire year!

Eventually, Audrey got fussy, and Gladys took her to a back room to nurse her. Alone with Emily, Lizzy was suddenly shy and nervous. What was she doing in such an expensive shop? She never should have agreed to this.

Levi suddenly appeared next to the table and asked, "So, how is the search going? I'm sure whatever you decide will look lovely on Lizzy - - I mean, I'm sure Henry will love it."

Lizzy blushed a bit, then said, "I think I have decided on this satin here, with lace for the sleeves and bodice. From what I remember, this lace almost exactly matches the lace on Gladys' veil. I guess we should have brought it with us to be sure."

Gladys came back with a sleepy Audry who Levi took back to the corner for a nap. "This is the one you want, Lizzy? Are you sure? I agree it is lovely."

"Yes, I believe so, although I'm sure it's way too expensive."

"Not to worry, remember? Why don't you go sit with Levi while we get this measured and cut."

Lizzy found a chair next to Levi and looked nervous again. He tried to calm her fears by saying, "I hope you don't mind all of this. It truly does make her happy to help you in this way.'

"I know, I just was brought up so differently when it comes to money, or the lack of it."

A few minutes later they were all loaded back into the buggy and on their way to the Grande Hotel for lunch and to meet Gladys' parents, Peter and Margaret Hanson. They were quickly seated in an area that seemed to be reserved for special guests.

"It is so nice to meet you Lizzy," Peter said. "Gladys has told me much about you and your upcoming wedding to Henry. He's a fine man, but also a lucky man to marry such a lovely young lady as you."

Lizzy blushed again, and then said, "Thank you so much for meeting us for lunch. I've never been in such a nice hotel, well, except for when I was in Chicago and doing laundry in the basement. I was never allowed upstairs."

Peter and Margaret looked quizzically at each other, and then turned toward Gladys. "Oh, it's ok." Lizzy continued. "We spent the winter in Chicago before we finished our trip here. I was just 17 and needed a way to make some money to help pay for our board and buy our land once we got here. It was a hot, sweaty job, but it paid well, and it gave me the satisfaction that I was helping my family."

"That's very admirable of you," Margaret said. "Most young people would not want such manual labor. Do you have other brothers and sisters? Tell us more about your family."

The waitress arrived to take their order, and Lizzy almost fainted at the prices listed on the menu. "Don't worry Lizzy–I'm taking care of everything," Peter said. "Call it an early wedding gift from us. You will almost be like family to us now."

Lizzy stared at the menu and was not sure what many of the items were. Levi leaned over and whispered, "I'm going to have the roast beef dinner with salad and soup, if that helps you decide. But any of the items are great."

Lizzy smiled in thanks and when it was her turn to order she said, "I'd like the roasted chicken with potatoes and peas, a green salad, and tomato soup." She tried to sound confident, and Levi winked his approval. Gladys was busy with her own order and did not see the exchange, but Margaret did, and she wondered if Levi was being a little too friendly to his soon-to-be sister-in-law.

Lizzy told them the story of her immigration, her mother's death and father's remarriage, and all the additional children. She relayed their adventures crossing the country, her snake bite and being snowed in last winter. She avoided topics such as Casper's death and the Indians shooting Adam. By the time she finished her tales, the food had arrived, and Lizzy was in awe of the number of plates and glasses, and the sights and smells of all the wonderful food. She unfolded her napkin to put in on her lap and had to smile as she held it in her hands. Downstairs in the basement was someone doing the same job she used to do. Never did she dream that one day she would be eating in the fancy dining room upstairs, instead of slouched in a corner of the basement eating cold bread and cheese brought from home.

The lunch was wonderful, but soon it was time to leave and head back home. The fabric and lace for her dress were tucked safely in a box and slid under their seat. Audrey was wide awake, and jabbered and laughed as they bounced along the city streets and then out into the country. They had about five hours before it would start to get dark, and Levi said he would have Lizzy home in plenty of time.

It was a pleasant drive for about two hours, and Lizzy was getting excited to be home. As nice as this day was, she missed her parents and the rest of the family. And she missed Henry. They passed through several small towns and then into the country again but were still around two hours from home. Suddenly, something spooked one of the horses and he darted through a ditch and into a field. The buggy tipped over and everyone was thrown to the ground. Lizzy landed face-first into a pile of rocks and felt blood running down her cheeks. She tried to move but feared that her wrist was broken. She did manage to see Levi and Gladys sitting not far from her, brushing the dirt off a scared but unhurt Audrey. Gladys ripped off one of her petticoats and handed it to Levi, who gently tried to wipe Lizzy's face. He went to get some water from the buggy, and that is when he saw that one of the wheels was broken. He looked around in a panic–hoping to see someone else on the road and then looked for the horses who had run away. It would be dark before long–what were they going to do?

"Does anything else hurt?" Levi asked Lizzy, trying hard to hide his worry.

"My wrist is sore, but I don't think it's broken. Are you all ok?"

"Yes, just a bit shaken up. It all happened so fast."

"MY DRESS!" Lizzy shouted. "Is it ok?"

"I'm sure, but let me look," Levi said as he rose stiffly and went back to the buggy resting awkwardly on its side in the ditch. He pulled out the box and found it intact and unharmed. "It's perfect," he said with a sigh of relief. Lizzy certainly didn't need anything else to go wrong right now.

"Levi," Gladys whispered. "What are we going to do? It will be dark soon, and we have a broken wagon, no horses, and Lizzy is hurt."

"We just need to pray that someone comes along to help us. I certainly cannot leave you here to go get help. Let me look in the buggy to see what supplies we have in case we end up here for a while."

"And Jakob? You know Lizzy needs to be home before dark. He is going to be furious."

"I know, and it's my fault."

"Well, you didn't spook the horses or turn over the buggy, but Jakob will not be pleased."

Lizzy's face had stopped bleeding, and she gingerly stood up and moved closer to the buggy.

"I heard what you said, Gladys, and yes, my father will be furious. But it was an accident–it's not like we were socializing and lost track of time. I'll pray that a good Samaritan comes along soon to rescue us."

Chapter 21

Jakob was pacing back and forth as he watched the sun set over his newly plowed fields. Lizzy was supposed to have been home by now–she knew the rules! Where in the world was she? Eventually he went in the house but continued his pacing.

About an hour later he heard a buggy in the drive, and ran to the door to lecture his daughter, but also to rejoice that she was home. Except it was Henry who walked in the door.

"So, they aren't here either? Levi and Gladys never came home, so I rushed over here. I think we need to go search for them–something must have happened. Levi is very conscientious and would have had her home long ago if he could."

"Help me hitch up the wagon in case we need to bring everyone with us. Clara–Henry and I are going out to look for Lizzy and the others. Hopefully we will be home later, but I honestly can't say when as we may have to go all the way to St. Paul to find them."

"Dear Lord, please protect Lizzy, Levi, and Gladys. And the baby–please don't let anything happen to the baby!"

Jakob and Henry quickly loaded the wagon with blankets, some food, and Clara's medicine box. They had no idea what kinds of injuries they might encounter. They lit two lanterns and hung them from posts on either side of the wagon and urged the oxen out into the dark night. There was no moon tonight, no stars, and it felt like a storm was brewing. "Please let us find them," Henry whispered.

Jakob wanted to push the oxen to go as fast as possible, but knew he needed all their strength for what could be a very long night. Henry called out to Lizzy and Levi but heard nothing but a few night birds and the occasional coyote off in the distance. "Lizzy where are you?" he asked the darkness, but no one answered.

Chapter 22

Levi had moved both Gladys and Lizzy to rest beside the upturned buggy as it sat in the ditch. They had no blankets except for a small one for Audrey, and the only food was some fruit that Gladys added at the last minute. The air was getting colder, and the group huddled together to try to keep warm. Levi was in the middle with his arms around both women in an attempt to give them shelter and warmth. Lizzy's face hurt and she was worried about the extent of the damage.

He looked at the two women beside him, both relying on him for protection. Gladys was a lovely lady, and he adored his baby daughter. They had different views on money and lifestyles, but he did care for her. On the other side was Lizzy, who was like a breath of fresh air to him. Tough, hard-working, frugal–her sturdy personality was so much more closely aligned to his. Henry was a very lucky man indeed to be marrying her and to spend the rest of his life with her.

"I'm afraid we are in for a long, miserable night," Levi said, "unless someone happens to come by, which I hate to say I honestly doubt. Anyone with any sense will be someplace warm and dry tonight, not out driving around in the dark."

"I've survived worse when we were coming here. And surely someone will be on this road in the morning–we'll just huddle together for warmth. Levi–do you have anything with you to make a fire?"

"No, I don't. But I'll start carrying a flint with me from now on."

"Well, I for one am cold and hungry and extremely uncomfortable," Gladys whined.

"I know, my dear, but what choice do we have? We will get through this, I promise."

Several hours passed, and Lizzy faded in and out of sleep. Every part of her body hurt, and she was cold and damp and pretty miserable. She prayed over and over that someone would find them before a wild animal did, or Indians. She tried to think happy thoughts, reliving her lovely day of fabric shopping and the most amazing lunch at the hotel. She drifted off to sleep and was soon dreaming of her wedding and Henry's smile as she walked down the aisle. It seemed so real, and she could hear him calling to her.

"Lizzy–Lizzy–where are you?"

Henry's voice–that wonderful voice. But why did he sound worried? Was something wrong?

She opened her eyes to see nothing except drizzling rain. She was so cold–and wondered how much longer it would be until sunrise. She could feel that her face was swollen and feared how horrible she looked. She was glad her wedding was several months away so she would have a chance to recover.

She had shoved the box with her wedding dress fabric behind her to try to protect it as much as possible. How horrible for this beautiful fabric to be ruined before she even got it home. She just prayed that it wasn't getting too damp and destroyed.

"Lizzy–where are you?" she heard it again. Was she imagining things?

Then far off in the distance she saw a light bobbing up and down and could faintly hear the sound of a wagon. She placed a hand on Levi's shoulder and shook him awake. "Levi!" she said excitedly, "I hear something!"

Suddenly, a light was shining on them from the road. "Lizzy–Levi! Are you there?"

"Henry? Is that you? Yes, we are down here!" Levi said. "Please hurry–it's been a rough night and I think Lizzy is hurt."

Levi and Jakob scrambled down into the deep ditch and quickly understood what had happened. Jakob rushed to Lizzy, so Henry went to Levi and Gladys.

"Lizzy–are you ok?" Jakob asked worriedly.

"Father, I'm so glad to see you. Something spooked the horses, and I was thrown from the buggy. I hit my face and I'm worried I maybe broke something. I can open my mouth ok, so it's not my jaw or teeth. I think the others are ok, though."

"Even the baby?" he asked. "I didn't see her."

"Yes, she's fine. She's wrapped up and Gladys has kept her warm and dry as best she could."

"Let me help you up. How long have you been out here?"

"It was before the sun went down–we had plenty of time to get home before dark. Father, how bad does my face look?"

Jakob held the lamp next to Lizzy's face and she could see the concern in his eyes. "It looks like maybe your nose is broken–and there is some swelling around your eyes. Let me get you up and into the wagon. We have blankets and a bit of food and water. I don't see any bleeding right now—let's just get you home so you can warm up."

"Father—don't forget that box behind me. It has the fabric for my dress. I pray it is ok."

Jakob and Henry got everyone loaded into the wagon and wrapped in blankets. Audrey woke up for a few minutes, but then settled back into a deep sleep.

"How far are we from home, Father?" Lizzy asked.

"Just over an hour. Try to rest and hopefully the ride is not too rough for you."

'You have blankets and food," Gladys said. "I'm better already."

Lizzy drifted off to sleep before long. Being cold and wet in the back of this wagon—the same wagon she had crossed the country in—felt very familiar and almost comforting.

Before long, the wagon came to a stop in front of Lizzy's home. Jakob helped her down and into the house while Henry loaded the others into his own waiting buggy. Before leaving, he came into the house to check on Lizzy one last time.

"I was so worried about you—I'm glad we found you before you had to spend the entire night outside. If you want, I'll ride into town in the morning to bring the doctor to check on you. I'm so sorry that you were hurt."

"I'm sure I look horrible—if you want to change your mind about the wedding I understand—maybe Gladys can get some of her money back for the fabric," Lizzy said sadly.

"There is no way that a broken nose or black eyes would ever keep me from marrying you. You are still the loveliest lady in the county, and I cannot wait to be your husband. Is the fabric ok?"

"I haven't had the courage to look yet. The box isn't too wet, so I am hoping so."

"I'll be back over in the morning to check on you. I pray you can get some rest."

"I will. Thank you for rescuing us."

"Well, your father played a big part as well. He was angry at first, but his love for you was bigger than any curfew that was missed."

"OK–get Levi, Gladys and the baby home. I'll talk to you tomorrow. Goodnight my dear Henry."

"Goodnight my sweet girl."

Chapter 23

It was almost noon when Lizzy opened her eyes. Every part of her body ached as she remembered the events of last night. She slowly crawled out of her bed and looked at herself in the mirror on her dresser. She was shocked to see that both of her eyes were blackened like racoons, and her nose had a slight twist to the left. She looked around her room and saw that Clara had already been there, filling her pitcher with warm water and leaving some fresh towels nearby. At the foot of her bed was the box with the wedding fabric, still tied with the bow from the store. With trembling hands, she removed the ribbon and gently opened the lid. Inside was her fabric, carefully wrapped in tissue paper, and the lace was wrapped separately in linen. Both were in perfect condition. She stroked the satin and tried to imagine how her dress would look. Then she noticed a slip of paper at the bottom—it was a note from Emily, thanking her for her business and wishing her a lifetime of wedded happiness. There was also an envelope that contained $10.00. Lizzy wanted to protest, but instead smiled at the kindness of this new friend. Henry would be excited with the news - $10.00 would go a long way at the new farm.

She got dressed and went downstairs to see Clara alone in the kitchen—Father was working outside, and Adam had taken the younger children to the Augustines to go fishing. Clara tried to hide her shock when she saw Lizzy's face, but Lizzy waved her away.

"Let me get you some cold water," Clara said. "It will help with the swelling. How are you feeling otherwise?"

"Like I was thrown into a ditch by a runaway buggy. I'm just so glad to be home."

"And your fabric? I do hope it is ok, after being out in the rain and all."

"Yes, it is perfect. I cannot wait to get started–it's going to be so pretty. The whole experience was overwhelming."

"Sit here and tell me everything while I find you something to eat. You must be starving."

"Yes, I am. Has anyone heard from Henry?"

"He stopped by early this morning to check on you, but I told him you were sleeping in. He did leave a gift for you on the front porch."

"A gift? Do you know what it is?"

"Yes, but he swore me to secrecy."

Lizzy slowly rose from her chair and walked gingerly to the front door. Sitting on the porch was a lovely box five feet long by two feet deep, and about 3 feet tall, made from planks of white birch. She lifted the lid to find a note inside. *My dear Lizzy–I know with all you have been through these past several years, starting a Hope Chest is not something you have been able to do. I finished this for you last night - I hope you love it as much as I love you. Henry.'*

"Oh, Clara–it's beautiful. I have been thinking about this lately–I have so few things to bring into the marriage to help get the house set up. Even basic things–towels, sheets, and dishes. I know he has a few belongings in his room in town, but almost nothing to bring to the new house, either. At least this gives me a place to put things, as few as they are."

"His timing is perfect. Marie and I were talking about this just yesterday while you were gone. There is a new thing that has started in the bigger cities called a 'bridal shower.' It's where friends of the bride have a party, and everyone brings a small gift–maybe an apron or some linens. The women at the church would love to do this for you if you are willing."

"A bridal shower? Why do they call it that?"

"I'm not sure–I think in places like London and Paris the women put their gifts into a parasol and when it is opened, the gifts rain out. What do you think of the idea of having a party?"

"It sounds lovely, but I know everyone is struggling. I would hate for people to feel obligated to bring us gifts."

"The pastor's wife has already said she would be in charge–all we need to do is pick a date and she will arrange the rest."

"Sometime early in September? I'm really flattered that they want to do this for me."

"Everyone loves Henry, and everyone loves you, so of course they want to help in any way they can. Ok, come back in and tell me about your day in St. Paul while I fix you some lunch."

Lizzy recounted the excitement of the day–the shopping, the elegant lunch, the generosity of Gladys' parents, and how strange it felt to be upstairs instead of in the laundry room downstairs. Clara brought her some beef stew that was left over from yesterday, and Lizzy cleaned the plate, obviously hungrier than she realized.

It wasn't long before Adam and the children came home, each one shocked at Lizzy's appearance. She knew the swelling and black eyes would eventually disappear, but her crooked nose would likely remain forever.

The pleasant summer days flew by quickly, with Lizzy working in the garden, helping finish building the house where she could, and slowly taking one stitch at a time to assemble her dress. Clara and Marie helped her cut the pieces and provided guidance along the way. Little by little, the dress started taking shape.

Henry stopped by almost every evening to visit and talk about wedding plans with Lizzy and politics with Jakob and Adam. Tensions were continuing to rise regarding the slave trade and the dangerous Indian raids that were taking place in the Dakotas and western Minnesota territory. Henry had been involved in several more transports for the underground railroad, but he kept many of the details from her as he did not want her to worry.

The first Saturday in September was Lizzy's bridal shower, and she was overwhelmed by the generosity of her friends and neighbors. Twenty-eight women and young girls were in attendance where gifts were opened, and they celebrated with cake and other pastries. The gifts were lovingly placed into the Hope Chest, and Lizzy felt much more prepared to enter married life. Marriage. Just a few weeks away now. She loved Henry and knew that he loved her, but this was a huge step. Was she really ready?

Chapter 24

Saturday, September 30, 1853. Lizzy opened her eyes to a beautiful sunrise and birds chirping outside her window. Today was the day. This morning, she was Miss Lizzy Kruse, but tonight would be Mrs. Henry Sauter. It all seemed so unreal. Not all that long ago she arrived here in a crowded wagon knowing no one. And now she had met a wonderful man who she loved with all her heart.

She looked around the room and saw her dress hanging on her closet door, the veil carefully wrapped in linen and her new boots cleaned and polished. The dress was exquisite–it fit her perfectly and the lace on the bodice and sleeves helped create a magical feeling when she tried it on.

The wedding itself was not until 7 pm tonight–what a long day stretched ahead of her! Except there were a lot of things to help keep her busy, such as making sure the church had all the food and flowers they had selected. The wedding itself would be quite brief with just 30 people in attendance at the most, but she wanted everything to be perfect. She thought again about Gladys and her offer to purchase the fabric–Lizzy could see now that this was going to be the most special day of her life. All she had to do now was keep busy and be ready to pledge her life, and her love, to Henry.

Clara knocked softly on the door and poked her head inside. "Are you awake? It's your special day! The weather looks perfect. Come on down for breakfast. I know you are probably too nervous to eat, but you really need to. Then I'll fix you a bath and you can wash your hair. Marie will be here after lunch to braid it for you in that special way you want. And then I'll help you dress, and we'll take you to the church by six. The cake and other food are to be delivered by four, and the pastor's wife will oversee that. The younger children will be picking flowers for you to carry and for Henry to wear in his lapel. Is there anything we are missing?

"I need to finish packing my bag, too. Henry said we will stay in the new house tonight but then travel to St. Paul to honeymoon for several days. I'm excited, but also very nervous, you know, about tonight after we are alone."

"I know it's difficult for us ladies to talk about. You know the basics, right?"

"Yes, of course, but………"

"Just follow his lead, honey. He knows you are not experienced in this matter and I'm sure he will be gentle. Try to relax–it will make it easier and at times enjoyable."

Lizzy blushed at the thoughts in her head, and knew she needed to change the subject.

"I'm so glad that the swelling and black eyes had a chance to resolve before today. The last thing I wanted was a wedding picture of me looking like I had been in a bar fight! But the bump on my nose is here to stay I guess."

"It's really not that noticeable," Clara answered. "Come on downstairs - I have some of your favorites waiting for you."

Lizzy dressed in a simple pinafore and entered the dining room to see platters of bacon, fresh bread, strawberry jam, and a bowl of freshly churned butter. Clara was just taking a pan of fried potatoes from the stove. Jakob poured her a large glass of milk and gave her a kiss on her cheek. "My little Lizzy–how you have grown. I remember the night you were born --- upside down and backwards, but an answer to our prayers. I knew that night that you were going to be someone special, and you are. I thank God daily that you found such a kind and upstanding young man, and that he found you! I wish you a lifetime of happiness, I hope you know that."

"Thank you, Father. Clara, this all looks wonderful, but I'm not sure I can eat anything. Just too excited and nervous, I guess."

"Well, try to eat something–it's going to be a really long day, I could scramble you an egg if you want?" Clara asked gently.

Lizzy declined, and instead had a few bites of bread with jam and a slice of bacon. "I probably should get in the bath, so my hair is dry when Marie gets here. Any word from Gladys this morning?"

"Levi came by a bit ago and said everything was on schedule and they would be at the church in plenty of time. He also said that he saw Henry earlier who looked happy and scared and excited all at once."

Lizzy found it hard to imagine him anywhere as nervous as she was, but finished her light breakfast and went into the small room they had designated as a washroom. Clara was insistent that this be included in their new home to provide everyone with privacy while bathing, instead of doing it in her bedroom or the kitchen. She sank into the warm water and washed her hair with the lavender soap Clara let her use. Soon she was out and wrapped in a robe while Clara combed out her long hair so it could dry. The little children were next into the tub, each taking their turn to wash off the dust of the week. Then they were dressed in their finest church clothes and Jakob lectured them not to go outside or get dirty.

Marie arrived just after noon and started braiding Lizzy's hair in the crown style she wore the day she knew she was developing feelings for Henry. But Marie also had some tiny pink flowers that she worked into the braid, knowing they would look nice with the pink roses she would be carrying. About 4:30 in the afternoon, Marie and Clara accompanied Lizzy upstairs to help her get dressed and finish packing. Marie handed her a gift that contained new undergarments and stockings. They carefully helped her into her dress and then Clara gave her a small, padded envelope.

"This gift is from your father and I," she said tearfully. "I understand it is one of the few things that he had left that had once belonged to your mother."

Lizzy unwrapped the package to find a comb for her hair that looked like it was made from ivory, although it probably wasn't.

"I thought maybe we use this to help hold your veil in place?" Clara asked. "I know your mother would be so proud of you and is watching you from heaven. This way you can carry a piece of her with you."

Lizzy's eyes filled with tears and knew this would likely be the first of many times today she would cry—mostly from joy, but also sadness that her mother was not there, nor the other children that had been lost.

"It's beautiful, Clara. Can we try it now?"

Clara and Marie unwrapped the veil and attached it to the crown of Lizzy's head, the comb fitting perfectly into the braid. Both women hugged her gently, so as not to wrinkle her dress, and then took the veil back off. Lizzy certainly did not want it to get damaged on the way to the church.

"Are you ready?" Clara asked as she finished lacing Lizzy's boots.

"You go on down–I need just one more minute. Could you send Father up?"

"Of course," Clara said. "I'll take your suitcase if it's ready."

"Yes, thank you."

Lizzy sat carefully on the edge of her bed and looked around her bedroom. Jakob knocked softly on the bedroom door, then opened it to find his beautiful daughter, ready to go to the church to be married.

"I suppose this is the time I should give you marriage advice," he said softly with tears in his eyes. "All I can say is to keep God as the center of your marriage, and never go to bed with hurt feelings. Talk things out and love each other, more every day."

"Thank you, Father, for everything you have given me over the years. I love you so much! Ok, I think I'm ready–are you?"

"Ready for my oldest child, my first daughter, to get married? I doubt we are ever truly ready, but it's time. Let's not keep Henry waiting another minute!"

After taking one final look around her room, Lizzy slowly descended the stairs and then went out the front door. Jakob helped her into the wagon, the bench having been padded and covered with several blankets. Her suitcase was in the back and Clara was tightly gripping the veil. Marie had gone ahead in her own buggy with the flowers the children had picked. Lizzy took one last glance at the new house she had barely lived in, then turned her attention to the road that would lead her to Henry. Her journey here was ending, but she was about to embark on a new one with Henry by her side.

Chapter 25

The wagon pulled into the driveway of the church, and Levi stepped outside to greet them. Lizzy glowed like an angel in the setting sun, and Levi felt a pang of regret as he watched her climb down. Clara helped her put the veil back on while Adam took the younger children inside. Gladys came outside wearing a pale pink dress and holding Lizzy's bouquet. She was just in time to see the strange look in her husband's eyes as he watched Lizzy adjust her dress and ascend the steps to go inside. It was obvious, however, that Lizzy was not aware and had only Henry on her mind.

"Henry is inside," Levi said, "and everything is ready. There is a side room where you can relax until it's time–Henry is safely locked away in the pastor's office so as not to see you until the correct time."

"You look lovely, Lizzy," Gladys said. "The dress is beautiful."

"Thank you again for this, and for the veil. It's perfect. Your dress is lovely as well."

The group went inside the church and into a small room just off the foyer. Lizzy could hear others starting to arrive, and before long the pastor's wife began playing softly. Lizzy was trying to calm her nerves, trusting that the other arrangements were taken care of, and her only job today was to pledge her life to Henry.

"OK, let's get this wedding started!" Jakob said. "Ready?"

"Yes, Father. Do I look ok?"

"You are beautiful–a very lovely bride."

"Thank you."

The music changed a bit as Levi and Gladys began their walk down the aisle as best man and matron of honor. Marie had offered to take care of Audrey, and Lizzy could hear "momma–dadda" while everyone chuckled. Then the music changed again to Lizzy's favorite song "Abide With Me" and she began her walk toward Henry. He could not take his eyes off her, and she felt like she was floating while holding her father's arm. When they reached the altar, Jakob pressed a small kiss onto her cheek and placed her hand into Henry's.

The pastor began, "We are gathered here this evening to witness the marriage of John Henry Sauter and Hattie Elizabeth Kruse. Marriage is a sacred institution- if there is anyone here who knows why these two should not be married, speak now or forever remain silent."

Gladys looked at Levi for signs of discomfort, but he was smiling proudly at his brother. Maybe she had just misinterpreted what she saw earlier?

No one spoke up, of course, so Pastor Clarke continued, "Who gives this woman to be married?"

Jakob rose and said, "I do," with his eyes filling with tears again.

"John Henry–do you take this woman to be your wife–to love her, honor and keep her, forsaking all others, for as long as you both shall live?"

"I do," he said as he looked deeply into her eyes.

"And do you, Hattie Elizabeth, take this man to be your husband—to love him, honor and keep him, forsaking all others, as long as you both shall live?"

"I do," Lizzy answered with all the love she had.

"Do you have the ring?" the pastor asked.

Levi had Lizzy's ring in his jacket pocket, and he handed it to Henry. It was a simple gold band that had belonged to his mother.

"Bless this ring, Lord, as a symbol of Your unending love."

Henry slipped the band onto Lizzy's finger and gave her hand a squeeze.

"Let us pray," the pastor said. "Oh, gracious Heavenly Father, bless this union of Henry and Lizzy. Fill them with Your love for each other and walk with them through both the good times and the bad. Help them to keep You at the forefront of all decisions and keep them safe for many years to come. Amen"

"Amen," the crowd responded.

"And now, by the power vested to me by God and this congregation, I now pronounce you husband and wife. Henry, you may kiss your bride."

Henry lifted Lizzy's veil and gently cupped her face in his hands. "I love you, my sweet Lizzy," he whispered to her and then gave her a gentle kiss. Everyone rose to their feet, clapping and cheering. Henry escorted Lizzy to the back of the church, followed by Levi and Gladys. The small group of attendees joined them for hugs of congratulations and well wishes. There was a cake and some finger sandwiches set up in the foyer and the party lasted about an hour. As it was getting quite dark, Henry cut the party short and grabbed Lizzy's hand and walked toward the door. "Are you ready to leave, Mrs. Sauter?" he beamed at her.

"Yes, Mr. Sauter. Goodnight, everyone–thank you so much for coming!"

"We need photos before you leave!" Clara called, and a young man named Kristof directed them to an area he had set up.

"This will take just a minute," he said as he took a few pictures of the two of them, and then one of just Lizzy. "I'll take this film into St. Paul for processing. They should be ready in a week or so."

After the photos and another round of well wishes, they walked toward Henry's buggy, and Adam stopped by for a quick hug. "Your bag is already in the back. Congratulations, Lizzy --- you are the best big sister I could have ever wanted. Take good care of her, Henry."

"Of course," he replied as he patted Adam's shoulder. "Always."

Lizzy hugged him tightly, then Henry helped her into the buggy. "Goodbye everyone," she waved. "Thanks again for everything!" and then they drove off toward the home that Henry had built for his bride.

Chapter26

Lizzy snuggled closely to Henry as they began the short drive to the new farm. She had not been there in several weeks, as Henry wanted to keep most of it as a surprise. She had made suggestions for the design, of course, but had no idea how far along it was. Henry had just said that it was almost done and certainly fine to move into.

Lizzy was suddenly very shy as they got closer to her new home. Having grown up on a farm, she knew the mechanics of mating, but had never even seen her father do more than kiss Clara on the cheek. Her mind raced as she tried to imagine their first night together.

Henry could sense her uneasiness and squeezed her hand gently while smiling down on her. "I hope you like what I have done inside the house."

There was a bright crescent moon this evening, and Lizzy could see the outline of the house as they pulled in the drive.

"Let me help you down and then I need to put the buggy away. Are you ok waiting out here for me?"

"Yes, that's fine. I love that you have rocking chairs on the porch."

"I'll be right back, don't move!" he said with a wicked grin.

It was only a few minutes before he was jogging toward her from the barn. "OK, Mrs. Sauter–welcome to your new home!" and he scooped her into his arms to carry her across the threshold. He put her down gently, then went back to the porch for her suitcase and flowers.

"Oh, Henry–the house looks great. I had no idea you had come so far."

He guided her through the rest of the main floor–the kitchen, dining room and living room.

"I do have a surprise for you," he whispered as he turned a corner into the parlor where there was an upright piano against the far wall.

"Oh, a piano? Where did you find it? And how in the world did you get it in here?"

"A long story for another time. Come, my dear wife, there is one more room to show you." He took her hand and led her toward their bedroom. Instantly very shy, Lizzy started to tremble a bit. "It's ok," Henry continued. "I'll leave you alone to change and then we will just rest together for a while."

"Thank you. But before you leave, could you help me unfasten this dress? I cannot quite reach all the buttons myself."

"Of course," he said as he gently kissed her shoulder. "I'll be back in a few minutes."

Lizzy's hands were shaking as she removed her dress and slipped into a soft nightgown. She pulled back the blanket and slid between the sheets, waiting for Henry to return. She truly had no idea what to expect next.

A few minutes later, Henry returned to the bedroom, having already removed his suit coat and tie and even his shirt. Lizzy blushed as he removed his trousers and then crawled into the bed beside her. He wrapped his arms around her and kissed her gently. "My sweet girl–I am the luckiest man on the earth tonight. I love you."

Feeling strangely safe in his arms, Lizzy felt herself relax a bit and returned his kisses. Henry leaned over and blew out the lamp beside the bed. And then with all the tenderness and respect he had for her, they discovered together the physical expression of their love.

Many hours later, Lizzy opened her eyes to see Henry sleeping beside her. Her cheeks burned red as the memories of last night came flooding back to her. This was very different from what she had observed on the farm, and she was eternally grateful!

Henry had been very tender and sweet all throughout the night. She loved him more now than before, if that was even possible. She stretched a bit and reached for her robe. Sliding carefully out of the bed without waking Henry, she tiptoed into the kitchen to really look around for the first time. Her Hope Chest had been brought over a few days ago, and Lizzy lifted the lid to see all the gifts her friends had given her. The house was quite chilly, and she wanted to start a fire, but didn't want to make any noise to wake him. They were not planning to leave for St. Paul until after lunch. She found a blanket and wrapped it around her shoulders as she went out to the porch to admire the sunrise. The house was on a small hill, and she could see for several miles in each direction. Little did she know that sitting on this porch, searching the horizon, would be something she would do for years to come.

She heard the screen door open behind her. "Lizzy, what are you doing out here in the cold? Come back inside and I'll build a fire."

Lizzy rose from the chair and smiled at her husband. "Good morning, husband. I didn't want to disturb you, or I would have built it myself." He held the door for her as they walked inside.

"Good morning, my love. I have no doubts you would have! How are you? Are you ok?" he asked gently. He never wanted to hurt her, and hoped he hadn't upset or scared her."

"I'm fine, my dear Henry. Better than fine," she smiled.

They walked together back into the house and Lizzy looked for something to fix for breakfast while Henry lit the stove.

"Do you know how to fix coffee?" Henry asked. "I know your parents don't drink it much."

"I've watched others make it, but never done it myself. Plus, it was not something we could afford most of the time. I've only tasted it once or twice."

"No problem, I will teach you. It's really very easy. I might even turn you into a coffee drinker!"

"I'm not finding a lot for breakfast, just some bread and cheese, plus some potatoes and onions."

"I know, I'm sorry. I just didn't want a lot of food here that might spoil before we got back from our trip."

"No, that's fine. I've learned to be pretty creative over the years. Living in a famine will do that to you," she said sadly, thinking of her mother and babies Anna and Louisa.

"The fire is going well, so I'll go to the pump and bring in some water. I do have a few chickens in the barn, so I'll go look for eggs if you want?"

"Oh, that would be perfect," Lizzy said as she started to unpack her Hope Chest and looked for a skillet and some dishes.

Henry returned with a large bucket of fresh, cold water and three eggs. "I wish I could take all those sad memories away from you," Henry said as he filled a pot with water to warm on the stove.

"It's the hard times where we gain our strength, right? God never left us, even on the darkest days. Henry, there is something I have been wanting to ask you. Father was always in charge of our religious training and upbringing. He led the prayers at every meal and did Bible readings each morning. That is something I want to continue, and hope you feel the same way."

"Absolutely I do. I have an old German Bible that I use each morning and prayer has always been a big part of my life. I'll go grab my Bible and we can start right after breakfast."

Lizzy brought the food to the table as Henry returned to the room. "Have I told you today how beautiful you are? Even in a robe with your braids falling down–you are the one for me!"

"Eat before it gets cold, you silly man. The water is warm enough for us to wash off later before we dress for the day and the start of our trip."

Henry sat next to Lizzy at their tiny table and held her hand softly in his. "Dear Father," he prayed. "Thank You for this day and the start of our married life together. Thank You for this food and bless the beautiful hands that prepared it. Guide us today on our trip and all the days of our lives. Amen."

"Amen," Lizzy whispered. Was this really happening? Here she was, sitting in her robe and messy hair, sharing eggs and potatoes with her new husband.

After breakfast, Henry picked up his well-worn Bible and opened the front cover. "Time to make this official," he said as he wrote their names and yesterday's date on the page for 'marriages.' Lizzy smiled as he turned to 1st John 3. "I'll pick up where I left off yesterday, if that's ok."

"That's perfect," she said as she admired the man who was now her partner.

Henry started reading from verse 1: "*See what great love the Father has lavished on us, that we should be called children of God! And that is what we are! The reason the world does not know us is that it did not know him. Dear friends, now we are children of God, and what we will be has not yet been made known. But we know that when Christ appears, we shall be like him, for we shall see him as he is. All who have this hope in him purify themselves, just as he is pure.*"

Lizzy had not heard the Bible read in German for quite a while, and it made her a bit homesick. "That's a lovely passage," she said softly. "I'm glad He chose me to be one of His children."

"Speaking of children, are you still wanting 10? If so, we are going to need a bigger house!"

"We'll see—let's just take one at a time for now, ok?"

Lizzy cleared away the breakfast dishes and washed them with some of the warm water. She took the rest and poured it into the bowl and pitcher in the bedroom. She took off her robe and began taking a quick sponge bath when she saw Henry watching her from the doorway. "Let me help you with that," he said wickedly, and took the cloth from her to gently wash her back. Lizzy leaned against him, then turned to kiss her new husband. She was going to enjoy married life.

Chapter 27

"Are you sure we have everything?" Lizzy asked as she climbed into the buggy.

"I have your bag and mine, plus some emergency supplies in case we run into trouble along the way. We shouldn't have a problem reaching town before dark. I can't wait to spend this time showing St. Paul to you. I spent quite a bit of time there when Levi and I first arrived in Minnesota. I asked him to check on the farm every day we are gone, and to help himself to any eggs he finds. It's nice to have him and Gladys so close.

The drive to the city was uneventful, and the couple chatted easily the whole trip. "I'm sorry I cannot afford a room at the hotel where you had lunch with Gladys," Henry said apologetically. "That's way out of my budget."

"We never really talked about money," she replied. "I know you plan to keep giving music lessons in Oliver's Grove, but until the dairy farm is up and profitable, what do you think about me taking a job in town a few days a week? I'm not afraid of hard work, and surely there is something I can do to generate an income."

"I know how hard you can work, I'm just not very comfortable with your taking on a regular job. It's my responsibility as your husband to provide for you and our family."

"Well, it's just us, at least for now. And I think we need to make more money before winter sets in. I certainly don't want another winter like last year."

"We can ask around when we get back—I don't want you worrying about it now. Let's just have a nice dinner tonight and enjoy this special week. There is plenty of time later to worry about money."

Dinner that night was at a small café, and then they checked into the Adams Hotel. It was clean and their room was on the 3rd floor, overlooking the river.

Lizzy was not nearly as shy when they got ready for bed, but was still a bit tentative returning his caresses. Again, Henry was patient and gentle, and before long they had drifted off in a contented sleep.

The next four days were filled with shopping and exploring the bustling city, eating a picnic at Como Park overlooking the Mississippi. They watched as steamboats and freighters chugged up and down, bringing people and products into town. They went to the theater one evening, and another day they visited Ft. Snelling. As pleasant as the visit was, the city held an undercurrent of unrest and even hate speech. The last day in town they were sitting in a restaurant and conversing in German. Behind them were several large men who had just come to town on a tugboat.

"Oh, great," one of the men said. "Just what we need is more immigrants! Dirty Krauts. Who said it was ok for so many of them to come here?"

"Easy, Sven," one of the men said. "Our families were immigrants too—remember?"

"Between them and now the darkies acting all uppity……. Minnesota sure ain't what it used to be."

Lizzy was shocked to hear such language, and Henry shrugged his shoulders. "Ignore them," he said softly. "Just bullies, picking on someone weaker. Try not to worry."

They loaded their things into the buggy for the four-hour drive home. It had been a wonderful time, but she was anxious to get things settled in the new house.

"I do have one stop to make before we leave town. It's with my contact at the Underground Railroad."

"Oh, I would love to meet him, if that's ok?"

"Let me go in first and see how things are going. Women don't normally go into barber shops, but I don't anticipate a problem. It's just around the corner."

Henry parked the buggy in front of 'Edward's Barber Shop' and went inside to speak to the owner. After a few minutes, Henry poked his head out the door and motioned for Lizzy to come in.

She climbed down from the buggy and Henry escorted her in. He introduced her to Edward Lawson, a tall thin black man around 50 years old. There were no other customers in the shop.

"Edward, this is my wife Lizzy. We just got married last week, so I'm still getting used to introducing her that way. She knows about my involvement in the cause and is very supportive. I know I've been unavailable to help lately but am ready to be of assistance however I can."

"However WE can," Lizzy corrected. "One of the reasons my father moved us to Minnesota was because it is a free territory, for now at least, and I hope to do all I can to keep it that way."

"I'm pleased to meet you, Lizzy," Edward said. "Henry has been a great help to us over the years, and knowing you are supportive is very important. As long as Minnesota remains a 'territory' and not a state, we are at the mercy of the Federal Government's establishing and enforcing their rules on us. What we need is statehood–a chance to take a stand on this issue for ourselves, and hopefully eliminate slavery altogether."

"What is the status on that?" Henry asked.

"It's gaining traction in the bigger towns, but with so many people working on farms or logging in the forests, politics doesn't always mean as much to them as it does to us. We are probably a few years away yet from a vote in congress."

"And what about the Indian situation?" Lizzy asked softly. "My family has had several interactions that were not positive, including the attempted murder of my younger brother."

"Another difficult situation for sure. This was *their* land first, but our government has continued to push them away from fertile fields and onto desolate reservations where almost nothing will grow. It's not hard to understand why they are hostile."

"My brother said a young boy showed up at his school one day, looking like he had not eaten in a week or two. He was begging for food, and fortunately the teacher was sympathetic, and all the children gave him food from their lunch pails. But so many of the confrontations have turned violent–what does the government plan to do?"

"I'm not really sure–I don't believe they anticipated this kind of resistance to the relocations."

"Well, I would love to stay and talk politics with you all day, but we have a long drive home," Henry said reluctantly. "Stay in touch using the usual methods, and we will help if we can."

"Goodbye Edward," Lizzy said as they stood to leave. "God bless you for the wonderful work you are doing."

"Safe travels Henry and Lizzy. I'll be in touch."

The pair went outside and climbed into the waiting buggy. Lizzy was silent as they started toward home. They passed many types of people–young and old, white and black, male and female. It was quite different from her all-white farm community. Lizzy felt alive here, filled with the excitement of helping to make a difference in her new soon-to-be state.

"Penny for your thoughts," Levi said as he turned the buggy onto the dirt road that would lead toward the farm.

"There is just a certain feeling I get when I'm here–an air of excitement and possibilities. But there is certainly the other side of the coin here, too: racism, poverty, arrogance. It's a fine place to visit, but I'm glad to be going home. It was a wonderful trip, Henry. Thank you."

They stopped at the trading post in Oliver's Grove to pick up some supplies. Lizzy saw a 'help wanted' sign in the newspaper office. "Can we just stop and ask?" Lizzy pleaded to Henry. "I'dw love to know what kind of help they are needing."

"OK, but don't get your hopes up. The owner, Graham Franklin, is pretty traditional in his values, and I'm not sure he would hire a woman, any woman, because he believes they belong at home being wives and mothers. But we can stop."

A small bell 'tinkled' as they opened the door to the newspaper office. "I'll be there in a bit," came a gruff voice from the back. After a minute or two, an older man perhaps 60 years old walked into the lobby, wiping his hands on his large white apron. "How can I help you?" he asked.

Lizzy looked around the office with excitement–the smell of the printer's ink was intoxicating to her.

"Good afternoon, Graham. I'm not sure you remember me–I'm Henry Sauter–I work at the trading post, and I give piano lessons. This is my wife Lizzy."

"Oh, yes–I remember now. Nice to meet you, Mrs. Sauter. What can I do for you?"

"We noticed your 'help wanted' sign in the window and wanted to inquire about it," Lizzy said boldly.

"You are looking for extra work Henry?" Graham asked.

"No, I am," Lizzy replied.

Graham let out a short laugh and said, "This position is for a part-time writer. I want someone to explain our changing times in language the locals can understand. I'm sure you have much more pressing duties in your home, taking care of your husband and children. I would prefer to hire a man for this position."

"And why is that?" she asked. "Women don't understand politics? Women can't write coherent sentences? Women should be seen and not heard?"

"Lizzy, I'm not sure this is the best way to go about this," Henry whispered.

"I just want to know why you would instantly write off an entire gender, Mr. Franklin. Why not give me a chance and if you don't like what I write, you don't pay me? I can make it more female-friendly if you want–gardening tips, food preservation, or sewing. Did you know I made my own wedding gown? "

"You've got yourself a wild one there, Henry. Sure you are up for this?"

"I knew her spirit when I married her–it's one of the reasons I love her, to be honest."

"OK, how about this. I give you two weeks to bring back to me a 200-word article about preserving food for winter storage. If I like it, I will pay you $5.00. We'll take it from there. How does that sound?"

"Perfect!" Lizzy said, with ideas already buzzing in her head. "But I hope you will let me move beyond homemaking tips to topics that really matter–slavery, race relations, the fight for statehood, gender equality."

"Hey, not so fast. One step at a time. No more than 200 words–that's all the space I can give you."

"You won't be disappointed, I promise!" Lizzy said as she skipped out the door.

"You had better hold on, Henry–it's going to be a bumpy ride with that one!"

"She's just what my life needed. We'll be back in two weeks. Thank you!"

Chapter 28

Lizzy was silent the rest of the drive home, and Henry could see the look of excitement on her face. He was glad that Graham had agreed to let her try her hand at writing, but hoped he would become more open to the idea of a female journalist.

After unpacking the buggy and putting the supplies away, Henry left to check in with Levi and Lizzy started organizing her kitchen. Again, she was so thankful for the gifts in her Hope Chest --- the kitchen would have been pretty sparce otherwise. She started cooking dinner for Henry and realized that this would be her first real meal for him. Wanting it to be special, she picked the last of the lettuce from the fall garden. She wanted to make a salad that her mother made as a child–could she remember all the instructions? She cut up a banana and made a dressing of sugar and milk. It was a strange salad, but one she loved. She then cooked some potatoes and a nice piece of pork they got in town. They had also picked up some carrots, so she peeled a few and put them in a pot to boil.

She set the table with the new linens she received but was sad that she did not have a complete set of dishes that matched. She heard the back door slam and knew Henry was home. She ran her hands through her hair and removed her apron and met him on the back porch as he was washing his hands.

"Something smells wonderful in here," he said with a smile. "Levi and Gladys send their love."

"I hope all is well with them. Anything happen while we were away?"

"Nothing special. Levi came over each day to check on things and took home about two dozen eggs."

"Good," she said as she placed a soft kiss on his cheek. "Dinner is ready."

Leading him into the dining room, she proudly stood and admired her lovely table setting and platters of food.

"I can't believe you did all of this while I was gone," Henry said. "Sure you don't want to just stay home and cook for me?"

"Funny. Let's eat before it gets cold."

"What is this?" Henry asked as he pointed at the salad.

"An old recipe of my mother's. I think I remembered it correctly–it's been a very long time."

Henry offered the prayer and then hungrily filled his plate. "This all looks amazing–I think I'm going to like having you here!"

He was a bit hesitant when he looked at the salad, but then admitted he was pleasantly surprised by the sweet taste. After dinner, Lizzy cleared the table and began washing the dishes. Henry went to the parlor and started playing the piano. Lizzy knew she would never tire of listening to him play.

"Are you still wanting to learn?" he asked as she walked into the room. "I'd love to teach you."

"Yes, that would be wonderful. But right now, my head is full of ideas for my first article. Do you have paper and a pencil? I should have had us pick up some in town while we were there."

"I have a little bit of both in the top desk drawer. Any ideas for your article?"

"I was thinking starting at the beginning, which is the root cellar. It's hard to store things if you don't have anywhere to put them."

"Makes sense. And yes, I'll pick up more when I go to town next."

"Thank you for letting me do this, Henry. It means a lot to me. And I won't neglect my duties here at the house, I promise."

The next two weeks were busy for the couple with Henry making the finishing touches on the house and Lizzy working hard to make the house their home. She made curtains from grain sacks and Kristoff the photographer stopped by with their wedding pictures, which she proudly hung on the parlor walls. Each afternoon after lunch she worked on her article, editing and re-writing until she felt it was the best she could do. Coming in at 187 words, she proudly tied the pages together with a ribbon and climbed into the buggy with Henry for the short ride to town. Walking boldly into the newspaper office, she handed the article to Graham and waited for a response.

"Sit here in the lobby while I go in the back to read this in private. I'll be back in a few minutes."

Lizzy had a hard time sitting and being patient–she paced back and forth and worried that she could have made it better.

What if he turns her down? After about five minutes, Graham walked back into the room.

"For a first article, I think you did a fine job. It could use a bit more polish, but I'm sure that will come in time. And now for the byline–I don't think I can use the one you provided–'Mrs. Henry Sauter.' I doubt my readers are ready for a woman author just yet."

"Well, I tend to disagree, but it is your newspaper. What about my initials–'H. E. Sauter'? That doesn't give my gender away, does it?"

"No, that sounds fine. Henry?"

"I would much rather it have her own name, and not hide behind initials. But if she's fine with it, so am I."

"Great," he said as he rustled around in a cigar box kept in his desk drawer. "Here is your first $5.00. Bring me an article by the 25th of each month because I go to print on the first. And I expect a one-month notice if you intend to quit when the babies come."

Lizzy took the money but was so disappointed in his attitude. Quit when the babies come? As if she was unable to work with children! How dare he treat her that way? She would show him!

Henry climbed in beside her and could feel her anger. "I told you he was very traditional. Don't let him upset you–prove him wrong, ok?"

"What shall we do with the $5.00? There are so many things we need for the house."

"I think you should spend it on *you* for a change," he replied. "What is something you want?"

"It's almost winter–I would love to use it to stock up on food, but maybe use a bit for some new mittens? Mine are pretty threadbare."

"New mittens it is! Let's head over to the trading post and see what we can find. I fully intend to support us, Lizzy. Your writing money should just be for you."

"Absolutely not. We are a team, and I plan to do my share."

"What about a compromise? You keep out $1.00 for yourself and the rest can go to the household fund. The money you keep is yours to do with whatever you want."

"I like the way you think, Mr. Sauter. It's a deal!"

The next few weeks flew by as they continued to finish the house and store food away for the winter. Henry chopped up more firewood than they would need, and Lizzy worked hard to make the home cozy and cook nutritious meals. They continued to go to her parents' home for Sunday dinner, and it was wonderful to see everyone and play games with the younger children. And she always made sure to play with Sunshine the cat, who was growing fat and sassy chasing mice and birds.

Much to her delight, Henry made good on his promise to give her piano lessons. Starting slowly with just a few simple songs and rhythms, Lizzy struggled to get her fingers to move confidently across the keys. Henry assured her that everyone started out as a beginner, but she started believing that maybe her talents lay elsewhere.

One Sunday about a month later, Clara pulled Lizzy aside and asked her privately, "You seem to be adjusting well to married life. But I'm curious–is there any possibility that you could be pregnant?"

"Pregnant? Already? I really doubt it. I mean………….." Her voice trailed off as she tried to remember the timing of her last cycle. Perhaps Clara was right?

"We mothers know how to recognize the signs in others. Have you been feeling ok?"

"Now that you mention it, I have been rather tired lately, but we've been working hard to get things situated for the winter. How soon did you know when you were expecting?"

"Usually within just a few weeks after missing a cycle. I guess you should go see Dr. Hampton?"

"Should I wait to tell Henry? I wouldn't want to get his hopes up if it's not true."

"Perhaps, but you would need an excuse to go to the doctor without him, and he would be suspicious anyway."

"True–I guess I'll tell him tonight and try to get to the doctor next week."

After a fun afternoon of board games, Lizzy and Henry headed for home. Once inside, Lizzy was pacing through the house like she was looking for something. Henry was confused and asked, "Did you misplace something? Can I help you look?"

"Perhaps," she said with a smile. "I am looking for the best place to put the rocking chair."

"Rocking chair? We don't even own one yet….why the need to find a place?"

"Because we may need one soon to go next to the cradle."

"The cradle? What are you telling me Lizzy? Are we having a baby?"

Lizzy smiled and said, "To be honest, I'm not totally sure, but all the signs are there. I want to go to see Dr. Hampton to confirm everything. We never really talked about how soon we would have children - I just figured God would give them to us when the time was right. Are you ok with this?"

"Of course! I've wanted a house full of children ever since I met you. Here, sit down and rest! Do you need anything?"

"No, I'm fine. Just a little tired. Can we drive into town tomorrow to see the doctor?"

"Yes, yes, of course. I'm glad winter is coming–it will give me more time to make furniture and for you to relax by the fire and maybe sew some baby clothes. Lizzy–I love you and our little baby already."

"Well, I'm not totally certain, so let's not get too far ahead of ourselves. But I could use a nap."

"Yes, rest my love. We'll head into town first thing in the morning."

Chapter 29

Dr. Hampton did indeed confirm the pregnancy with a due date around the 4th of July, 1854. Lizzy spent most of the winter inside the house preparing for the baby and resting when she could. Henry worked doubly hard finishing the barn and stocking up on hay when he could. There were many Sundays when he went to church alone because the weather was too cold or the roads too dangerous. Lizzy had already had one buggy accident, and certainly didn't want another.

She tried to be happy about the pregnancy, but in the back of her mind she kept remembering Casper: how it felt for her to hold him, rock him, and then for him to die in her arms. She certainly didn't want to bother Henry with her worries, so she kept the fears to herself. He was very devoted to her, making sure she rested as much as possible and did not do any heavy lifting. But he had no idea how much Casper's death still affected her. This winter was much milder than the last, and before long the first signs of spring arrived. She loved relaxing on the front porch, watching the world come back to life, and feeling the life growing inside her. She had no idea that she could love this little person so much—someone she had not yet seen or touched. The thought of something bad happening made her physically ill. How in the world did other parents bear such a loss?

Clara and Marie came over to help plant the garden, along with giving her motherhood advice and preparing for the baby. They both noticed Lizzy's lack of enthusiasm as the pregnancy progressed, and correctly guessed at her depressed mood.

"Lizzy, dear, please try to remember that the majority of pregnancies end with healthy moms and babies. I know you have had some bad experiences, but let's try to think positively and pray for this little blessing, ok?"

"I'm trying, Clara, I really am, it's just so hard–he died in my arms! I will never forget that feeling."

"My poor girl–I'm so sorry you had to experience that. You are young and healthy, and there is no reason to expect anything but a positive outcome and delivery."

As Lizzy got closer to the time of delivery, her fears increased so that even Henry noticed and was concerned about her. Each evening, he would make her comfortable on the sofa and then play relaxing music for her. He tried to convince her that each kick or movement of the baby was a sign that all was well, but she seemed to pull further and further away from him.

Early on the morning of July 10th she awoke with sharp pains and cramping. Henry rode quickly to Levi's house and begged him to ride into town and bring the doctor. Henry rushed back home to find Lizzy on her hands and knees in the bedroom, crying in pain. He helped her back into the bed and rounded up towels and put water on to heat. He brought in a pitcher of cold water and dipped a rag into it, wiping her face and neck.

"Hold on, my sweet girl. Levi went to get the doctor and they will be here soon. Please just try to relax–I know it's hard, but I'm right here. I'll never leave you."

"It hurts so much—I just know that something is wrong."

"Just hold my hand, squeeze as tight as you want—the doctor will be here soon."

Time seemed to drag while they waited for Dr. Hampton. Eventually they heard Levi's buggy in the drive and the sound of footsteps rushing into the house.

"We are in the bedroom!" Henry called. "I'm so glad you are here—she is in an awful lot of pain."

"Hello, Lizzy. How are you doing?" Dr. Hampton gently asked.

"I was fine when I went to bed but woke up in pain. I have a terrible feeling that something is wrong."

"Let me examine you and we'll see what is going on. Gentlemen, do you mind waiting outside?"

"Of course," Henry and Levi said. Henry gave Lizzy's hand a squeeze and then left with Levi and closed the bedroom door. They exchanged concerned looks.

"I know it's hard to wait," Levi said, "but it's just the way it is. The doctor will take good care of her, I'm sure."

Dr. Hampton opened his medical kit and took out his stethoscope. He listened for the baby's heartbeat but was having trouble finding it.

"Tell me about how active the baby had been lately," he said as he continued to search for a heartbeat.

"Last night for sure, but I haven't really noticed this morning. Tell me, doctor, is something wrong?"

"I'm not sure just yet. Let me finish my exam and then we'll bring Henry back in."

Lizzy started to cry and whispered, "I knew it, I just knew it. God, why are you doing this to me?"

The doctor brought Henry back in and delivered some devastating news. "I'm so very sorry, but I am unable to find a heartbeat or any movement. You have progressed in your labor almost to delivery, and we need to continue. But I'm afraid the baby is no longer alive."

Lizzy closed her eyes and tried to comprehend what the doctor was telling her. Her baby was gone, before even having a chance at life.

"Ok, Lizzy, I know this is hard, but you are going to have to push for me --- push as hard as you can. Lizzy–can you hear me?" the doctor asked worriedly.

She heard him but did not have the strength or desire to continue.

"Lizzy, my love, I'm here," Henry added. "You are strong, and you are brave–we need you to do this."

She opened her eyes to look at him–he looked as devastated as she felt. Another strong contraction came, and she bore down and pushed with all her might.

"Keep going, Lizzy," the doctor said. "One or two more of those and then you can rest." She had one more contraction, and then it was over. The doctor was holding a perfectly formed baby girl, but who was not moving or breathing. He cut the umbilical cord and then unwound it from around the girl's neck where it was tightly knotted. This appeared to be the cause of her demise.

"Do you want to hold her?" the doctor asked gently.

"Yes, please," Lizzy said with tears streaming down her cheeks. "Henry–she is beautiful. Oh, my heart is breaking!"

Henry sat beside her and gently stroked his daughter's face. Her features were a mirror of Lizzy, along with a full head of auburn hair. He felt completely empty inside–how could this have happened to them–and especially to Lizzy?

Chapter 30

Word of the loss of Lizzy and Henry's baby spread quickly throughout the community. Even Mr. Franklin sent his condolences. Lizzy's articles had been popular from the start, and he was hoping to expand her word count and allow her to write about other things besides home and garden.

Pastor Clark and his wife Lillian were some of the first to visit her. Henry was trying to be strong for his wife, but his heart was breaking as well. The pastor asked about arrangements for the baby, and if they had selected a name. Lizzy was wrapped in a blanket despite the 100-degree heat and appeared not to be listening.

"Have you selected a name?" he asked gently.

"Mary Elizabeth," Lizzy whispered. "And I want her buried next to Casper."

"That would be fine," Henry agreed. "You can make the arrangements, just as you did with Casper?"

"Yes, I'll handle everything and get back to you later today or tomorrow. Henry and Lizzy, I am so very sorry for this devastating loss. Life's mysteries are difficult for us to understand this side of Heaven, but one day we will be reunited with those who have gone on before us. God will give us the strength to bear the trials of life, if we but trust Him."

"Amen," they both said softly.

The next few days were a flurry of visitors offering condolences and bringing food. Lizzy had no appetite and stayed in the bedroom most of the time. On the day of the burial, Henry helped her dress and then into the buggy for the short drive to the small cemetery. She was numb as the pastor read many of the same passages as he had done just over a year ago for Casper. One lone tear trickled down her cheek as they lowered the small casket into the ground and covered it with dirt. They rode back to their home in silence and Lizzy went straight into the bedroom. Henry had no idea how to comfort her.

Several days passed, and Lizzy rarely left her bed. Severe depression was setting in, and Henry again asked Levi to bring the doctor out from town. When he arrived, he gently knocked on the bedroom door and poked his head inside. "It's me, Lizzy, Dr. Hampton. I'd like to check on you if that's ok."

"Fine," came a faint voice from inside. The doctor went in and shut the door before sitting on the side of the bed.

"Lizzy, let me say again how very sorry I am. You have been through a lot in your young life and it's hard to understand. Sometimes bad things just happen."

"I feel like God is punishing me for doing something wrong. I tried to eat well, get plenty of rest….she was so beautiful."

"Yes, she was, but Lizzy you must understand. You did nothing wrong here. There are times that the baby just gets tangled in their cord, and it has nothing to do with you. Please try to be gentle with yourself."

They visited a bit longer, and the doctor examined her to make sure she was recovering from the childbirth.

"Lizzy, would you like me to help you get dressed so you can sit in the parlor or maybe outside on the porch? Or would you like me to send Henry in?"

"Yes, I would like your help. I know I cannot stay in bed any longer, hiding from everyone and their sadness."

The doctor eased her from the bed and handed her the items she requested. His kindness affected her greatly, and she gave his hand a gentle squeeze. "Thank you," she whispered.

Soon the bedroom door opened and the doctor escorted Lizzy into the parlor where Henry and Levi were waiting. Henry jumped to his feet and helped her get comfortable on the sofa.

"Lizzy, dear, is there anything I can bring you?"

"Just some water, and maybe some fruit and cheese? I am a little bit hungry."

"Of course, whatever you want."

"I'm going to head home," Levi said, "but Gladys wants to know when it would be a good time for her to visit."

"After lunch perhaps?" Lizzy answered softly. "I would love to see her, too."

"I'll check back with you in a day or two," the doctor said as he moved toward the door. "Henry, may I talk with you a moment?"

"Of course," he said as they left the room.

"Henry, I think your wife is suffering from what they are now calling post-partum depression. It's fairly common in women with normal deliveries, but this case was especially traumatic for her. She blames herself for the baby's death, which of course is not true. You need to be especially gentle with her, but don't hesitate to contact me if the depression worsens. I don't want to start her on any medications, but there are things I can give her if they are needed later."

"Thank you, doctor. I'll be in touch."

Gladys arrived shortly after lunch, and Henry left the two ladies to talk in private.

"I'm so glad you are here," Lizzy said softly. "I have so many questions."

"Lizzy, I am so very sad for you and Henry. I understand that Mary was a beautiful baby, perfect in every way."

"Yes, she was. But I need to know—how did you bear it? Henry said that Reuben died shortly after birth? How did you cope with such a huge loss? How did you find the strength to go on? And to be brave enough to have another child?"

Gladys took a deep breath and said, "I never would have made it without Levi, I know that for sure. He was kind and supportive, but I needed to remember that he was grieving also. I was not the only one who had lost a child. Like Mary, there was nothing outwardly wrong with Reuben, and that was very hard to accept. Time will lessen the pain, and you *will* get through this. And eventually, and only you know when that will be, you will want another baby. And while you will be scared and worried, eventually you will hold your baby in your arms and know the joy of being a mother. Right now, all you know is pain. But that will change someday - I promise."

They chatted about other matters for a while, and Gladys mentioned her writing for the newspaper. "I've been hearing a lot of positive comments about your articles. Are you going to go back to writing, once you feel up to it, I mean?"

"I want to. Mr. Franklin sent his condolences along with a note that said he would welcome me back whenever I wanted to return. I think there is a nice old man under all that gruff exterior."

"I've only seen him a few times in town—he seems to keep pretty much to himself. But I'm glad he wants you to come back. You do have a gift for writing."

"Thank you. It feels good to be creative in a different way from just cooking or gardening, although those are wonderful things. I know I'm not up to it yet, though."

"Of course not. Well, I should head home and back to Audrey. She is probably awake by now. You get some rest. I'm glad you are feeling a bit better."

"Thank you for talking with me about your experience—it really helped me."

Lizzy's strength came back slowly over the next several weeks, and the devastating pain she felt started to ease to a dull ache. Henry's dairy business was starting to be more profitable as he took several gallons of milk into town each morning. Lizzy finished harvesting the last of the fall garden and again preserved as much as she could for the upcoming winter. She wanted to return to her writing, but the words just didn't come. She and Henry had settled into a comfortable routine, but without returning to the physical aspect of their relationship, she knew their marriage was not as complete as it should be.

As their first anniversary approached, Henry suggested that they try to get away for a day or two. He wondered if she wanted to return to St. Paul or try somewhere else?"

"St. Paul would be lovely. Perhaps visit some new places? I know you don't want to be gone very long from the farm."

"Levi can handle things for a few days, but I don't want to ask too much from him. He's been such a big help these past few years. I never could have gotten the house done in time without him."

"He has been a huge help to all of us. You are blessed with such a wonderful brother."

"Have you ever ridden on a train?" Henry asked. "I heard St. Paul has an excursion train that lasts a few hours and even provides dinner. Sound interesting?"

"Yes, it really does. I think trains are fascinating. You have been on a train?"

"Only once, when we immigrated. We rode from Chicago to St. Paul."

"I'm so ready for a change of scenery. I think the dinner train sounds like fun."

"Then it's a date!" he said as he kissed her gently on the cheek. How he loved her, and wished he could take away her pain. *Their* pain.

Two weeks later they left the farm early in the morning for the four-hour trip to St. Paul. They arrived just in time for a quick lunch before boarding the excursion train to Eau Claire, Wisconsin. Once settled in a passenger car, Lizzy rarely took her eyes off the passing scenery and marveled at the amount of open farmland just waiting to be settled. Would this really fill up with people someday?

The trip lasted almost three hours before pulling into the station. There was a lot of hooking and unhooking of cars before an engine was placed at the other end and the trip back to St. Paul began.

They were escorted to a dining car where they were fed a lovely chicken dinner. A railroad employee stood at the front of the car and explained the history of steam trains in the US and their expansion west. There were even plans to extend the trains all the way to the west coast in the next few years. Lizzy had a great time and thanked Henry for suggesting it.

The train returned to the St. Paul terminal, and they retrieved their buggy from the livery and drove the short drive to their hotel. It was the same one they had stayed at last year, and Lizzy found the familiarity comforting.

They dressed for bed and Henry climbed in beside Lizzy, pulling her close in his arms. "Happy Anniversary, Mrs. Sauter. Marrying you was the best decision I ever made."

"Happy Anniversary," she replied, feeling warmth and safety within his arms. He kissed her gently, and she felt the old passionate feelings returning. Yes, she was still dealing with her grief, but she wanted, no, *needed*, to be a complete wife again. "I love you, my dear husband," she said softly.

Chapter 31

The autumn months were especially glorious with leaves of red, gold, even purple. Lizzy returned to writing, but this time she felt her words held a bit more maturity. So much had happened in her life since her first root cellar article.

1855 began with a blizzard that snowed everyone in for several days. How different it was for her to live in a house with plenty of food and firewood, after the horrible time in the little cabin just two winters ago. By the end of the month, Lizzy realized she had missed her cycle. At first, she wondered if things were still irregular after Mary's birth, but she was feeling some other familiar symptoms. Was it possible that she was pregnant again? Did she have the strength to go through this? All she knew was that she needed to tell Henry.

That night over dinner she told him about her suspicion of being pregnant again. She wanted to be happy and excited, but the old fears had come roaring back.

After praying for strength and clear thinking, Henry pulled her close as she wept for Mary, and Casper, and all the other babies she knew that never had a chance.

"We'll go into town as soon as the roads are clear enough to see Dr. Hampton and get confirmation. Then we'll pray every day and do all we can to ensure a healthy baby and delivery. And put the rest in God's hands."

It was a week before enough snow melted that Henry was comfortable taking Lizzy to town, but they were thrilled to learn that she was indeed pregnant, with the baby due in August.

"Can we keep the news to ourselves for a while? I'm not sure I'm ready for everyone to know just yet." Lizzy said softly. "They have just now stopped looking at me with pity."

"Of course," Henry replied. He knew the coming months would be extremely stressful for everyone.

They spent the next few weeks adjusting to the thought of another baby. Not a replacement for Mary, but a beautiful baby with its own future and story.

Easter Sunday after dinner, they announced to the family that they were expecting again. Everyone was excited and pleased that Lizzy seemed to have turned the corner with her grief and moved forward with her life.

She had frequent visits with Dr. Hampton who assured them that all was progressing normally. On the afternoon of August 27, Frederick Henry was born. Labor went quickly, and soon Lizzy was holding her son in her arms. He had a lusty cry and voracious appetite like his father, but blue eyes and auburn hair like his mother. Lizzy had never known such contentment. Finally, she felt that she had acclimated to her new country and life in Minnesota and had no desire to return to Germany. Her life was here with Henry and her child.

She immersed herself into motherhood, doing all she could for young Freddy. Taking care of the home and her child gave her immense satisfaction, but she continued her writing for Mr. Franklin and branched out into more current events. There was increasing talk in town of the Minnesota territory becoming a state, and for Oliver's Grove to change its name at that time. Four founding fathers of the town put their names in a hat, and the name 'Hastings' was pulled. Lizzy wrote numerous articles about the process, riding to and from town with Freddy at her side. The week after the name change, she suffered a miscarriage before she was even sure she was pregnant. The doctor could give no reason but doubted that riding in a buggy was the cause. Although very sad, she knew that God was in control and there would be more babies if it was in His will.

Henry continued his work with the Underground Railroad and was often gone overnight. When that happened, he took his family down to Levi's house for safety reasons. Their long-time friends the Bakers were growing older and experiencing some health problems, so they were looking to step back from the actual transports. Lizzy's writings became a bit more controversial when she let her abolitionist feelings be known, urging for statehood so they could decide for themselves the issue of slavery.

1858 brought the admission of Minnesota as a state and another baby to the family—Hanna Marie. Lizzy stayed quite busy helping on the farm and caring for the two babies. Her writings were taking on a more political tone, and she was starting to feel the disapproval of her neighbors who had figured out that she was H. E. Sauter. She was constantly reminded that as a woman, she had no place in politics or voicing an opinion on national issues.

Henry's dairy farm was becoming more and more profitable, and he even hired Adam to come over each day to help with the milking. They had over 100 cows now, and Lizzy was so used to the farm smells she didn't notice them anymore, although everyone else did. Adam loved playing with the babies, and had started courting a lovely lady named Amelia, who was from a wealthy family from Germany. He was anxious to make as much money as he could so he could purchase his own land and build a home for her.

The other Kruse children were growing and thriving, and Lizzy enjoyed spending each Sunday afternoon with her father and Clara. There were still reports of various Indian interactions that turned violent, but they were mostly confined to the west side of the state.

Things were extremely tense as 1860 started with numerous southern states threatening to secede from the union if a Republican was elected President. Lizzy's writing took on an even more urgent tone as the rhetoric on both sides grew louder. Another son, Casper Jacob, was born to the family in December. Lizzy seemed to easily juggle the farm, three children, and becoming a leader in the area for her anti-slavery stance. When Abraham Lincoln was elected that fall, 11 southern states voted to secede. Splitting the country in two was unacceptable to most northerners, and the streets were filled with talk of war. Who could have imagined a Civil War that would pit brother against brother, father against son? President Lincoln waited a month after his inauguration before deciding to send provisions to Fort Sumter in the harbor of Charleston, South Carolina. On April 12, 1861, Confederate guns opened fire on the fort, and the Civil War began.

News of the war spread quickly across the country. Both Henry and Levi felt strongly about fighting for the end of slavery but dreaded leaving their wives and children for months or years, or even forever. While Lizzy was very outspoken about the sin of slavery, she still didn't want Henry to go. How would she and the children survive while he was gone? Henry told her that he had already fulfilled his military required service in Germany before immigrating, but that he was willing to serve again. She felt like a fraud, urging the fight for reunification, but not wanting her husband to be the one to do it.

On June 15, Henry and Levi went into Hastings to meet with other German immigrants to discuss enlisting in the war, if Minnesota was asked to join the fight. Lizzy was home with the babies and Gladys and Audrey were at their home at the other end of the property. Gladys was lighting a fire to fix dinner when there was a loud explosion, and burning embers covered both she and Audrey. Lizzy could hear the noise and rushed out the door to see flames and smoke pouring from the house. Not even thinking of her own children, she ran as fast as she could to the burning structure, only to find that another neighbor had gotten there first and was pulling Gladys' badly burned body from the home. Lizzy rushed in and found an equally burned Audrey on the floor. Carrying her outside, she could hear Gladys' anguished cries. "Please save my baby!" she shouted over and over. As if by a miracle, Henry and Levi were on their way home from their meeting and saw the flames. They rushed to the scene and Levi cradled Audrey in his arms as she took her last breath. Gladys was hysterical from the pain and loss of her child, and faded into unconsciousness. Just a few minutes later she died.

Lizzy sat there on the ground, covered in smoke and ash, the palms of her hands burned, and she cried for the loss of her friend. Then she saw Levi's devastated face and suddenly remembered that she had left her own children at home unaccompanied. She begged for someone to help her get to them. Henry needed to stay with Levi, so another neighbor rushed her home, where she found her own three precious babies sleeping soundly.

Chapter 32

Lizzy found herself again in the grove of white birch behind her family's original cabin. Beside the tiny markers for Casper and Mary were two more freshly dug graves—one small one for Audrey and a larger one for Gladys. Levi had wanted them buried here instead of on his own farm. Once again Pastor Clarke read the familiar verses and recited the usual prayers. How many more times were they going to have to do this? How much grief can one family take?

Levi's home was too badly burned for him to remain there, so he moved in with Henry and Lizzy. He had almost no belongings that survived the fire, and he spent most of his time sitting in a bedroom, staring out the window toward his farm.

Just a few weeks later, Lizzy learned that she was pregnant yet again. How could she and Henry be excited about this new baby when Levi had lost so much? Talk of Minnesota joining the Union forces was increasing each day, and just before Christmas both men went to St. Paul to enlist. Levi felt he had nothing to live for and was eager to leave Minnesota to fight for the abolition of slavery, but was devastated when he failed the physical due to having flat feet. Henry passed with flying colors and was told he would start his service in February. Worried about his wife and children, he asked Levi to continue living at his farm to keep an eye on things for him. He would have both farms to work–grain in one and the dairy cows on the other. The income from the two properties should carry them through what everyone felt would be a very short war.

Clara and Marie came over as often as they could to help her with the children and preserve food for the winter. They hoped the next baby would be born before Henry left to join the 5th Minnesota, but on the morning of February 19, 1862, Henry kissed his very pregnant wife goodbye, hugged his other children, and then asked Levi to drive him to Hastings where he would meet up with the other soldiers. Henry tried to show more bravery than he felt as he gave the care of his precious family over to his brother. "Please take care of them–they are all that I have," Henry begged.

Levi returned to the farm and put the horses in the barn along with the buggy. He checked on the cows and tried to wrap his head around this new responsibility he faced. Only six days passed before Lizzy gave birth to Adam Reuben. She now had four small children and no husband at home. Although she tried to keep up with the housework and caring for the babies, she cried herself to sleep most nights–would she ever see Henry again? He had promised to write when he could, but letters would take weeks or even months to reach her. One evening she walked into the parlor and sat down at the piano. She tried to play a few lines from a song Henry had taught her, but the memories were too painful–the presence of the piano seemed to taunt her and was a constant reminder of all that was missing from her life.

Spring turned into summer, and Lizzy was busy enlarging her garden and working from sunup to sundown to ensure food for her family. She loaded the children into the wagon once a week and went into town to learn the latest war news and submit an article to Mr. Franklin. He had expanded the publication of the newspaper to each Monday and circulation increased as more people wanted updates on the fighting. Her earnings were used for items she could not produce at home, and she was thankful to be able to purchase shoes and clothing for her growing children. In late summer, she noticed that many items at the store were becoming scarcer or were so expensive she could not afford them. Death notices started coming in, and Lizzy raced to the trading post to search the list of names, relieved to see Henry's name was not included, but sad for those that were. The lists seemed to get longer each week, and Lizzy's fear increased.

In October, Mr. Franklin received a telegram stating the 5th Minnesota was involved in the Battle in Corinth, Mississippi, where 355 union soldiers were killed, 1,848 wounded and 824 listed as captured or missing. Lizzy tried to contain her fear that Henry was killed or injured, but it would take a week or so for the lists to arrive and be posted. She did receive her first letter from him, dated one month earlier. He said he was keeping a diary to track how far they marched each day, what they ate or what the weather was like. His Company E was made up of primarily German boys and they were led by Captain Sterling. He was particularly close with local men John Karels, Anton Lipke, Hans Schuster, and David Vollmer, whose wife and children lived near Hastings. Henry asked Lizzy to check in on her if she got a chance, as she was quite young and alone.

He asked about the children, of course, and the new baby. He wished he could be home with all of them. He recounted a few of the horrors of war, and how hard it was to watch his friends killed or injured. The worse part for him was retrieving the bodies of his friends from the battlefields after the fighting was done. The memories of those mutilated bodies haunted his dreams. Everyone was starting to believe that the war would not be over as quickly as their leaders had predicted. He ended the letter reminding her of his love, and to keep praying for him and for the war to be over soon.

Levi did his best to manage both farms and take care of Lizzy and the children. Her brother Adam had married Amelia and was too busy with his own property to help, but Levi did find a few men in town who, like him, were unable to serve due to health issues. One group came early to help with the morning milking, and another group came in the late afternoon. Levi was transporting close to 100 gallons of milk into town each day and was being paid well.

However, as the war continued throughout the year, meat became scarce and Levi had the opportunity to sell off a big part of the dairy herd for food. Lizzy wasn't sure Henry would approve, but understood that people would give up milk before giving up meat. As winter approached, the herd was down to 60 and his usual milk buyer in town decreased his purchase price so it was almost not financially responsible for Levi to continue. He let the evening workers go, opting instead to milk the remaining herd himself. It had been a very dry summer and the wheat crop on his own farm did not do well. He was worried he would not have enough grain or wheat to feed the dairy cows, and without the extra milk income, he could not afford to buy more. He and Lizzy sat down at the table one night to talk about the challenges.

"I'm struggling to know which path to take," Levi said worriedly. "I hate to sell off more of the dairy cows, since Henry worked so hard to establish this nice herd. But I'm having trouble selling the milk, and also having trouble feeding so many cows. Should I sell more beef while I can and just hang onto the money? I wish this horrible war would end and the economy could return to normal. I hate making these decisions without Henry being here. I heard talk in town that there was no end of the fighting in sight, and we need to figure out how to survive another year, or maybe two."

After much consideration, Lizzy said, "What's crazy is that families in the south are starving and would love to have our milk or beef, but the rail lines are mostly destroyed and it's impossible to get any food to them. Since their economy was tied up in slavery and cotton, people are dying of hunger. But I agree, if we cannot afford to feed the cattle and there isn't really any profit in milk anymore, the best thing would be to sell the cows for whatever we can get for them. Hopefully the war will end before we run out of money."

"Sadly, I agree," Levi said. He looked across the table at the woman he had come to admire over the years. Not only was she lovely, but she was smart and strong and determined to do whatever was needed for her family. There was no comparison between her and Gladys, who he still missed dearly. But would she have been able to survive these difficult times without the finer things in life her money allowed? He was sure she could not.

"I'll go into town tomorrow and see what I can arrange. We can keep the chickens and the few goats we got last year. They will provide us enough eggs, milk and even meat if things get desperate."

"I pray it won't come to that, and that this dreadful waste of life and our country can stop."

Within a week, the cattle were gone, and Levi was given a large sum of money. He worried about putting it all in the bank, as there had been rumors of an increase in robberies around the south. But he certainly didn't want all of it at home, either. Lizzy suggested they divide it up into several envelopes and then put them in fruit jars she could hide in the root cellar.

The money was not the only thing he brought home from town, though. He also had two letters from Henry—one for him and one for Lizzy. His letter was graphic and horrible, and his heart broke for all the soldiers on both sides of the battlefield. Lizzy's letter, however, was less grim and talked more about the day-to-day routine of military life. He asked lots of questions about the children and hoped Lizzy was holding up alright. The South was losing more battles than they were winning, and everyone hoped the fighting was nearing the end.

President Lincoln signed the Emancipation Proclamation in September, which declared the freedom of all slaves on January 1st of 1863. Surely the war would end soon after that?

Sadly, the fighting continued all through 1863. Casualties continued to mount on both sides. In July, the country was shocked when it learned of the fighting in Gettysburg, Pennsylvania, and the President's speech a few days later. Mr. Franklin's paper could hardly keep up with the battles and the numbers of the dying, and he asked Lizzy to help run things in the office. She said she would, only if she could bring all four children with her. By now, Graham was pretty used to her bringing the children in when she dropped off articles, and they were very well behaved.

And his heart was softening a bit toward her, knowing how difficult it must be for her while Henry was gone.

Things were getting stressful on the farm, as it was all across the country. The money they made selling Henry's dairy cows was soon to run out, and they had even had to butcher a few of the chickens and one of the goats for food. But even if they had money, there were limited items available for sale. A few local merchants would make the long drive to St. Paul to try to purchase anything they could find, but whatever they found was grossly overpriced. As fall approached, and then winter, Lizzy fell into a deep despair. She received a letter from Henry just a few days before Christmas, and as the family was huddled around the table near the fire, Lizzy read Henry's letter to them, skipping over the more gruesome parts. She had no gifts to give to the children, so they decided just to skip the holiday and the younger children didn't notice. Freddy noticed, however, but also knew that there wasn't even money for food; there certainly wasn't money for gifts.

The winter seemed to last forever, and there were no more letters from Henry until late in June, 1864. Lizzy could barely force herself to go to town to check the death lists that seem to arrive almost daily now. But Henry's letter said that he had been granted leave and would be home sometime in late July, depending on availability of transportation. Lizzy was excited to see him and was hoping that this meant that his time in the Army was over.

Levi told Lizzy that he should leave while Henry was home, so they could have time together as a family. She refused, of course, and said that *he* was family, too. But Levi had to be honest with himself–he had fallen in love with Lizzy and was afraid that Henry would notice.

"I'll try to make myself scarce," he finally agreed. "I can always stay out in the barn, since there are no cows there anymore."

"Absolutely not!" Lizzy countered. "I never would have made it through these past two years without you - you are staying!"

Lizzy cleaned the house and scrubbed the kids and tried to find as much food as possible so Henry could have good meals while he was home. It had been so long! And she was nervous to see him again. He had been gone for over two years–would things be different? Would *he* be different?

On the 9th of July, Lizzy was taking a brief rest on one of the rocking chairs on the front porch. She closed her eyes and felt the warm breeze lull her into a nap. Suddenly she heard a noise and jumped up to see Henry in the back of a stranger's wagon. "HENRY!" she yelled excitedly as she ran down the road to meet him. He was really home!

Chapter 33

The wagon came to a stop and Henry climbed wearily from the back. He thanked the driver who urged his team down the road. He saw Lizzy running toward him and tried to force a smile. She was so lovely, even after all this time he knew she was the one and only for him. But every time he closed his eyes, he saw the mangled bodies of his friends and the piles of dead along the roads. Lice and bugs and cold and fatigue and hunger–he had experienced it all. Even though he wanted to be home forever, he dreaded telling Lizzy that he planned to re-enlist but as a bugler. It would keep him mostly off the front lines, and he believed he needed to continue fighting for the cause of reunification of the country.

Lizzy threw her arms around Henry's neck, crying his name over and over. Oh, how she had missed him. But as she hugged him, she noticed how thin he was, how his dark brown hair was now starting to get grey, and there was a strange far-away look in his eyes.

They walked slowly up the drive and toward the house. Four children came rushing out to meet them, including 2-year-old Adam Reuben who Henry had never met. Lizzy lifted him and introduced him to his father. The child was hesitant, of course, of this strange man, and Henry's heart broke a bit. Lizzy noticed how slowly Henry climbed the steps and was worried about him both physically and mentally.

Levi stayed upstairs to give the family some privacy. Henry sat in the living room and tried to relax, but it was difficult with the children running around excitedly, dancing and yelling. The older children, Freddy and Hannah, kept climbing on his lap and hugging him–so happy to have their father home.

After things finally calmed down a bit, Lizzy put lunch on the table and called everyone to wash up and get ready. She opened the door at the foot of the stairs and called up for Levi to come down and join them.

"Levi has been here this whole time? Why did he not come down? I just figured he was in the barn or maybe out in one of the fields."

"He wanted to give us time as a family first. Let's have a nice lunch and then the two of you can talk about farming. There's a lot that as happened over the past two years."

"I'm sure. Everything has changed…" he said as his voice trailed off sadly.

Levi came sprinting down the stairs and gave his older brother a big hug. "We are all so glad you are home! For good, I hope?"

Henry looked around at the house he built with his own two hands, his children, his beautiful and strong wife, his faithful brother….how he wished he could stay.

Lizzy brought food from the kitchen and Henry moved stiffly to his usual seat at the head of the table. Everyone held hands as he led the prayer, "Dear Heavenly Father–there is so much in my heart I do not know where to start. Thank You for this wonderful food and the people gathered around this table. Thank You for safe homes and shelter from the weather. Thank You for friends and neighbors who help in times of need. Please care for those who are struggling and please intervene to bring an end to this horrible war. Help our country recover from its wounds and we can again be one nation, indivisible. Amen."

"Amen," they whispered as Lizzy dried her eyes. Her family was finally back together, and she never wanted them to be apart again.

After lunch, Levi took Henry out to the barn and explained what had happened to the dairy cows and the financial state they were in. He worried that Henry would be angry but was surprised by his attitude.

"You did what you felt was best, and I'm not angry. These past two years have broken all the rules for the entire country. Once the war is over, things will get back to normal, and maybe even better. Well, for us in the north anyway. The southern states have been devastated and there is very little infrastructure left --- roads, railroads, even whole cities have been burned to the ground."

"I've seen some news photographs and drawings–is it as bad as they make it seem?"

"It's 100 times worse–there is no way to describe it or capture it on paper."

"But at least you are home–you came back to Lizzy and all of us. You can put those memories behind you."

Henry did not reply, and Levi looked at him worriedly. "You are home for good, right?"

"No, I have decided to re-enlist and I must leave in about three weeks. Please don't tell Lizzy–I'll find a way to do it, but for now, I can't break her heart again."

Henry asked Levi if he was ok staying here to help his family until the war was over. Levi agreed–mostly out of loyalty to his brother but also selfishly because of his growing feelings for Lizzy. He would never act on them, of course, but knew that he wanted to be a part of her life, if possible.

Once back in the house, Levi went upstairs, and Henry begged for a nap. It had been a grueling trip home on boats and wagons, and he had not slept in a real bed for two years. Lizzy sent the children out to play as she quietly went to the parlor to write her next article. After several hours, the children came in for afternoon naps and Lizzy started dinner. Henry was still asleep, and Lizzy tried not to worry. She honestly had no idea what he had endured all these months, so she let him nap. Even on his first day home, she knew she needed to be patient. What she really wanted was some time with him–no children, no distractions, just the two of them, alone.

It was almost dark when Henry emerged from the bedroom, looking somewhat rested and energized.

"Wow–you have no idea how much I missed sleeping in an actual bed, instead of on the ground or in the back of a wagon if I was lucky. A few more days like this and I'll be back to normal. I have missed you all so much."

"Not as much as we missed you," Lizzy whispered to him softly. She was so thankful that her husband was finally home!

Chapter 34

Once the children were in bed and Levi had gone to his room upstairs, Lizzy lit a few lamps and took a quick bath. She put on her nicest nightgown and slid into bed next to Henry. He wrapped her in his arms and sighed, "I have missed you, my sweet girl."

Several days passed, and Henry was ready to visit people at church and then Lizzy's parents afterwards. He met Adam's new wife Amelia, and they announced that they were expecting their first child early next year. He was enjoying his time on leave, but he almost felt like a stranger in his own home. He was certainly a different man than he was when he left, and people had grown and changed as well while he was gone.

As his second week at home started, he knew it was time to tell Lizzy that he was re-enlisting. He dreaded her reaction but felt a commitment to see the war to its finish. They were sitting on the porch, rocking in the chairs, and enjoying the summer evening, when he finally took a deep breath and said, "Lizzy, there is something I need to talk to you about, and wanted to wait until we were alone."

"Yes, my love? If it's about restarting the dairy herd, I'm just not sure when the right time will be."

"No, it's not about the cows. Before I came home on leave, my commanders offered to extend it to three weeks if I agreed to come back as the bugler. It should keep me off the front lines, and I really don't think it will be for much longer. The south is on its last legs and surrender will be soon. But it's a chance for me to make extra money and a larger pension down the line. And it's a fight I want to finish."

Lizzy was stunned and her rocking chair came to a halt. "How can you even consider leaving us again? Thank goodness Levi was here–I don't think we would have survived without him. I've already almost gone mad with worry–must you really go back?"

"Yes, I must. I've already signed the papers. I head back early next week."

"And you didn't think you should discuss this with me first? What are we supposed to do while you are gone? We are almost out of money and don't have more animals to sell. If it weren't for my newspaper money, we would have starved months ago. I just cannot believe you are doing this. Please–can you reconsider?"

"I'm sorry, but no. I honestly think Lee will be surrendering soon–there's already been talk about it and the south can't hold out much longer. Please–trust me that this is a good decision for us down the road."

Lizzy went into the house and started getting ready for bed. Levi was in the parlor reading and saw the devastated look on her face. His heart broke for her–how could Henry be so cruel?

Henry came inside and went into the bedroom and softly closed the door. He sat on the bed next to Lizzy and tried again to explain. She cried on his shoulder and said, "If you must do this, then please, let us make the most of this time together. Let us be together in every way until you go."

"Of course, my sweet girl. I love you now, and I will love you when I return in a few months."

The week went by quickly, and soon Henry was loading his backpack and Levi had hitched the wagon to take him into town to join a few other soldiers for the trip back south. He was told to meet his regiment just outside of Memphis, so the trip would not be too difficult once they got to St. Paul and then could travel down the Mississippi on a barge. Lizzy and the children stayed home–she could not stand to have them see her cry and possibly fall apart. Henry was leaving her, and this time she felt like she would never see him again.

Once he was gone, Levi returned to the farm and things seemed to quickly settle back into the routine of a month ago. Lizzy wrote articles and did her best to feed the children with their dwindling supplies. Levi worked the fields in an attempt to have a bit of grain to sell. The few chickens and goats were the only livestock they had left and would certainly not last much longer. And after about a month, Lizzy learned that she was pregnant again. Would Henry be home for the birth of this baby?

Winter came early to Minnesota, and the situation was truly serious. Lizzy's parents were struggling as well but did bring over a deer or some fish occasionally. Levi had again chopped plenty of wood for the winter, but once the snow started, it seemed like it would never end. Day after day, blinding wind and snow drifts kept the family inside. Levi had spent the last of the dairy money on oil for their lamps and some flour and bacon. The only other food they had was what Lizzy had been able to preserve over the summer. There was obviously not enough food for everyone for very long, and certainly not for a pregnant woman.

Then came news of a battle in Nashville where there were over 3600 killed or injured. Henry's name was on the 'injured or missing' list and Lizzy collapsed on the floor of the trading post, sobbing in grief. Why did he have to go back to the war? How long would it be before she knew his fate for certain? She cradled her pregnant belly and mourned that this child would probably never know its father. Was he injured or ill, or possibly taken as a prisoner? She had heard horrible things about prison camps such as Andersonville in Georgia or Elmira in New York.

1865 started with Levi, Lizzy and her children huddled around the fire in the kitchen, eating the last of their food. Their clothes were in tatters and the smallest children were crying with hunger. Snow was piled up outside the door making getting to the outhouse a challenge. There were only two chickens left— the last of the goats had been killed before Christmas. Lizzy worried about her unborn baby who didn't seem to be moving as much lately.

One of the things Lizzy was missing the most was Henry leading their family devotions each morning. She went into the bedroom and found his old German Bible. She needed some encouragement and turned to Isaiah 41:10 *"Fear not, for I am with you; be not dismayed, for I am your God; I will strengthen you, I will help you, I will uphold you with my righteous right hand."* She needed His strength because she was completely out of her own. The entire country's economy was in shambles, thousands of men had been killed or seriously wounded, thousands more who survived physically were haunted by the memories of the brutal war and came home with 'shell shock' as the doctors were calling it. Some were reserved and isolated, while others turned angry or violent with the slightest provocation. She also heard stories of soldiers who took their own lives because they could not cope with the memories. Lizzy was worried about Henry, of course, and the personality change she saw during his leave. Would it continue to get worse the longer he was gone, if by chance he was only injured and able to come home?

There was an unusual noise outside, and Levi opened the door to see Adam's wagon struggling through the snow. In the back were two deer and several racoons. Levi rushed out to help take the animals to the barn where he began skinning them and preparing them for dinner or preservation. Lizzy could barely find the words to thank him for saving her family. He was just glad that he could help–there was no food left in town even if someone had money. This war needed to end before the whole country died of starvation or exposure to the cold.

Spring finally arrived in late March, and with the new life in the ground, Lizzy gave birth to another son, Albert, on April 8, 1854. A week later they received the notice that Henry had died of his injuries he sustained last fall. Lizzy was a widow at age 29 with five children under the age of ten. The future was dark and bleak, and she struggled just to get out of bed each morning.

Just one month later, General Lee surrendered, and the war was officially over. It took some time for the news to reach across the country, and the fighting actually continued until the fall. But to Lizzy, the war was never going to be over, because Henry was never coming home.

Albert was a fussy baby, and Lizzy had difficulty bonding with him. To her, he was a constant memory of what she and Henry had together, and a reminder that he chose the war over his family. She was sitting on the edge of the bed, sobbing and mourning her husband, when Levi came to the door.

"Lizzy, may I come in?"

"Of course," she said between tears. "I just got Albert to sleep, but I'm so exhausted. He looks so much like Henry, and the pain is overwhelming."

Levi put his arm around her shoulders—how he wished he could take this pain away from her, from both of them. She rested her head on his chest and felt safe for the first time in a long while. He had been such a steady constant in her life for many years now.

Levi kissed her forehead gently and she lifted her tear-stained face to his. He loved her so much and he wanted to protect her—to give her the life she deserved.

He took a deep breath and softly said, "I love you Lizzy—I always have. I am so very sorry this has happened to you. Please know that I will stay here and help raise Henry's children in his absence. You are an amazingly strong, smart, and determined woman. I am honored to be your friend."

"Oh, Levi. I never would have survived these past horrible years without you! You have so many of Henry's good qualities, yet you are different in how you view the world, and me. I have always been fond of you, too."

He kissed her gently at first, and then with more passion as he felt her responding. They clung together in both their shared grief for Henry but also the expression of affection for each other.

Chapter 35

Only a few weeks passed before Lizzy realized she was pregnant yet again. Levi was thrilled, of course, to have another chance at fatherhood. She had not yet told her family, fearing they would label her a fallen woman and a disgrace to the memory of her newly-dead husband. She did miss Henry terribly, and while at times felt like she was being disloyal, she also honestly cared for Levi and knew that his feelings for her were sincere. Henry was gone, dead, never coming home. She could not mourn him forever.

In early September as she was hanging laundry out to dry, she heard a buggy coming down the road. It stopped at the edge of the property and Lizzy watched as a disheveled man managed to climb down with some help from the driver. His leg was missing below the knee. Lizzy had no idea who this poor man could be, or why he was stopping at her farm. Then she heard his voice.

"Lizzy --- Lizzy my sweet girl–I'm home!"

The only person who ever called her that was Henry, but he was dead. What was happening? She was frozen in place, unable to move toward this stranger. Surely her mind was playing tricks on her.

He limped slowly toward her, relying on crudely constructed crutches. "Lizzy–it's me! Henry! I finally made it home!"

"Henry–is that really you?" she called. "That's not possible–they told us you died from your injuries."

Henry was finally standing in front of her, and there was no mistaking that it was him. "So, no one told you? There was a mix-up with the death notices and my name was confused with another soldier named Hans Schuster. He was in the same hospital room and passed away a few months ago. My captain found the error and they were supposed to notify you."

"No, no one told me," she said, suddenly very self-conscious of her growing belly. "I still cannot believe you are here."

"I have so many questions–how are you? Levi? The children? I will need Levi's help to get the dairy farm up and running again."

"A lot has happened since you left after your leave," Lizzy said softly. "Including the birth of your son Albert. He was born just days before we were told you died."

"Another son? You got pregnant while I was home on leave? And you faced it alone!"

"I didn't want to tell you in a letter, to add stress to you. But Levi was here. He took care of me, of all of us."

It was then that Henry took a good look at his wife and his eyes were fixed on her abdomen.

"I'm confused......I haven't been home in over a year, and Albert was born several months ago. What is this?" he asked angrily as he pointed to her pregnant belly. "Are you expecting again? Obviously, this child isn't mine–what has been going on?"

Lizzy was filled with so many conflicting feelings–relief and happiness that her husband was home, and shame for being pregnant by Levi. How was she going to explain this to him? As she struggled to find the right words, Levi came running from the barn.

"Henry --- Henry ---- is that really you? We were told you did not recover from your injuries. What a miracle this is!"

"I trusted you!" Henry yelled at Levi. "I asked you to take care of my wife and family. How long did she wait before sleeping with someone else?" Glaring at Lizzy he yelled, "Did you even mourn for me? Who was it? Who did this to you?"

There was an awkward silence when Lizzy and Levi exchanged nervous glances. Henry's eyes opened in horror as he put the pieces together. "No–please don't tell me that my own brother is sleeping with my wife? I'm going to be ill."

"Henry, please–let me explain!" Levi begged.

"I don't want to hear anything either of you have to say. Levi–get your belongings out of my house and leave immediately. I don't care where you go or what you do–I no longer have a brother." Levi hung his head in shame and slowly walked away.

"And as for YOU," he turned his attention to Lizzy. "I cannot even look at you. How could you have done this? For months all I could think about was getting home to you and the children. It was your memory that kept me going all those horrible days and nights on the battlefields and in the hospital. And I come home to find this–this–debauchery."

"Please!" Lizzy begged. "You don't understand."

"Oh, I understand completely. I suppose he has been sleeping in our bed?"

"Yes," Lizzy said softly. "But it's not like you think."

"Well, the bedroom is yours now–I will never sleep in there again. I'll fix up a place in the barn. And under NO circumstances are you to say the baby is Levi's–I'm not going to lose my reputation because the two of you had no self-control."

"Please, Henry. Let's go for a walk and let me explain. I don't want the children to overhear."

Henry suddenly stopped and softly said, "My children.... how are they?"

"They are all doing fine–they will be so excited to see you! The youngest ones didn't really understand what happened, or rather, what we were told happened. But Fred and Hannah were devastated. They tried to be brave and strong for my sake, but they are still in mourning for you."

Henry was unsteady on his crutches, and Lizzy helped him to the porch where he sat in one of the rockers. "Please, Henry–I know you are upset and shocked, but let me tell you all that happened. We received the notice that you were injured and in the hospital in St. Louis. I was raising four small children and pregnant. The previous winter weather had been awful, and we ran out of food more than once. Thankfully Levi was here to care for us, and my family helped as well. But after we heard you had died, I just couldn't go on. The notice was on official government letterhead–we had no reason to doubt the accuracy of the letter. Albert was a newborn, and I was about to give up completely. Your brother is a wonderful man and cared for all of us. It wasn't until just recently that things became more serious between us–please don't blame him. We only acted on what we believed to be true at the time."

"My head understands what you are trying to tell me, but this is going to take a long while for me to adjust to, or to forget. How am I supposed to watch your growing belly, knowing that the child you carry belongs to my brother? This is NOT how I envisioned my homecoming!"

They sat in silence for a few minutes, each wrestling with the sudden change in their circumstances. Finally, Lizzy spoke, "Henry–one thing I know for sure. You are the love of my life, and we have been given a second chance. I hope we can get past this and can become a family again."

"You are asking a lot of me, Lizzy–I need some time to think. I have listened to your side of things, and part of me understands. But I need to be alone for a while."

"I understand. I'm so sorry, Henry. I prayed for you so many times, sitting here on this porch, scanning the horizon, looking for you. I had dreams about you walking in the door and our lives returning to what they were before the war. But that all died when I was told you were gone. I need to go back inside and check on the little ones, Albert especially. He looks so much like you–I cried every time I looked at him, missing you so much."

Just a minute or so after Lizzy went into the house, Henry heard the laughter of children drifting on the breeze–he realized it was his older children on their way home from school. How he ached to hold his children in his arms! But how would they react to seeing him?

Suddenly the voices stopped, and Fred was standing in the middle of the road, trying to make sense of what he was seeing. "Papa?" he asked timidly. "Is it really you?"

"Yes, son–it's me. I've missed you so much."

"But what–how–I don't understand."

"There was a mix-up at the hospital–my ID got switched with another soldier. I'm so sorry I have been gone for so long, and there was such confusion. I had no idea that you all were told I was dead."

Fred stood frozen for a few more moments, then rushed toward his father and threw his arms around him. "Papa --- this is such a dream come true for me, for all of us."

Hannah and Casper were not far behind and ran up the porch steps to hug their father. Lizzy heard the commotion and carried babies Adam and Albert out to meet their father. Henry was overcome with emotion as he marveled at the changes in his older children and then picked up Adam, who he had only seen for a few short weeks while on leave a year ago. He saw Albert sleeping in Lizzy's arms and broke down and cried. He was home, and all his children were safe. The only thing ruining this reunion was the slight expansion of his wife's waist and the knowledge that this latest baby she carried was not his but belonged to his brother.

Chapter 36

After several minutes of reunion on the porch, Lizzy helped Henry into the house and onto the sofa in the parlor. Making sure he was comfortable, she went to the kitchen to start fixing dinner. The Minnesota economy was beginning to recover a bit, and she had been able to plant a garden and buy a few supplies in town. Levi was farming again and had even bought a few dairy cows and chickens. She heard movement behind her and turned to find Levi walking silently toward the front door, a small bag in his hand filled with his belongings. Lizzy had tears in her eyes as she watched him silently mouth the words "goodbye Lizzy" and quietly head toward the barn to hitch his horse to the buggy. She understood why he needed to leave, but her hand went protectively to her belly and the growing baby inside her. How was she going to raise this child and never let anyone know the real story? Levi was losing his third child, and her heart was breaking for him.

She called Hannah into the kitchen to help set the table and asked Fred to help Henry into his chair. She then asked everyone to wash up while she put the food on the table. She still could not believe that this was happening–that Henry was home, and they were gathered as a family for this special meal.

Once everyone was seated, Lizzy looked to Henry to offer the blessing. They all held hands, including baby Albert, and bowed their heads. Henry took a deep breath and said in a soft voice, "Dear Father, we are gathered here together, finally, as a family to offer our thanks to You. We have so very much to be thankful for—this food to nourish us, this home to protect us, and this land to provide for us and others. Although our separation was long and full of trials and difficulties, You never left us, and for that we are eternally blessed. Help our country during this difficult time of Reconstruction and protect us in the years to come. Amen."

"Amen" everyone echoed, and Lizzy wiped the tears from her eyes. When she got up this morning and started what she thought was an ordinary day, she never could have imagined that they would be here like this. She squeezed Henry's hand just as she had years ago when they were first courting. It felt familiar, but so much had changed.

During dinner Lizzy noticed how frail Henry was - he was just skin and bones in his army fatigues, and his hands shook a bit as he passed the food around the table. Although he ate with a good appetite, it was not with as much enthusiasm as she would have expected after so much time away. But what bothered her the most was the far-way look in his eyes, almost like he was not really here with them but somewhere else. Albert dropped a cup from his highchair, and it clattered on the wood floor. Henry jumped and winced at the sound—it was obvious that the loud noise startled him now more than prior to the war. Lizzy could only imagine the horrors he had witnessed and the sounds that must have haunted his dreams, and probably still did.

After dinner, Lizzy and Hannah cleared the table and started the dishes. Fred helped Henry back to the parlor and the other children played with blocks on the floor. What would have looked to outsiders like a perfect family picture was anything but. Henry was home but was a very changed man from the one who willingly enlisted three years ago, emotionally as well as physically. Lizzy was pregnant again, but the baby was not her husband's. How soon would everyone notice and put the pieces together? Three of her five children barely knew their father and had no idea about the vibrant, strong man he used to be. The two older children did remember him but were having trouble adjusting to this new reality. Everything was strange and felt very temporary.

As she was finishing the dishes, she heard the familiar sounds of the piano coming from the parlor. She hid out of sight as tears streamed down her face–how many times she had prayed for this, but not like *this*. What was going to happen to her family? Would he ever forgive her and get past this? She carried baby Albert into the bedroom to get him ready for bed and was surprised when Henry gently knocked on the door.

"Lizzy, may I come in?" he asked gently.

"Of course," she answered, and she helped him to sit on the edge of the bed.

"First of all, I just want to thank you for taking such wonderful care of the children. I cannot imagine how hard it was for you to have been left to provide for them and protect them while I was gone for so long, and with no idea when or if I would return. It would have been hard enough during normal circumstances, but we both know things were far from normal for both of us. But as for your relationship with Levi and now the baby, well, it's a lot for me to wrap my head around. Did I hear Levi leave earlier?"

"Yes, while I was fixing dinner. Neither of us dreamed this would happen, I hope you can believe me. We never would have hurt you this way if we thought there was any chance of you coming home."

"I know, it's just…" his voice trailed off and he seemed at a loss for words. Eventually, he continued, "I don't think we need to make any final decisions tonight. I'm exhausted and I imagine you are as well. I'll have Fred help me make a pallet in the barn."

"But how will you explain it to him? He's 10 years old—he knows enough to know that you should be here with me, with us."

"He also knows where Levi has been sleeping, right? I'm sure he is full of questions. I'll think of something. May I hold Albert before I leave?"

"Of course! He's almost asleep and extra cuddly right now. Oh Henry, he looks so much like you, like I imagine you looked as a baby."

Henry gently cradled his newest son and tears filled his eyes. He had seen so much death and destruction and had lost all hope of ever holding his children again. But what kind of father was he now --- disabled in both body and mind? What did he have to offer them, or Lizzy for that matter?

Chapter 37

After about 30 minutes, Fred returned to the house and knocked on Lizzy's bedroom door. Lizzy opened it and slipped outside. "I just got Albert to sleep. Did you get your father situated in the barn?"

"Yes, but I don't really understand…"

"I know, it's all very complicated. I appreciate you helping him, though."

"I hope he's ok out there—it feels like it might storm tonight."

"The air does seem strange, but I figured it was just me, with all the surprises we've experienced today."

Almost on queue, there was a loud rumble of thunder off in the distance and it started raining. Lizzy looked anxiously out the door towards the barn, wishing she could convince Henry to come back inside.

"Thanks again for your help, and I promise I'll fill you in someday. It's been a long day for everyone."

Fred went upstairs to his bedroom and Lizzy went back in and looked at Albert. "Your father is home," she said softly.

About two hours later Lizzy was jolted awake by crashes of lightning and thunder and the sound of tree branches breaking.

The house seemed to be straining to stay together. She jumped from her bed, grabbed Albert, and ran into the kitchen. Fred came rushing down the stairs carrying Adam and leading the others.

"We have to get in the root cellar!" Lizzy yelled over the noise. "We need to be below ground! Hannah, take Albert while I find some lamps and matches."

Soon the small family was safely tucked into the dark and musty cellar, and the winds continued howling above them. Suddenly Hannah said, "Mother, what about Papa? Is he going to be ok?"

"I don't know, Hannah. He's been through tougher things than a thunderstorm–I'm sure he will be fine." Of course, Lizzy feared that after all of this time, after finally getting him home, they might lose him all over again on his first night home.

The storm continued for several minutes, and the noises were almost unbearable. The three younger children were crying. Fred and Hannah were doing their best to help keep them calm, but Lizzy could see they were terrified as well. They heard a loud crash as a tree slammed into the house. Lizzy began praying as loud as she could. "Dear Father in Heaven, please send Your angels of protection to cover us. We are trusting You to keep us safe."

Suddenly there was a banging on the cellar door, and they could barely hear a voice calling out to them. "Lizzy–are you down there? It's me, Levi! Help me with this door!"

Lizzy and Fred jumped up and helped Levi open the cellar door. The wind continued howling as Levi descended the steps with Henry in his arms. He sat Henry down on a box and then helped Lizzy as she struggled to pull the door shut again. When they got it latched, they both collapsed on the ground exhausted.

"Levi–what are you doing here? And Henry–are you ok?" Lizzy shouted over the noise.

"I had just gotten into town when I realized the storm was coming and it looked really fierce," Levi answered. "I was just too worried about all of you and came back as fast as I could. I saw a light in the barn and went there to investigate–that's where I found Henry. I knew we would all be safer here in the cellar, so I brought him back. I'm glad you are already down here."

Lizzy sat next to Henry and held his hand. "We were so worried --- thank you Levi for saving him. I've never seen a storm like this before."

"Yes, thank you Levi. The sounds of the wind and crashing trees was deafening."

They remained huddled together for another 30 minutes before the storm lessened and then all was quiet again. Levi and Fred managed to get the door open, and Lizzy handed the sleepy children up to them. She turned to Henry and started to help him stand. Suddenly Levi sprinted down the steps again and picked Henry up to carry him upstairs and into the dining room. Lizzy followed behind, bringing the lanterns to help light the house a bit. To everyone's surprise, there was just one window that was broken by a fallen branch and the back door had been ripped from its hinges. Otherwise, things looked remarkably intact. That is, until Henry looked out the front door toward the barn and saw that it was gone. Nothing but a few splinters of wood remained. No cows or chickens. No hay from the loft. Nothing. Lizzy's eyes were wide as she realized that Henry would have died had he remained in the barn during the storm. Tree branches, and in some places complete trees, littered the yard and pasture. The outhouse was blown over and pieces were scattered into the garden, which was totally flattened by the wind and rain. The sun was peeking over the horizon, and Lizzy just wanted to cry. So many times she had struggled to establish a life for herself, only to have it ripped out from under her or blown away. How were they going to feed their growing family now, with no garden and no milk or meat? Feeling defeated, she went back into the house, lit a fire, and started to make coffee.

"Remember how I had to teach you to make coffee?" Henry asked gently.

Lizzy smiled at the memory. "Yes, it was the first morning after our wedding. Life held so much promise for us then–the future was wide open with possibilities. Little did we know…" and her voice drifted off.

"Levi, will you join Lizzy and me in the kitchen?" Henry asked. "Since the children are all asleep, perhaps now is a good time to talk?"

"Of course," Levi said with a nervous glance towards Lizzy. Henry could hurl all kinds of hateful words toward him and that was fine–he deserved them. But he was hoping Lizzy would be spared.

Lizzy brought steaming cups of coffee to the table and the three of them looked at each other in silence, each wondering what to say or who would go first. Henry finally broke the silence.

"First off, I want to apologize for some of the things I said yesterday. I was angry and was harsher than I should have been, and I could have been more willing to listen to your side of things. Please forgive me."

Lizzy felt a tear slide down her cheek and she reached for Henry's hand. "You don't have to apologize, Henry. You came home to a situation you knew nothing about, and honestly, I probably would have said more if the tables had been reversed."

Henry nodded, then turned his attention to Levi. "My dear brother. We have been through so much together over the years. I was angry with you for many reasons, but mostly my pride was hurt. I was coming home wounded and maybe half the man I used to be, and I saw that you had taken my wife and my children and started a new family of your own. I expected you to care for my family, but not to care *that* much, even after I was presumed dead. I think we all understand that the old rules of etiquette and decorum became obsolete during the war. Please forgive me. But what is the most amazing, is that even after I said those horrible things and kicked you out of my house, you still came back and saved my life. I will be eternally grateful to you for protecting my family while I was gone, and then saving me once I got home."

The room was silent for a minute or so, then Levi said, "Henry, my big brother, the one I have looked up to all these years: I was honored that you entrusted me with your family when you went away to the war, and mourned for you when we heard you had passed away. When I saw you today, I was filled with such joy and happiness for Lizzy, because I knew she never stopped loving you. I know the situation is one none of us ever would have expected. I will move into town but of course will help you here on the farm in any way you might want. And I will respect your wishes about the baby."

"Yes, the baby. That's what we need to clarify today. I want the three of us here to pledge and promise that **NO ONE** ever learns that I am not the father. I know I am only a shell of a man both physically and emotionally, but I cannot deal with people knowing our complicated situation, and then treat me with even more pity. Can we all agree on that?"

Lizzy and Levi exchanged glances, and Levi nodded his head 'yes.'

"Henry," Lizzy finally said, "Levi and I will do as you ask. Nothing would be gained by others knowing the truth, and it would only harm the child down the line. But I am almost three months along, - I'm not sure how we will be able to fool everyone for the next six months."

"You'll just have to do your best to keep it hidden until it would be logical to announce to your family and pray it's not a 10-pound child when born in the spring. And Levi, I appreciate your offer to help with the farm. I'm certainly not going to be able to work it as I used to. We'll have to sit down in a few days and honestly evaluate what is the best course of action now that the storm has destroyed so much. What has happened with your land since I left?"

"I tried to keep both places up for a while, but it just got to be too much, and there was no market for the grain anyway. So, it has sat idle for the past year."

"That's too bad, but I do understand. I have one more thing to ask, Levi, if I may? I have only one set of clothes that I brought home with me, and everything is shabby and worn out. Do you have anything extra I could have?"

"I'm sure I can find a few things—I'll bring them the next time I come back --- two days from now?"

"That would be fine. Lizzy, how about some breakfast? We all have some long days of cleanup ahead of us, and I think

I see the back door laying in the garden. If it is, we can get it rehung this morning."

"Of course, but first I have something for you," Lizzy said as she stood and walked into the bedroom. She returned with a grain sack filled with Henry's old clothes.

"I was saving these for you, of course, for when you came home. When we heard you had passed away, I bagged them up to donate in town, but somehow, I just could not bring myself to do it. I'm so glad I saved them."

Henry peered into the sack to see his old shirts and pants, and even a pair of shoes and several socks. New socks–he wasn't sure the last time he had new socks.

"Thank you, Lizzy. Levi–would you mind helping me wash up and change? I'm still not very good handling things on just one leg."

"Of course. And then we can get to work on the back door."

Lizzy went to the kitchen to fix a breakfast of eggs, potatoes, and the last loaf of bread she had made yesterday. She had no idea what they would eat later today or in the future.

They had just finished their meal when a wagon rumbled to a stop in the driveway. Jakob and Clara came rushing in, worried about the family after last night's storm. They froze in their tracks when they saw Henry sitting in his usual chair.

"Oh, merciful God in heaven–Henry, you are home? But we thought…" Jakob was unable to finish his sentence.

"Yes, it's me. There was a mix-up at the hospital, and you were misinformed about my passing. I just got home yesterday."

"Well, I certainly am glad you are home!" Clara exclaimed as she gave him a hug. She noticed his missing leg and undernourished body. Sadness flashed across her face, but she quickly forced a smile and sat down beside him. "You have no idea how much we all missed you, how we mourned for you."

Henry shot a quick glance at Lizzy, who was trying to hide her growing belly from her parents and keep the charade alive. "I'm just glad I'm home. The experiences of the past three years --- they haunt me at night. I just want to return to a normal life, whatever that is now. But it looks like we have got to start over–again. I assume you noticed the barn is gone, along with the few animals that were left."

"That's another reason we are here," Jakob said. We have the wagon loaded with some extra vegetables Clara preserved and several squirrels and ducks we shot yesterday. I can reach out to the church to see if anyone has things they can share, especially milk or eggs for the babies. No offense, Henry, but it is obvious that you haven't been eating well. We'll do our best to get you back to health quickly."

"Thank you. I'm sure you heard some stories about what life in the Army was like, but there is no real way to explain the daily misery and discomfort. I kept a diary, as a way to tell the real story. Lizzy–maybe you could include some of it in your articles? You are still writing, I hope."

"Yes, I am. I am so very thankful that Graham decided to take a chance on me and increased the number of articles I could write, along with my pay. I'm sure he would be excited to include some of your diary entries."

"Good. I'm glad it's in the backpack that Levi and I grabbed last night from the barn, or it would have been lost in the storm."

"Speaking of storms," Jakob said, "I heard it was a huge tornado. We didn't really have much damage except lots of broken tree limbs. The grove of white birch behind the old cabin was almost flattened, but the cemetery is fine. The barn was spared, and we didn't lose any animals. Once we get some sort of shelter built here, I'll bring a few chickens and a goat over for you. It's too late in the fall to replant any of the garden—that's going to be the hardest part. But now that the war is over, we are all hoping that the economy starts coming back as some basics of life are restored."

They visited a few more minutes while Levi helped Henry get dressed, then the men went to retrieve the back door and try to get it reattached. The older children came downstairs and had breakfast before going to unload the wagon. Lizzy started washing dishes but noticed that Clara was watching her with a suspicious eye. Lizzy knew that Clara was always the first to notice her pregnancies, sometimes even before she did herself. Concealing this one from her was going to be difficult.

Of course, Clara had noticed from the minute she walked into the house. Lizzy had been pregnant six times before, and each one looked basically the same. Henry had just gotten home, which left only Levi to be the father, and Clara could not let herself believe that. And maybe she was wrong this time…but she doubted it. Did Henry know? He miraculously comes home from the war after being presumed dead, only to find his wife pregnant by another man? No, it couldn't be.

Chapter 38

Several weeks passed as the cleanup on the farm continued. Word of Henry's amazing return home from the war quickly spread, and the family was surrounded with love and care from their friends and neighbors. Levi continued to come to the farm each day to help with the repairs and to build a new but smaller barn. It was obvious to everyone that Henry was physically struggling and was not going to be able to return to farming or running a dairy barn as he had before the war. He was emaciated and frail, and many times seemed to be lost in his memories of the war. He often had a far-away look in his eyes, and Lizzy knew he was reliving the painful war experiences. Graham was excited to publish parts of Henry's diary which turned out to be wildly popular with the readers.

As the weeks turned into a month, it was obvious that Lizzy could no longer hide her pregnancy and decided it was time to announce it to her family. After finishing their traditional Sunday dinner with her parents after church, Henry struggled to stand and said, "The Lord has been very faithful to me, and to my family. These past several years were not what any of us could have imagined, but God never left us or failed us. And as such, life goes on and I wanted to announce to all of you that coming early summer next year will be the next member of the Sauter family --- Lizzy is again expecting."

The family all jumped to their feet and hugged them both excitedly. Lizzy took a quick glance at Clara, who seemed to be doing the math in her head. She was right–Lizzy was expecting, and there was no way that this was Henry's baby. She locked eyes with Lizzy, who was silently pleading with her to remain quiet. "Later" Lizzy mouthed the word and Clara nodded.

After dinner, Lizzy and Clara, along with a few of the older children, started clearing the table and washing dishes. The younger children went outside to play, and the babies Adam and Albert were asleep in a back room. Once they were alone, Clara asked the question that Lizzy knew was coming, but that she dreaded hearing.

"Very exciting about another pregnancy–how have you been feeling?"

"About the same as usual," Lizzy answered very nonspecifically.

"Lizzy–I have known you for almost all your life. Even though I am not the one who gave birth to you, I figure I know you as well as anyone on this earth, maybe more. Whatever you say will stay in this kitchen. The baby isn't Henry's, is it?" Lizzy silently shook her head 'no' and then suggested they go for a walk so she could explain in private.

"…And that's the whole story," she said sometime later. "Neither of us expected this, and certainly never dreamed that Henry would come back from the dead after all those months. But you MUST keep this a secret–we have all agreed that this is our private situation and refuse to have Henry's reputation tarnished."

"I understand—we have all had to make allowances and adjustments during these trying times. Just be careful, ok? And stay healthy. I love Levi like he was another son, but I don't know how he is going to handle seeing his child raised by another man, after losing two of his own."

Fall turned into winter, which thankfully was not as harsh as those in the past, and Levi continued to come almost every day to help with things around the farm. He tried to push his feelings for Lizzy to the background, but it was difficult as he watched her pregnancy progress. *Their* baby, but one he would never be able to claim. It was eating him up inside, but he felt he owed it to his brother to keep his promise.

Early in April of 1866, Rosa Margaretha was born. The birth was uneventful, and luckily baby Rosa weighed just less than seven pounds, so no one was overly suspicious. Henry had hoped that he would be able to love this little girl but found that his heart was completely hardened toward her. She was a lovely child, a mirror image of her mother, but Henry wanted nothing to do with her.

The economy was improving while the south underwent reconstruction. The logging industry exploded as the railroad continued its expansion west. Freed blacks moved into the bigger cities in droves, along with immigrants from France, Britain, Italy, and Sweden. The diverse culture was exciting and vibrant. Even smaller towns like Hastings felt the influence and Lizzy enjoyed her weekly trips to town with her articles.

Lizzy and Henry slowly worked their way back to each other emotionally and physically, and in October of 1867, Bertha Helena was born. Elizabeth Louise followed in February of

1869. Things continued to be difficult on the farm with Henry's declining health. He never fully regained his strength, and the local army doctor felt he would have a lifelong deterioration due to poor nutrition and exposure to the elements and infectious diseases while away. He also seemed to be losing his eyesight. Levi had been working at the local lumber mill part time and was finding it difficult to help as much on the farm as he previously had. He had been offered a supervisory position but was struggling with the decision to accept it or not. After Elizabeth was born, Henry and Lizzy sat down with him for another difficult conversation.

"Levi, my dear brother. Never would I have survived these past several years without your help, but I think it's time we reconsider our long-term goals and plans. I'm thinking, maybe it's time to sell the farm and move into town. Then you would be free to pursue a career with the lumber mill."

Lizzy felt tears in her eyes as she realized what all the war had taken away from them. Where was the vibrant man she had fallen in love with and married just 15 years ago? They were supposed to have a lifetime of memories together, but no one imagined that so many of their dreams would become nightmares.

Levi was silent for a few minutes, but then agreed. "It makes sense. My property has been vacant for years, and yours is but a shell of what it used to be and could be again with different owners. Let me talk to some folks in town—there are new people arriving in Minnesota each week and I'm sure we can easily find a buyer for both properties. And of course, it has been difficult for me to be here each day to see Rosa grow and thrive. Being away more is a good idea for all of us, I think."

"Then it's settled," Henry said softly. "But I'm thinking St. Paul would be better for us–more opportunities for the children with schools and the arts, and avenues for your writing, Lizzy. Graham has been wonderful, but you have made a name for yourself in the region, and I think you deserve more than just a local newspaper and a few dollars per week."

"Would you be happy in St. Paul?" she asked. "That's an awfully big change from the farm life you have known forever."

"I think I need the change. Looking at this farm everyday just makes me feel like a failure."

Lizzy and Levi exchanged sad glances, then Levi said, "Ok, I'll go into St. Paul in the next week or so and talk to a friend I have at the land office. He'll know the best course for us to take, I think."

"Then it's settled," Henry said dejectedly as he hobbled towards the bedroom, defeat written on his face.

Chapter 39

Levi was amazed at how quickly he was able to find someone who was willing to purchase both properties 'as is'–totally sight unseen. The price was quite generous, much more than what they originally spent all those years ago. The next step was to find a suitable house in St. Paul, which turned out to be a bit more difficult. Not much was available that was large enough for a family of 10 that was also accessible for Henry with his health issues. They eventually settled on a multi-story home on Elwood Street and Lizzy started work for the St. Paul Pioneer Press with a weekly column at triple the pay she was earning writing for Graham. They joined the local Lutheran Church, and Henry met several people who wanted music lessons for their children. Though it was not the life either had envisioned, they settled into a routine.

In late summer of 1871, she was pregnant again, but spent most of this pregnancy in bed with fatigue and pain. In April of 1872, she received word that her father was very ill and not expected to live much longer. Against her physician's advice, she made the long wagon trip to Jakob's farm and arrived just minutes before he passed away. Devastated and exhausted, she decided to remain a few days and try to be of support to Clara. Two weeks later, Clara died in her sleep. Just like that–both her father and his long-time wife were gone. Lizzy was too emotional and exhausted to return home just yet, and on May 22 her son Louis Luther was born. The local doctor who assisted with the delivery strongly counseled Lizzy not to have more children as it seemed her body was having difficulties.

After a few months staying with her brother Adam and his family, Lizzy finally had the strength for the trip back to St. Paul. Everyone was excited to see her and the baby, and Lizzy told Henry what the doctor had said. Although chemical contraceptives were not available at the time, Lizzy's doctor told her of various herbs used by the Native Americans that seemed to be fairly effective. She faithfully drank the tea each night and prayed for no more pregnancies.

The children were growing and doing well at school and taking piano lessons. Casper and Adam, especially, were proficient in music and were well on their way to becoming concert pianists. Bertha had a beautiful singing voice already evident at age 5. Things may have seemed normal on the outside, but behind the closed doors of their home, life was anything but. Henry's health continued to deteriorate, and his eyesight was rapidly fading. He still jumped every time there was a loud noise or one of the children slammed the door. Henry maintained a good relationship with all his children, except for Rosa. His hostility toward her seemed to grow each year, and she had no idea the cause. She watched her father play with the other children, tell them stories, play piano for them. But when she tried to get his attention, he just turned away from her. Several times she tried to ask her mother what was wrong, but Lizzy just begged her to be patient and try to be understanding.

The next two years passed uneventfully. Lizzy continued writing, and some of her articles were picked up for national publication in such magazines as Better Homes and Gardens and Harper's Monthly. One of her more popular articles was an interview she did with Edward, the freed slave turned barber who had been so instrumental in the underground railroad. The money they had received from the sale of the farm was long gone, so things were tight financially. The older children were working part-time jobs after school. Life in St. Paul was now very different from the town where they celebrated their honeymoon or where she went dress shopping. There was such a larger mixture of cultures and races, and the town was bustling with excitement and growth. Lizzy cherished the times she could leave the house and visit people who would tell her what was happening across the state and the nation. She continued her interest in local politics, even though as a woman, she was not allowed to vote and her presence at political rallies was frowned upon. Henry's health had deteriorated to the point that he rarely left the house, and his doctors came to visit him at home. So, much to everyone's surprise, in January of 1875 Lizzy suspected that she was pregnant again. The herbal tea she was drinking each night was supposed to be exceptionally effective, but not 100%. She told Henry, who was only mildly excited, but after about six months she miscarried a son they named Eddie. It was impossible to take him back to the old homestead that her family no longer owned to have him buried next to Gladys and the three children. Instead, they opted for the cemetery beside their Lutheran church. She was 39 years old, and this was the second of her babies she had to bury, along with numerous other family members and friends. How much grief was one heart supposed to bear?

But there were good times as well. Fred married a lovely girl named Susan and soon they had children of their own. Hannah married Edward just the next year, and Lizzy found joy watching her family expand to new generations. Henry was pretty much a total invalid now, and Lizzy had begun the process of filing for a pension for him. Like all government bureaucracy, it seemed to be taking forever.

Christmas of 1876 was a busy one with the older children visiting with their families, and other children still at home. The local veteran's society had given Henry a wheelchair which offered him some independence and improved his mood somewhat. Most of his time, however, was spent sitting by the window, reliving the battles and the horrors he witnessed. Most physicians knew little about how to treat the condition other than with strong opioids or narcotics. Henry was 52, but his body matched that of a man of 80. Regardless, he was the love of her life, and Lizzy was dedicated to caring for him, for as long as she had the opportunity. But each day was getting harder.

The dinner table was overflowing with meat and fruits and desserts, but for some reason, Lizzy was not very hungry. In fact, her stomach was a bit upset and she found herself just nibbling on a few crackers. The last time she felt like this… surely it wasn't possible that she was pregnant yet again? Between the herbal teas and Henry's frail health, neither one of them could have imagined this. But thinking back over the dates of her cycles, the timing was correct for her to feel the symptoms she had felt so many times before. As much as she loved being a mother, she wasn't sure she could do this yet again, especially since the last pregnancy ended in a miscarriage. She kept her feelings to herself until she could talk to a doctor.

Of course, her doctor confirmed the pregnancy and set a due date of next summer. She would be 42 when this child was born, and she was already a grandmother. Finances were tough and her husband was an invalid. "Please God," she prayed. "Please help me during this difficult time. I have trusted You through the famine, our immigration and settlement, the loss of so many children, the blizzards and even a tornado. Please don't leave me now."

Within a few weeks, it became more obvious to everyone that she was indeed pregnant. This was her 13th pregnancy, and she certainly hoped it was her last. One night as they were preparing for bed, Lizzy told Henry that he was going to be a father yet again, probably in May or June. He smiled slightly, then looked away. Lizzy wasn't sure he totally understood what this meant for them for the next 20 years, and she sighed with the weight of all the decisions that were on her shoulder more and more each day.

Fortunately, the pregnancy was uncomplicated, and Franklin Henry was born in June of 1877.

"Another son, named after me?" Henry asked weakly. "May I hold him?"

"Of course," Lizzy answered. Henry was almost completely blind now, so Lizzy placed the baby carefully into his arms.

"Describe him for me," Henry asked.

"Well, he looks a lot like Fred did as a baby --- long legs and arms, bright blue eyes, but not much hair. It's hard to tell what color it will be."

"I do hope it's a deep auburn like yours," he said sweetly. "One of the first things I noticed about you, all those years ago."

Lizzy smiled. Henry did have lucid moments occasionally, where she could get a glimpse of the man she fell in love with. Sadly, those moments never lasted long before he faded back into his memories. But she cherished them when she could.

Life for Lizzy and her family was about the best that could be expected for a disabled veteran and his wife, along with their numerous children. Not many people in the country had much money, but St. Paul was growing every day and there was a feeling of optimism in the air. Lizzy was now one of the most well-paid authors at the paper, and she was blessed to have a creative outlet. Being a wife and mother was still the most important thing to her, but writing about the political issues of the day was what brought her alive. Besides Henry's illness, her biggest cause for concern was the growing resentment and hostility between him and Rosa. He often lashed out at her for no reason, and Rosa cried herself to sleep many nights, wondering what it was that she had done wrong for so many years. Lizzy wanted to comfort her daughter, to let her know that it was not her fault, but of course could not do that without spilling the secret, and Henry would never forgive her.

She had received several letters from Levi over the years—nothing personal, just news about the lumber mill and asking how Henry was doing. Levi had never married again or had more children. He had resigned himself to being a bachelor living in the woods—cutting down trees and floating them down the rivers. No one reading the letter would ever have guessed the secret they were all straining to keep.

In early 1881, Henry's war pension was finally approved, and Lizzy received $12 per month on his behalf. It wasn't a lot, but she was glad for the help. Henry could no longer give music lessons or do any other sort of manual labor. Living on Lizzy's newspaper salary was extremely difficult, especially with so many children still at home.

The fights between Henry and Rosa continued to escalate into 1882. After one particularly loud argument, Rosa was crying on the outside steps as Albert came home from his afternoon job at a shoe store. He and Rosa were very close in age and were always together. After she told him of the latest fight, Albert devised the plan for them to run away to Canada. He had noticed for years the strange way that their father had treated her, and never understood it. His questions about it to their parents were ignored. He pulled a few dollars out of his pocket and figured they could stow away on a train bound for Ontario, where he was sure they could find work. At first Rosa thought he was crazy, but then realized that she could no longer live here where she was so unwanted. They made their plans, and within a week they were gone.

Chapter 40

Lizzy awoke to the sound of footsteps rushing down the stairs and shouts of "Mama–Papa! Come quick!" Lizzy jumped from her bed and ran to the hall to find Bertha and Elizabeth in a panicked state.

"What in the world is wrong?" Lizzy asked, confused that her normally levelheaded daughters were in such distress.

"Mama–Rosa and Albert are missing. Rosa left this note on her pillow," Elizabeth said in a rush.

Lizzy grabbed the note and then sank into the nearest chair. *"Dear Mama–I'm sorry that it has come to this, but I cannot live here any longer with the hateful way I have been treated, while the others are treated normally. I have no idea what I did that was so terrible, but it doesn't matter anymore. Don't come looking for me, not that Papa cares enough to anyway. Albert is with me; we will be fine. Rosa."*

Lizzy was sobbing as she read the note the second and third time. How could her children have just up and left like that? Had she failed that badly as a mother? Where were they going, and how were they going to survive? They were just 16 and 17 years old–much too young to be travelling alone. And how was she going to tell Henry? Albert was the one of all the children who was the most like Henry in both looks and disposition. And she also needed to find a way to tell Levi. This was going to crush him.

She took the girls in her arms and tried to calm their fears. She fervently prayed, "Father, we come to You in this time of distress and need. We don't quite understand what has happened, but please protect Rosa and Albert–keep them safe and bring them home to us soon. Wrap Your arms of comfort around them and guide them back to us. Amen." She then rose and went back to the bedroom to tell Henry.

"Lizzy, what is going on? I heard quite a commotion."

"Henry, I'm not sure how to tell you this, but Rosa and Albert have run away. She left a note asking us not to try to find them. My heart is broken–what if something terrible happens to them? How will we ever know? Two more of my babies…gone!"

"I suppose you blame me for this," Henry said angrily.

"Well, as a matter of fact I do. I don't know why you had to be so hateful to her. You could have just ignored her, but no, you had to be so angry about things she had no control over that you drove her away. And Albert went with her! I'm not sure I can forgive you for this."

"Forgive me? Have you forgotten who got us into this mess in the first place? Every time I looked at her, all I could see was your betrayal."

"It wasn't betrayal, Henry! We had been told you died. Did you expect me to live like a nun the rest of my life?"

"Of course not. I just never thought you would turn to *him*, my own brother. And so soon! Have you heard from him lately?"

"Not in several years," she lied. No sense telling Henry that Levi checked on them several times per year. "Last I heard he was logging up near the Canadian border."

"Good. Now can you help me get dressed?"

Lizzy helped him dress and pushed his wheelchair to the dining room, placing him near a window where he could feel the sunlight. She went to the kitchen where she sat in a chair and wept.

Months passed with no word from either of the children, and Lizzy's heart was broken. Henry actually seemed to be in a better mood without Rosa's presence being a constant irritation to him. Lizzy kept busy with the smaller children while still writing for the newspaper. Even though the war had been over for almost 20 years, there was still tremendous interest in Henry's diary, and she had even been approached by a publisher who wanted to print it as a book. As more of the children got married and left home, Lizzy felt freedom to pursue her own interests more than she ever had before. One of those was politics, of course, and she found herself immersed in local and state issues. While still not accepted due to her gender, the local business leaders grew accustomed to her presence in town hall meetings and even at the state capitol.

In 1895, Bertha met a dashing young man named Christopher and they moved first to New York City and then Philadelphia, Pennsylvania. He had made quite a name for himself in the steel industry and was influential in the railroads as well. Lizzy was sad for her to move so far away, and figured it was unlikely that they would ever see each other again.

The whole country was excited for 1900 to arrive—a new century full of promise and excitement. Lizzy wanted to celebrate with Henry but knew the sounds of the fireworks would likely trigger an episode of his anxiety. Lizzy and the children enjoyed the show, however, and eagerly anticipated the future.

A few weeks later, a letter arrived in the mail addressed to Lizzy. It was from Canada, and Lizzy recognized Rosa's handwriting. Was this the news she had been waiting for?

Chapter 41

Lizzy lit a fire in the living room and situated herself into her favorite chair. "Please, God, let her be ok. I have missed her and Albert so much–please help me bear whatever news this is."

Lizzy carefully opened the letter and unfolded two pages of writing. *"January 10, 1900. Dear Mama–I hope this letter finds you and the others well. I know I should have written years ago, but at first, I did not have much to tell. Albert and I arrived safely here in Canada, and both found jobs rather easily. I worked as a maid in a hotel–imagine that! Albert went to work with a group of loggers and sent money to me each month. We lived together for several years when he was between logging jobs, until I met a nice man named William and we decided to get married. We have one daughter–Elizabeth Mary–and she is two years old. The main reason I am writing now is that I just received word that Albert is missing from his work crew. They are not sure what happened to him, but he had been working near a flooded river and perhaps got swept away. I wish I had a real answer to give you. I know you loved him.*

There is no need to try to respond–I am happy here in Canada and I am sure things were better for you and Papa after I left. Again, I will never understand. Rosa"

Lizzy read the letter several times, hoping to find some hidden clues about where in Canada she was or what had really happened to Albert. She closed her eyes and the vision of her son being swept away by floodwaters was more than she could bear. She knew she needed to tell Henry but wondered how to do that without upsetting him by including news from Rosa. Thinking about it further, she decided that there was no real reason to tell Henry anything at all. It wouldn't bring Albert back and could possibly make things worse if he became angry talking about Rosa. She folded the letter and put it into her apron pocket. "I'll pray about this later, maybe write to Levi and see what he thinks I should do." she said softly to herself.

Eventually, she did write to Levi and was relieved that he agreed with her about not telling Henry that Albert was missing. Henry's lucid moments were coming less frequently now, and there seemed no real reason to risk upsetting him.

A few more years passed, and more children left the home to make lives of their own. In 1904 there was a knock on the door, and Lizzy opened it to find a young man on a bicycle, holding a telegram in his hand. "This is for Mr. and Mrs. Henry Sauter—is that you?"

"Yes, thank you," Lizzy said as she took the paper from the boy. Once alone inside the house, she opened it to find a message from Bertha's husband Christopher. *'Sad to share the news that Bertha passed away yesterday. She developed a fever and died within a few hours of being hospitalized. Doctor is not sure the cause. I'm sorry for your family's loss."*

Another child—gone. This is *not* how it was supposed to be. She did a mental checklist of her children:

Mary—dead

Fred—married to Susan

Hannah- married to Edward

Casper–married to Clotilde

Adam–married to Maria

Albert–missing in Canada

Rosa–ran away to Canada, married to William

Bertha–dead in Pennsylvania

Elizabeth–married to James

Louis–married to Cyrilla

Franklin–alive, not married

And then there were her 2 miscarriages

How she loved each of them, and missed the ones who were gone. She prayed she did not have to endure the loss of any more children–she doubted her heart could stand much more. But more than anything, she was watching her dear Henry slip further and further away from her --- and that was the ultimate pain of all.

Chapter 42

The next decade went by quickly without a lot of change in the household, other than the need to take in boarders to help make ends meet. The first to arrive were Ira Huntsberger who was a cook at a local hotel, and Benjamin Nicholson who had just arrived from Norway and was working odd jobs. Later they added William Rothman to the group. He was a paper hanger by trade but was often unemployed and had trouble paying his rent. He did not stay with them very long.

One fall evening she was sitting on the front steps when she heard the cries of a kitten. Hidden in the bushes was a pure black male kitten that looked hungry and scared. She picked him up and carried him inside, fixing a bite of food for him and trying to clean him a bit with a damp cloth. She decided to name him Amos, in honor of the runaway slave who had saved her brother's life all those years ago. Finally, she had the kitten she had wanted all her life and spent many hours stroking his black fur and finding comfort in his antics. Amazingly, Amos took a liking to Henry as well, and often curled up on his lap as he sat in his wheelchair.

There were more grandbabies, of course, and Lizzy loved it when the house was filled with children. Henry seemed weaker each passing year, and Lizzy wondered how much longer he would be with them. In January of 1913 they celebrated his 90th birthday with most of the children and grandchildren in attendance, along with many of Lizzy's friends from the newspaper world. He was one of the older living Civil War veterans from the area, so one of the papers did a nice writeup about him.

Once the party was over, his condition began to decline rapidly. His new doctor, Dr. Thiele, was a kind man who specialized in treating older people, especially veterans. He had a calming effect on Henry who seemed to respond positively to his presence. But it soon became clear that the end was not far away. One more serious infection or trauma, and Henry would not likely survive.

Lizzy rarely left his bedside now, opting instead to sit in a rocking chair next to him. She would read aloud from the newspaper and tell him about the latest local elections or the efforts for women to have the right to vote. Day after day, week after week, she was totally devoted to the man she had loved almost all her life. Yes, things had been difficult, and she had endured more death and hardship than most women her age. But this is where she belonged.

In November, he took a turn for the worse—coughing and gasping for air. The weather had been cold and rainy, and Lizzy feared he had caught pneumonia. She asked a neighbor to find Dr. Thiele and beg him to come as soon as possible. She did not see how he could last much longer.

Chapter 43

Lizzy closed her eyes and settled back into her chair. The rain had turned to snow and was falling softly onto the ground outside the bedroom window. "Oh, my–I never intended to talk that long. What time is it?"

"It's about 8 PM," Dr. Thiele replied.

"Henry --- how is he?"

"It won't be long now. His breathing is quite shallow, and his heartrate has slowed."

"Is he in any pain? Is there something more we can do?"

"No, he's not in pain. I gave him some medicine to help him relax, but I think hearing your voice these past several hours has also kept him calm. Do you want me to leave you with him now?"

"Do you mind? I'd like to say goodbye, alone."

"Of course. I'll be right outside if you need me."

Dr. Thiele stiffly rose to his feet, realizing he had been sitting for way too long. As he closed the bedroom door behind him, he heard Lizzy's soft voice.

"My dear Henry --- my life will not be the same without you. What a time we had together! But I know you are tired, and it's your time to go. And it's ok. I love you, Henry–I always will."

"Lizzy?" Henry softly moaned.

"Yes, my love?"

Henry turned his face toward Lizzy's voice, and with trembling hands brushed his fingers against one cheek, finding the small bump on her nose. With his last breath he whispered, "Lizzy, my sweet girl–I LOVE YOU."

And then the doctor heard the soft cry of heartbreak from one of the strongest and most courageous women he had ever met.

Epilogue

Dr. Thiele's eyes squinted a bit in the late afternoon sunshine. It was October 1ˢᵗ, 1916. The sky was crystal blue, and the air was crisp. Rows of trees lined the cemetery driveway, and each was more splendid than the last with their leaves of red, gold, and mauve shimmering in a gentle breeze. He was standing off to the side while the family was saying their last goodbyes.

Lizzy's casket was gently lowered into the ground beside her dear Henry, and they were together again at last. After Henry died, she had moved back to Hastings for a few years to live with one of her sons, and the doctor had lost track of her. He was saddened to hear that she had developed pneumonia three weeks ago and passed away a few months after her 80ᵗʰ birthday. She had been a celebrity of sorts in St. Paul due to her involvement in politics and national issues, and her death had been covered in the local newspapers. Dr. Thiele had read in the obituary that the family was bringing her back to St. Paul for burial, and although not many of the mourners knew him, he felt he had to be here. One by one, the children and grandchildren passed by the casket, including a woman he did not immediately recognize. He saw several of Lizzy's close friends and someone he learned was Henry's brother Levi. Knowing what he did now about the family dynamics and history, he was finally able to put faces with some of the names he had heard about.

He thought he heard the name "Rosa" and immediately thought of Lizzy's estranged daughter who, other than the one short letter, still had no contact with the family. Lizzy's other children—all middle aged and with children and grandchildren of their own—were crying and hugging each other, although there seemed to be some underlying tension with this strange woman.

Everyone except Rosa moved toward their cars or buggies, while she walked closer to the gravesite. Dr. Thiele heard her say, "Mama, Papa - I'm so sorry that I never came back. I wish I knew what happened, why you both treated me so differently from the rest of the family. I should have tried harder to understand. My life was so miserable all those years, feeling on the outside of your love and never being accepted. I wish I knew why—but now we will never know."

Levi stood next to his car, watching the scene at the gravesite. Dr. Thiele could see the anguish on his face and sensed the conflict he felt. Would he approach her? Would he tell her the truth, now that Lizzy and Henry were both gone? The doctor was totally caught up in the drama before him, since he was one of only a few people who knew the whole story.

After several moments, Rosa dropped a few rose petals on the coffin and rejoined her husband William at their car. Levi quickly turned his back to them so they could not see the tears in his eyes. Once everyone else had left, Levi approached the grave and Dr. Theile could faintly hear him say, "Goodbye my sweet Lizzy. I kept our secret—rest well my love."

And then the doctor was alone in the cemetery—alone with his thoughts and memories of the woman he had recently come to know and to admire. It was such a beautiful day, and he strangely felt at peace.

"What an amazing journey you had, Lizzy," he said to her gently. "But rest now, your journey is finished."

List of Characters
*early death

Germany:
- Kruse, Jakob and Margaret
  - Anna*, Lizzy, Adam, Louisa*
- Kruse, Jakob and Clara
  - Rosina, Hannah, Casper* (born in Minnesota)
- Dr. VanGruber

New York City:
- Walz, Hans and Susannah
  - Gretel
- Pulcher, Fritz

Chicago:
- Koehler, Johannes and Eva
  - Lydia
- VanDussen, Emil and Antonia
  - Kurt, Erik
- Johannson, Gertrude
  - Augusta
- Miller family
- Bauer family

On the Road:
- Blakley, George
- Lee, Albert
- Doc Parsons
- Doctor Nilan

Minnesota:
- Augustine, George and Marie
  - Fred, Sebastian, Sarah
- Sauter, Henry
- Sauter, Levi and Gladys
- Baker family
- Pastor Clarke and Lillian
- Amos (slave)
- Ruby (slave)
- Lawson, Edward (freed slave/barber)
- Dr. Theile
- Dr. Hampton
- Dahl, William and Emily
- Hanson, Peter and Margaret
- Franklin, Graham
- Ira Huntsburger
- Benjamin Nicolson
- William Rothman

Civil War 1862-1865

5th Minnesota:
John Karels
Anton Lipke
Hans Schuster
David Vollmer

- Sauter, Henry and Lizzy
  - Mary*, Fred, Hannah, Casper, Adam, Albert, Bertha, Elizabeth, Louis, Edward,* Franklin

- Sauter, Levi and Gladys
  - Reuben*, Audrey*
- Sauter, Levi and Lizzy
  - Rosa

Maps, Pictures, and Extra Information

Bremen, Germany

Potato Famine 1845

Typical Immigrant Ship from Germany 1800's

Slavery Map 1850

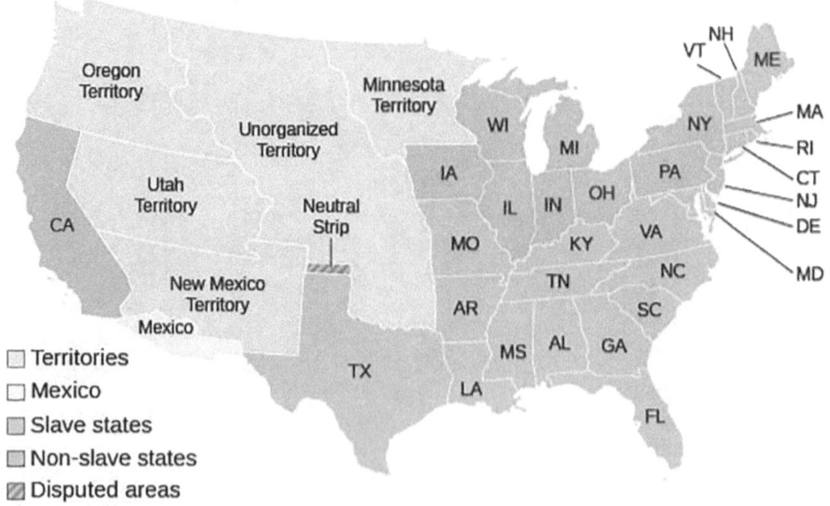

Underground Railroad

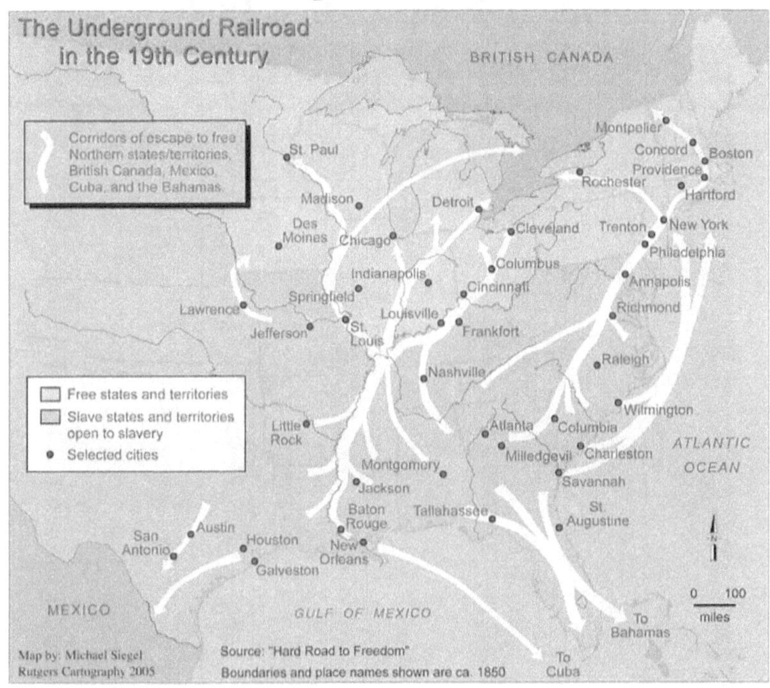

Hastings, Minnesota

Infant Mortality 1800-2020

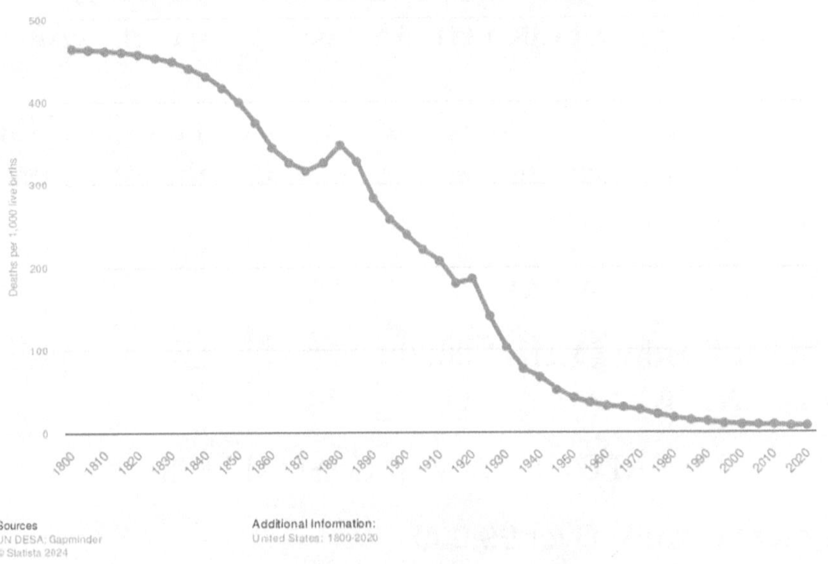

Civil War Field Hospital

CIVIL WAR CASUALTIES

CASUALTY NUMBERS AND BATTLE DEATH STATISTICS FOR THE AMERICAN CIVIL WAR

Though the number of killed and wounded in the Civil War is not known precisely, most sources agree that the total number killed was between 640,000 and 700,000.

UNION CIVIL WAR CASUALTIES

Combat Deaths: Over 110,000
Other Deaths*: Over 250,000

CONFEDERATE CIVIL WAR CASUALTIES

Combat Deaths: Over 95,000
Other Deaths*: Over 165,000

(*Other Deaths include, among others: disease [by far the most common cause of death], accidents, drowning, heat stroke, suicide, murder, execution.)

Researchers have increased this number an additional 50,000 for civilians who were killed. Binghamton University historian J. David Hacker believes the number of soldier deaths was approximately 750,000, 20 percent higher than traditionally estimated, and possibly as high as 850,000.

St Paul, MN 1900

Other Books by this Author

Gate to Gate Trilogy [Boarding Pass, Future Flights, Wheels Down] (2020)

An architect. A young boy from a broken home. A bride on her honeymoon. An Iraqi war vet. What could these people possibly have in common? Absolutely nothing, except they shared the same airplane seat throughout the course of one particular day. Everyone has a story, but those stories don't always take the course we planned or end how or when we had hoped. Each person we cross paths with is at a different place in their own personal journey, but these seemingly random meetings have the potential to alter our course and take us to places we had never imagined. Pack your bags, settle into a comfortable chair with a bag of pretzels and a cold drink, and let your imagination soar along with our eight passengers. Your flight is just beginning.

A Home for Molly (2019)

Molly is a young stray cat that is adopted and learns what it is like to have a home for the first time in her life. She explores her new world and finds love for the lady who adopted her. Quirky and mischievous, this children's book is filled with fun actual photos of Molly in her new home.

Serenity Secrets (2021)

Lacy Mason, investigative reporter for Channel 11, has gone undercover in search of answers to strange happenings at Serenity Springs Memory Care and Hospice. What she discovers is a dark web of lies, deceit, and retribution that threatens the lives of all the patients, including her own mother. With the help of her former boyfriend from the St. Louis police department, Tony Malone, Lacy puts her own life on the line in a race against time to uncover the Serenity Secrets.

A Life of Devotion (2022)

This is a collection of 52 weekly devotionals to reflect on God's love and provision for our lives. It has been my pleasure to share my memories and the teachings of my parents and others who shaped me. My prayer is that you find them enjoyable to read and relatable to situations in your own life.

It is also my desire that these short devotionals help start a habit of weekly Bible reading or will supplemented the other readings you already do. I hope you will find time to memorize the verses that mean the most to you–I'm so thankful for the times God gives a verse back to me just when I need it.

May God richly bless you in the years to come.

Oh To Be Like Him (2023)

My desire for 2024 (and beyond) is to be more like God. But what does that mean? How do I achieve that? Join me as we journey through this collection of weekly devotionals to discover the attributes of God and his faithfulness to help us learn and grow into a reflection of him.

Oh! to be like Thee, blessed Redeemer, This is my constant longing and prayer;

Gladly I'll forfeit all of earth's treasures, Jesus, Thy perfect likeness to wear.

Refrain:

Oh! to be like Thee, oh! to be like Thee, Blessed Redeemer, pure as Thou art;

Come in Thy sweetness, come in Thy fullness; Stamp Thine own image deep on my heart.

Thomas O. Chisholm (1897)